Viking Wolf

Book 5 in the Dragon Heart Series

By

Griff Hosker

Viking Wolf

Published by Sword Books Ltd 2014
Copyright © Griff Hosker First Edition
A CIP catalogue record for this title is available
from the British Library.
Cover by Design for Writers

Dedication

Thanks to all the Time Team programmes! You keep me straight on most things. And thanks to my readers who also make sure that I am as accurate as possible.

Contents

Prologue

Cyninges-tūn

It was the coldest winter we had ever known. It was even colder than the harsh winters of Norway. Some of those who had chosen to live beyond the walls of our settlement were found frozen to death. When my hunters went out they discovered cold and empty halls filled with the frozen dead. And it was the year of the Wolf. We heard them howling in the long winter nights and Kara and her mother were fearful. Their noises seemed so close that they sounded as though they were in our walls. The snow was so deep and frozen that, at times, we could not open our gates. We were trapped within our wooden walls. We were in a prison of snow and ice. My wife, Erika, was a good wife and a good provider for the people. We had laid in plenty of supplies both food and firewood and we ate. We did not eat well but we had food. Those beyond the walls did not. Those beyond the walls who did not freeze, starved to death. My wife was the heart of our people. She had been teaching my daughter, Kara, to become a volva like her. They had visited all those who had been sick inside both our villages during the winter. I only allowed them across the frozen lake when the storms had abated and I sent them well escorted. They saved many lives in Cyninges-tūn. Had they not gone then I fear that we would have become the villages of the dead. Kara was becoming as skilled as her mother although she still wished to have the second sight her mother had. That was the sign of a true volva. Erika had cuddled her, "When you are a woman then it will come. In the spring or the summer, you will dream and when you wake then you will have the sight."

We had two walled settlements which were separated by the Water. Within our walls, we had shelter from the wind and my men cleared the snow so that we were snug behind our wooden defences. The turf on our roofs kept us warm but we could not hunt and food ran short. When my people did not eat they succumbed to many small illnesses. Our two settlements had been built to the east and west of the Water.

I lived in the smaller one which was on the hill and restricted
by the ground. The larger one was to the west and had much
flat land. The ice on the Water aided us for we could walk
between them and ensure that all of our bounty was shared.
If it had not been so then many more would have died. When
there was a slight thaw and we were able to open the gates
and move around I took Arturus and my Ulfheonar to find
those who lived beyond our walls. It was the worst journey
of my life. I had been a slave and taken from my home. I
would relive that journey a thousand times before I would
repeat the walk to Lang's Dale and Windar's Mere.

Arturus had grown considerably. Soon he would be old
enough to become a warrior although Erika thought not.
Indeed there were many youths the same age as Arturus who
were not as big and they had taken the sword. He was
desperate to impress me so that I would allow him to join me
on my next raid He made sure that he obeyed Haaken and
Cnut and he emulated them in every action. He had many
skills. He was almost as good at tracking as Snorri and he
could handle a sword with the best of them. Haaken and
Cnut had taken to aiding Snorri with his training. They were
my oldest friends and the ones I trusted the most. This would
be his last winter in my home. Come the spring he would
join the warriors in the warrior hall.

We found Lang and his family or, rather, we found the
remains of Lang and his family. We had saved them some
years earlier from a wolf attack. We had thought that we had
destroyed the nest of wolves but we were wrong. It was a
sign from the gods. The wolves had returned. They had
descended again to feast on flesh. They had somehow gained
entrance to the farm and the fur and pieces of bone told their
own story. Lang and his son had defended themselves and
their family but they had perished nonetheless. The tracks of
the pack led east towards the wide water that was Windar's
Mere.

We found no living person between our home and
Windar's Mere. There were dead, frozen corpses now and
there were carcasses or parts of carcasses showing the trail of

the wolves. When we reached there, Tostig Red Hair was so cold that he was actually blue. Windar refused to let us leave until we had eaten and warmed through. He told me tales of those around the mere dying; some frozen to death and others devoured by wolves. When we had warmed through, a day later and tried to leave we were trapped in his hall by a snow flurry for a further two days. When the storm abated we left and headed home. We hurried to avoid the icy wind and sleet which chilled us to the bone despite the layers we all wore.

I had no idea if we would survive in our newly conquered home. Had we made the right decision when we had left our island in the west? I doubted it. There the winters were gentle and there were no wolves. The gods were playing with me and the Norns were spinning their webs. I could not even begin to envisage the plans they had for me. We huddled in our turf-roofed hall by the Water of Cyninges-tūn and we heard the wolves howl in the hills. Death now stalked our land. We were no longer the hunter; we were the hunted. The land and the wolves were conspiring against us. We had fought our enemies and now we had to fight against Nature herself.

Chapter 1

It was a sombre spring. And it proved to be a late spring. Normally it would be a joyous time for the new growth and new births made everyone feel alive. The only animals which had survived were the few that we had kept within our walls and they were perilously small in number. Although the snow had gone the ground was still hard. No crops could be sown. This would be a late, hard spring.

"I will take my drekar and we will raid. I will feed those for whom I am responsible."

My wife, Erika, was a wise woman. "The people are hungry but they fear the wolves more. If we are hungry then they will be too. The wolves are the greater danger. We can live on the food we still have."

It made sense. We thought that we had destroyed the pack in the hills above Lang's Dale. They had returned. "I will take my Ulfheonar and we will hunt them."

My oathsworn were all as eager as I was to do something. We were in our prime and it did not sit well to rest, eat and drink while outside our walls women and children were dying of starvation, disease and now wolves. It was not our way. We could not fight nature but we could fight the wolves.

Haaken rubbed his eye socket. It was a habit he had and it showed he was concerned. "We need to know where the wolves are. Windar said that many of his people to the east of the mere suffered. We should first go to Lang's Dale and see if they are there and if not we can track them and hunt them elsewhere. I agree with your wife, Dragon Heart. If we are hungry then the wolves will be too. We need to find the wolves."

Others banged their ale beakers to show their agreement. We spoke openly in the warrior hall. We had no rank.

Beorn stood. "Jarl Dragon Heart, there is still snow on the hills. Snorri and I will seek tracks above Lang's Dale. We can leave now and be back before dark. If they are not there and have moved further west it will allow us to prepare better."

I nodded. We would need time to gather weapons. Snorri and Beorn were the two best trackers and hunters that we had. If they found tracks above Lang's Dale then we could eradicate this threat quickly.

They returned, chilled to the bone, with the news that there was no sign of the wolf. There were neither tracks nor spoor. We would have to seek them closer to Windar's Mere. This was a different pack.

We had spent the day preparing supplies for a week. I took only four of my Ulfheonar and Arturus, my son, and our dog, Wolf. We had kept alive six ponies which also determined our numbers. The others had been eaten during the exceptional cold.

I knew my family would be safe as we left to go hunting wolf. We took spears, bows and arrows. I had Ragnar's Spirit strapped around my waist for I needed the comfort of the blade touched by the gods. Over my shoulders, I placed the wolf cloak from my first kill. I wore it, always in combat, and when hunting wolves. It told my enemy who I was. I was Ulfheonar.

My trackers had decided that, as there had been wolf tracks heading north from Windar's Mere, we would begin our hunt there. "The settlement at the Rye Dale will be a good place to begin. There is high ground to both sides and that seems to us like wolf country."

I would not argue with such wisdom and Snorri and Beorn led us northeast. We would bypass Windar's mere and save time.

Arturus had grown. He was now almost a man. He stood as tall as my shoulder and he had filled out. He would come with us on my drekar when the summer came. He had been the ship's boy but he was now old enough to row. I knew he wished to speak with me when he kept looking at me and then looking away.

"You will learn, as you grow older my son, that it is better to say the words in your heart and not keep them imprisoned within. If you do so then the words will change and they will eat you up. Let them out; they need their freedom."

"I was thinking of the treasure at the Roman fort, when will we go for it?"

We had discovered, in a chest, a message from the past which directed us to a hidden place in the old Roman fort far to the north. It had eaten Arturus up all winter. "We have more important tasks before that one, my son. We have a responsibility to our people."

"What of us? When do we think of our needs?"

"When the people are happy."

That did not please the impetuous youth. "That does not seem fair. If it was not for us the people might be slaves or dead. They should be grateful."

I heard Haaken snort. "Your son has much to learn, Dragon Heart."

I nodded, "As we had to learn." I turned to Arturus. We had spent the winter making a shield for him to use. It had taken a great deal of care and attention to detail and I knew he would understand what I was to tell him. "We are like your new shield. We are a circle. Each part is as important as the rest. The Ulfheonar and I might be the metal boss in the centre but if the rest of the shield is destroyed then we cannot survive. We all depend upon each other." I could see him reflecting on that. He was a thinker. Aiden, my Irish mystic, had seen to it that he learned to think. "We will deal with the wolves and then take to our ships. When we have fed the people then we will journey north."

He seemed satisfied and then plagued Snorri and Beorn with questions on the hunting of wolves. We followed the little bubbling stream which would lead us to the small group of huts that was Rye Dale. It was the place we grew our rye and also guarded the entrance to the valley of Windar's Mere. Further north there was the water of Rye Dale and then the Grassy Mere. Rye Dale was the furthest north we had settlers.

The lack of smoke and noise told us, long before we reached the halls, that there was nothing left alive. Two of the smaller homes had gaping doors and, inside we saw the remains of gnawed bones and shredded clothes. The families had died. The main hall had a barred door. We banged upon it and shouted, "Dargh!"

Dargh had been with me since we had left Hrams-a. He was an older warrior but he had come to this dale to be a guardian of the valley. He did not answer.

"Break down the door." The door was well made and it took us some time but eventually we broke it down and were greeted by a sad sight. Dargh and six warriors lay dead. Their bodies, although partly decomposed were thin and emaciated showing that they had starved to death. There was neither water nor food within.

Cnut pointed to the door. "They barred the door against the wolves. They must have been close to death else they would have faced them and died as warriors."

"Aye. They were loyal and faithful warriors. They deserved a warrior's death. Come we will send them to Valhalla. Find some firewood."

There was none within the hall. That had been another cause of the death; the cold. Nature was exacting a terrible vengeance for our settlement. We gathered the old wood from inside the huts and made a pyre. As we stood around, saying goodbye to our friends the smoke spiralled to heaven taking the spirits of the dead with it.

Haaken looked angry. "Come let us avenge our dead and kill these wolves!"

Snorri put his arm on Haaken's shoulder. "Never hunt with a hot head, always use a cool mind. We will find these wolves but we will be careful."

"He is right, Haaken. Lead on Snorri. We obey you."

"We leave our ponies here. They will alarm the wolves and tell them that we are coming." We tied our ponies to the trees which ran along the river. They could eat and drink safely. If the wolves were ahead of us, as I thought, then they would have to pass us if they smelled the ponies. Snorri knew how to hunt. He turned to Arturus. "Tell your dog to hunt. He will pick up any scent."

Arturus and the dog we had named Wolf were inseparable. He was as intelligent as any animal I had ever seen but had a stubborn nature. The only one who could always make him obey was Arturus. "Wolf, hunt!" he waved his arm north of us and the dog raced off to the undergrowth. We waited while it sniffed here and there. It darted to a bush and sniffed again. Then the sheepdog went to a patch of dead bracken and turned, its ears erect. It gave one shrill bark.

"He has found something," said Arturus proudly.

We ran to the dog and while Arturus fussed him Snorri knelt down and sniffed. "He is a good hunter. There is wolf spoor." He nodded to Arturus.

"Wolf, find!" He waved it away again and the dog ran to the north west. There was a craggy ridge which ran alongside the two waters. He went unerringly up the trail through the trees.

I loped along at the rear. It allowed me to see ahead. The others could worry about the trail I wanted to see what was ahead. I saw that the trees ended some mile or so ahead. It was the steep black crag which showed me the direction we would take. It loomed up above the trees and, as we climbed steadily, I saw a dark shape beneath. It was a cave of some description. The others were all focussing on the ground beneath their feet and none were watching for danger ahead.

"Halt!" I hissed.

Arturus whistled and the dog stopped too. They all looked at me expectantly. I did not want to shout and I walked towards them and spoke quietly. "There is a cave a mile or so ahead. I have seen it. It may be that the wolves are some way ahead but I remember the last wolves we found had a lair such as this one. I think we proceed as though this is their home. If I am wrong…"

Haaken gave a quiet chuckle. "I have yet to see you make a wrong decision." He slipped his bow from its case and strung it. "Better to be prepared."

Viking Wolf

Cnut, Arturus and Beorn had spears. Snorri, Haaken and I had bows. Our arrows were the barbed ones. These were wolf killers. I strung my bow and gave it a tug to test the tension. I held an arrow in my right hand and we set off again. My caution was justified for Wolf suddenly went down on his haunches and his ears went down. There was something ahead.

Arturus hissed, "Stay!" to the dog. A wolf would soon take down a sheepdog.

We spread out in a half circle. Beorn was in the centre. I stood next to Arturus and we moved towards the tumble of rocks which lay just ahead. We could all see the dark mouth of the cave above us. We would have to climb up the jagged teeth of rocks to reach it. Snorri held up his hand and disappeared around a rock to our right. He came back and said, quietly, "There is a path to the right. Those with bows can use the path. Beorn, you and the others climb the rocks slowly and watch the cave mouth. Your spears should protect you. Try to give us time to get into position."

He nodded and I turned to my son, "Be careful, my son and if you have to strike then strike true."

We followed Snorri and when we began to climb we could smell death. The wolf lair was close. The path gradually rose to the level of the shelf on which the cave lay. When Snorri reached the top he turned around quickly and waved us up. We were at the side of the cave. The entrance was twice the height of a man. It opened some forty paces from us. Snorri gestured for us to spread out. I notched my arrow.

Suddenly I saw a Beorn's spearhead rise from the cliff and I heard growling echoing in the cave. We had found the wolves, or at least, some of them. The question was how many were there? A second and a third spearhead appeared. We moved a little closer. We could not see the entrance of the cave that was hidden.

Two things happened at once: Beorn sprang onto the rock shelf and two wolves hurtled from the cave with slavering jaws and a roar which echoed like thunder from the cave's roof.

Snorri had the fastest reactions and his arrow thudded into the side of the nearest wolf. Haaken and I were a heartbeat later. My arrow flew into the head of the wolf wounded by Snorri and Haaken's struck the rump of the second. The first wolf fell and tried to get up. The second hurled itself at Beorn who threw himself at the wolf with his spear held before him. The spear went down the open mouth of the wolf. The beast tried, even as it was mortally wounded to reach Beorn. Its dying teeth clamped onto Beorn's hand.

Cnut and Arturus joined their wounded companion and Cnut dropped his spear to prise apart the jaws before they stiffened in death. The three of us had each notched another arrow and we headed for the entrance to the cave. There was a howl which chilled my blood and then a huge male wolf flanked by two young wolves charged towards the nearest hunters, my son, Beorn and Cnut. The three of us let fly. I dropped my bow and drew Ragnar's Spirit even as the arrow was in the air.

My brave son stepped in front of the wounded Beorn and held his spear before him. I saw that he had braced the end against the rocks. One of the younger wolves had been struck by arrows and had turned his attention to Snorri. He raced towards him. Haaken desperately notched another arrow to loose it at the young wolf leaping at Cnut. I only had eyes for the enormous male wolf which was about to devour my son.

The wolf had tried to clamp his jaws around Arturus' head and his exposed chest struck my son's spear which drove deep into the beast. It missed his heart and the wolf's teeth snapped towards Arturus' head. He jerked it out of the way but the weight of the wolf and his motion made him overbalance and he fell backwards, the wolf's teeth sinking towards his unprotected throat.

Ragnar and my mother gave my legs added strength as I prayed for help. I swung my sword back as I flew over the ground. I struck with all of my might and the sword bit deeply into the back of the wolf's neck. My sword was sharp and the head was severed. I arrested my motion before my blade struck my son. The wolf's teeth had left a red mark on the throat of Arturus. Another heartbeat would have seen the end of my son.

We had no time for self-congratulation. Behind me, I heard howls as the rest of the pack emerged from the cave. Although five lay dead there were four females and three large cubs which charged from their lair. The winter had been good for them and they were not lean. They were muscled and they were savage. Snorri took out two cubs in two arrows. While Arturus struggled to his feet, Cnut stood before Beorn with his spear ready. Haaken, like me, had drawn his sword.

Two of the females leapt at me and Haaken at the same time. Out of the corner of my eye I saw Cnut spear a third female. As I slashed at the she wolf I saw, with sinking heart, the last female leap at a shaky Arturus. My brave boy had drawn his seax. My inattention meant I caught the wolf on its shoulder. It did not die immediately but, as it fell to my feet, the beast fastened its teeth around my ankle. I chopped off its head. Turning quickly I saw that Arturus had a hand beneath the throat of the she wolf while he was stabbing her in the side with his seax. I stabbed forward with Ragnar's Spirit and the tip went through its eye and into its brain. It shuddered and died.

And then it was over. The pack was dead. I was shaking. My son had nearly died twice and in those moments I had felt my world end. I lifted him to his feet. "Are you wounded or injured?"

He rubbed his neck and shook his head. Then he threw his arms around me, "You have saved my life…twice! I am your son by birth and now I am your oathsworn by choice."

I nodded. I was too upset for words. I saw Beorn rising. Cnut was tying a bandage around his left hand which had been savaged by the wolf.

Haaken said, "Anyone else hurt?"

We all shook our heads. Snorri said, "Haaken, come with me and we will see if any survived in the cave."

"Arturus are you able to fetch the ponies or do you need to rest?"

It was a test for my son. Was he a warrior? "I will go, Father." He looked at Beorn. "What of Beorn."

"Cnut and I will see to our friend." I smiled for my son had become a man in those few moments.

He disappeared down the path and I went to Beorn. Beorn was a little pale. "Thank you, Cnut, I owe you my life." He looked at his hand. Two of his fingers were mangled. He nodded at them. "They must come off, Dragon Heart."

"I know. Cnut, light a fire. Beorn, you had best sit down." As he sat down I took the skin I had with me. In it was the liquor of distilled mead. "Drink some of this."

"The cave is empty." Haaken and Snorri wandered over to us.

"He will have to lose some fingers. Begin to skin the wolves. It is getting late. We will need shelter and food."

When the fire was burning well I took my dagger and placed it into the fire which Cnut had started. It needed to be hot enough for the grim task ahead. We heard the whinny of the ponies as Arturus led the beasts, preceded by Wolf, up the path. Arturus took the ponies into the cave where there was a large pool of water and he took off their saddles and they drank.

Haaken had skinned the huge male wolf first. He did it well away from the nervous ponies. When he had finished, Haaken held up the skin of the beast slain by the two of us. The head was not attached but it was still a magnificent skin. "There, Arturus Wolf Killer, you now have your wolf skin. When you have passed the tests then you can join the Ulfheonar."

Cnut shook his head and pointed to the teeth marks on my son's neck. "When you are bitten by a wolf and do not die then you need no test. Arturus Wolf Killer is Ulfheonar. The wolves chose him."

It made sense to me. Haaken nodded. "You are right. Welcome to our ranks!" And so my son joined the Ulfheonar and was given his new name. Over the years it was shortened to Wolf or at least in the heat of battle men called out Wolf. The fact that the dog, when present, responded too never seemed to matter.

Arturus seemed quite touched by the gesture. I smiled at him. "Of course you will need a better sword. The seax is a fine weapon for a boy but a warrior needs a blade. We will see Bjorn Bagsecgson when we return." I turned to Beorn. "And now, my friend, let us see to you."

Haaken held his shoulders while Snorri held his maimed hand. Arturus just stared. He had never seen an amputation from close up. "Arturus have water ready." He went to the pool and brought a horn of water. It kept him occupied.

Cnut held a burning branch. He blew on the end to make it hotter. Beorn nodded. I took the red hot knife from the fire ignoring the heat from the bone handle. I sliced down and severed the little finger and the third finger as close to the palm as I could manage. As I drew back Cnut applied the burning brand and sealed the wound.

"Arturus, water!" As the stumps were doused I saw the relief on Beorn's face.

Haaken clapped him about the back and said, "Well Beorn Three Fingers, you and Wolf Killer here have given me a tale to tell. While we eat tonight I will compose."

We hacked one of the cubs into manageable pieces and roasted them over the fire. The cub meat was sweeter than the tougher, older meat of the larger wolves. We would take back the older carcasses for Windar's Mere and Cyninges-tūn. The meat would be cooked slowly. We had enough to feed both settlements for a week. The wolves may have killed many of our people but they would save the survivors. The Norns spun complicated webs!

As we ate in that huge cave Haaken composed his saga about the fight. We all helped for, when we returned to the hall then our people would wish to hear the tale. When we were satisfied we lay down on our cloaks. We had built a large fire and we would be warm.

"We have lost many fine warriors, Dragon Heart, in this harsh wolf winter."

"I know Haaken One Eye. We have also come closer to death this winter than I would have liked. We will need to raid and raid soon. Our people will starve else. I know that winter's icy hold still grips the land but we must go to Úlfarrston and see how our drekar have fared." Our boats had all been drawn out of the water and left close to the sea. The winter snows had cut us off. Even now the pass south was still treacherous but we would have to try it.

In the fire lit cave I heard Haaken chuckle. "Then let the sheep further south worry for the Ulfheonar now have another wolf and he has something to live up to."

I could not see his face but I knew that Arturus grew as the words were said.

Chapter 2

Windar and his people had been saddened by the deaths of Dargh and the farmers of Rye Dale. They accepted the wolf meat as weregeld for the deaths and Windar was determined to rebuild. "This is our land, Lord Dragon Heart and we will defend it; even from nature itself. We need those farms for food."

With leaders like Windar I knew that my people would survive no matter how severe the winters.

Erika had a mixture of concern and pride when she heard of Arturus and his brush with death. I smiled as I saw her examining the red puncture marks on his neck. She gave an accusing look at me before she said, "That is a sign, my son, that you need to take care. I am no longer around to watch over you as I once did."

Arturus had grown up over the winter and he detected the criticism in his mother's voice. He knew it was directed at me. "Father saved my life, twice!"

She was not mollified. "Perhaps had he not taken you then he would have had no need to!"

I had learned not to argue with my wife. You never won. Prince Butar had said much the same about my mother. "We will leave on the morrow with the shipwright to see how our drekar fare. We will need to raid sooner rather than later." I risked censure from Erika when I added, "Should I leave Arturus at home in case he slips on the ice?"

Laughing she said, "No, he had better be with you in case you slip, old man!"

Ragnar Bollison was our shipwright. He was an old man now but he had overseen the construction of all of our boats. He had been training his son Bolli Ragnarson to take over. The two of them would be able to tell us if the winter had damaged the ships.

Before I left I visited with Rolf. He was one of my most trusted jarls and had been badly wounded the previous year. His wounds meant that he would never fight for me again. His wounds had made him too slow; in battle it was the quick or the dead. I had worried about him during the winter as he had brooded about his two oathsworn who had died protecting his wounded body. Aiden, my Irish healer, had been looking after him. I found them in the small hall we had attached to the warrior hall. The two of them lived within.

Rolf, still suffering from the wound his leg had suffered, tried to rise. I waved him to his bed. "We go to the ships. Rolf, could I ask you to watch over our people while I am away. Aiden can aid you."

He smacked his injured leg. "And what use will I be? I cannot fight."

"No, but you can use your mind and that is a powerful weapon is it not Aiden?"

"It is, my lord." I saw that I had said the right thing for Aiden nodded. He had something of the second sight about him. I was convinced that he was some sort of Irish magician, a gladramenn. I was just grateful to have him as one of my followers.

"I want you to organise the warriors I will be leaving and train the new ones. We have lost Dargh and the men who defended Rye Dale. When I go raiding I will not have you by my side but I will sail happier if I know that you are here." He still looked doubtful. "Do you wish me to release you from your oath?"

Had I slapped him across the face I could not have had a more extreme reaction. "No, my lord! I beg you. My life is service to you. You took me from Frankia where I had no hope and gave me honour and a purpose. I will do as you ask. Please do not think to release me."

Aiden's smile confirmed that I had said the right thing.

We left before dawn. I hoped that we would be able to do some work before it became too dark. Ragnar Bollison and his son would need all the light we could get. We trudged down the valley. The sun would warm the land a little later but we found it slippery. We wore pieces of leather over our boots. The leather had iron studs in the body to give us grip but it was still a treacherous trail. When we passed

Backbarrow it began to get easier and we were all relieved when we saw the sea in the distance.

'*Wolf*' and the other drekar had been drawn up on the banks of the river. I left the men with Ragnar and his son while I took Arturus to meet with Pasgen, the headman of the nearby village.

Although they were not of our people the villagers had given their allegiance to me. I wondered how they had fared. This was not our first winter here and we were always surprised by the difference in the weather. Sometimes Úlfarrston had no snow at all. We were recognised as we walked up to the gates we had helped to build. Pasgen, the headman, came to speak with us as we entered.

"Lord Dragon Heart, we worried about you. This was a fierce winter. Even here we suffered with the snow."

I nodded, "I did wonder."

He took me into his hall. "The few ships which visited this winter told us of a terrible famine all over the Saxon kingdoms and in Hibernia."

I wondered how Jarl Erik, Erika's brother, had survived on Man, our former home. Many of his men had chosen me as a leader and there was little love lost between us now. "Did you have many deaths?"

"No, we were fortunate."

"We had many. It was not just the cold, we had an invasion of wolves."

"I am sorry."

"If any of your people arrive looking for homes then send them north. We need settlers."

"Of course. You will be looking to your ships I expect."

"My men are looking at them now to see what repairs we need."

"The river was frozen and we could not venture out to watch over them."

"I would not have expected you to. We will leave you now for I am anxious to know what work we need to do."

The sun had finally peered from behind the clouds as we headed up the river. Haaken and Cnut walked down to meet us. They both looked unhappy.

"Is there a problem?"

"Aye Dragon Heart, the hulls have the worm!"

The Norns were indeed mischievous. Arturus looked confused, "What is the worm?" I believe he thought it was some sort of dragon.

I smiled, "I am afraid it is a tiny creature which eats a ship from the bottom up. It means we have to build new ships." I looked up and saw Ragnar and Bolli coming towards us. "Tell me the worst."

He spread his arms and I could see that he was upset. The ships had been his babies. He had built them all. "The keels have gone on all of them." I nodded. "We can use the masts and the mast-fish. I think that two of the steer boards and two of the rudders can also be reused."

I had to make the best of it. "That is better than I could have hoped. Then we build two ships."

He brightened a little. I think he thought I would want all four replacing. "Just two?"

"Aye for you will just need two keels. The rest can be salvaged and that may be enough." I paused. "I would like at least one of them to carry seventy men. Can you build one that size?"

I saw the shock on the faces of Haaken and my Ulfheonar but Ragnar just stroked his beard. "If we can find an oak long enough then I will say aye."

I rubbed my hands together. "Then let us find an oak or two." He seemed happy and he gathered his tools. "One more question. How long will it take you?"

"If you give me twenty men I can have the first one ready in a month."

"Good then my new drekar will sail in a month and a day!"

Bolli threw me a shocked look but Ragnar just said. "We will make it happen, Jarl Dragon Heart, just so long as you allow me to name the ship."

This time it was my oathsworn's turn to look surprised. The naming of a ship was normally left to the leader. "Of course but satisfy my curiosity please, why?"

"I have now outlived all of those with whom I once sailed. I have outlived my ships. I will go to the Otherworld soon and this ship will live when I am gone. I would like to leave part of me in the vessel."

"Then you shall name it, Ragnar Bollison."

Snorri remembered a stand of oak trees and led us to them. Most were unsuitable, they had the girth but not the height. It was Haaken One Eye who spotted the ones that would be perfect. "There I can see two that appear to be straight enough and tall enough."

We eagerly hurried through the woods and found that my old friend was right. There were just two which were suitable. Haaken grinned at everyone. "I may only have one eye but at least it works!"

The axes were soon set to work on the two trees. Ragnar made sure that they cut them in the correct way so that they did not break on the way down. We held our breath as the first enormous oak came crashing to earth. The side branches broke on the way down but the mighty trunk was intact. The second fell in the same manner. As the branches were cut off I left them. "I will send the men from the hall to help you."

"Good. We will build shelters. If we are here for a month we would be dry at least."

"Good. I will be away for a month at least. I hope to see a drekar on the water when I return."

"And you shall. That I promise."

"Ulfheonar, we have a job to do."

I knew that they were all filled with curiosity as we headed north but I kept my own counsel. I would tell them when we reached my hall and not before.

After my spare warriors were sent south I sought my wife. "I will take Arturus and we will seek the treasure from the chest."

"I thought you had forgotten that."

"I had but Arturus reminded me."

She nodded, "The spirits must want you to have it then. How long will it take?"

I shrugged. "Two or three days to get there and two or three to get back."

"Then you had better hunt on the way back for the wolf meat will have disappeared by then."

"Of course."

I gathered the Ulfheonar around me. "We go north to the Roman Fort to find the treasure." That delighted them all, not least Arturus. "I will take just ten and the rest will stay here to guard my family and the settlement. We have sent many men to build our drekar."

They saw the wisdom in the decision but they did not approve. They all wished to come.

Later that night I took out the letter and map again.

I write this record knowing that my death is close at hand. I have served my masters well: I devoted my life to God, I helped King Coel and King Urien to protect the frontier and I kept alive the Roman ways. I have done my duty.

The barbarians are coming and I fear that the Warlord will not be able to hold them back forever. I believe with all my heart that there will come a hero as Lann of Stanwyck came from obscurity to hold back the Angles and the Saxons. It will not be in my lifetime.

To that end I have hidden the treasure of Rheged in the old Roman fortress of Luguvalium. The map will help someone to find it. I believe that God will direct some unborn hand to this end. I have buried it with St. Brigid's hand and ring as a way of telling the finder of the treasure. If the hand is not with this map then the barbarians have won and the treasure of Rheged is lost forever. The priests

*in this church know not what I do and when I
return north they will still be none the wiser.*

*The true hero will be from the same stock as Lann
of Stanwyck and, in him, is the hope for Britannia.*

I go to God with a clear conscience,

Osric of Rheged

The map would only help me when I found the Roman
fort. If truth be told it had been on my mind for some time.
This was a quest into the unknown. No-one had been further
north than the Grassy Mere. There were two passes further
north and our scouts had stopped at both of them. We would
be treading new paths.

As we climbed over the col at Rye Dale we saw Windar's
men already at work repairing the winter damage. We waved
as we headed into the unknown.

We had two ponies with our supplies. The Ulfheonar I
had chosen were Haaken, Cnut, Beorn Three Fingers, Snorri,
Harald Green Eye, Tostig, Erik the Tall, Thorkell the
Tall, Sigtrygg Thrandson and Arturus Wolf Killer. Arturus
was not yet a true Ulfheonar. We had not had the initiation
ceremony but I could not leave him at home. Sigtrygg was
the newest member of my oathsworn and he had been a
refugee from Audun'ston. His father had been headman and
he had died at the hands of the Saxons. His son wielded a
mighty sword called Saxon Killer and he was already held in
high esteem by my warriors.

We travelled the old Roman Road. It had fallen into
disrepair but we knew it would lead us to the Roman Fort we
sought. When we passed Grassy Mere we halted to view the
land to the south. "This would make a fine settlement."

"Aye Dragon Heart but for that we need more people."

Haaken laughed, "Well I am doing my best, Beorn Three
Fingers. I have one son already and my lady is with child

25

already. Dragon Heart here has sired two and another will be born before summer. It is about time you began to become a warrior in the bedroom too!"

Everyone laughed for Beorn was known to be shy around women.

"It is good to know that we have land and room to grow. It is why Prince Butar brought us west."

We dropped down the rise and headed north. "Aye, he would have loved this land."

Prince Butar had seen the land and knew that it promised much but he had been treacherously slain. I missed him still.

The land opened up and we saw the next hills rise like a wall in the distance. "Look my lord."

I followed Snorri's finger and saw, perched precariously on the sides of the hills little white dots. They were sheep and they had lambed. "You have good eyes Snorri. When we have this treasure we will gather those animals and begin to restock our fields."

We camped in a narrow valley with a small stream which bubbled close by. Snorri and Arturus went hunting while we made crude shelters and prepared food. The four pigeons augmented the stew of dried meat quite well. Thorkell the Tall found some wild garlic and thyme while Sigtrygg found some early mushrooms. We ate well. Normally we did not eat as well as this. I can still remember sucking on some dried meat for a whole day while at sea. We learned to take pleasure when we could.

Before we turned in for the night Haaken told some of the tales of Ulfheonar now dead. My dreams that night were of battles past and fallen brothers. It was a ritual which kept alive the dead.

We left the hills and headed across a fertile land. We became more wary for we could see in the distance the tell tale smoke rising from homes and farms. They were the first we had seen since leaving the Rye Dale. There were people. We knew not if they were hostile or friendly. Arturus sent Wolf ahead. He would alert us to any danger. We reached the settlement in the late afternoon. It straddled the road.

There was no palisade but it looked to have thirty or so huts.
I assumed our destination was beyond this. The Roman forts
we had seen had all been made of stone. They had ditches
and stood proud in the landscape. These were primitive huts.
Our halls were superior in every way.

"We will skirt the village."

"That will add time to our journey."

"You have somewhere else to go Arturus Wolf Killer?"

My son blushed and my men laughed. We used the
woods and hedges to move unseen around the village. When
we heard anyone we halted and so we reached the river
without being spotted. It was getting dark when we headed
east towards the fort we assumed would be close to the river.
Aiden had spent some time studying the maps we had found
and he had given me a good idea of where we might find the
fort.

Knowing that the village was less than two miles away
we camped without a fire close to the river. It was a damp
cold night and none of us slept well. When we rose we found
a misty morning. We could not even see the river which we
knew was but twenty paces to our right.

We made our way along the river bank with drawn
weapons. We sought stone. Stone meant Rome and Rome
meant the fort was not far away. It was Wolf who found it.
He ran back to Arturus and he led us to the stone wall which
went from the half destroyed bridge to the gate of the fort. It
was obvious that this had seen battles. The marks of
weapons still scored the walls. I took out the map. The river
and the bridge were marked. I waved us forward. Haaken
and Cnut brought up the rear while Snorri and Sigtrygg led
the way.

The gates were torn from their mountings and lay
discarded in the ditch. Inside we could see that many of the
stones had been looted but the buildings still retained their
shape. I pointed to a building. "That looks like it. Two of
you watch this gate and another two the far gate." I knew all
would wish to be there when we uncovered this treasure but
they obeyed.

The room we sought was a side one off from a large room. Having found the hidden door in the chapel before we knew what we were looking for. There was a stone in the floor of the room with a dirty line towards one end. I gave the map to my son and knelt down. Taking my dagger out, I scraped away the dirt and dust of ages and found the metal handle which I prised up. It resisted but after some gentle coaxing popped up. I sheathed my dagger and took hold of the metal. I pulled. Haaken and Cnut put their daggers under the sides and slowly but surely the stone began to rise.

When the stone was removed we saw a black hole. Once again we remembered the chapel and I put my hand into the void. I felt around until I found a chest. This was a larger one that the one we had found in the church. I needed two hands to raise it. It felt much heavier too and I struggled to lift it. Cnut aided me and the well made chest was carefully hoisted from its tomb.

I tried the top and it was locked. I lay down again and felt around. I felt nothing for a while and then, suddenly my fingers brushed something small and hard. I put my hand around and pulled it out. Regardless of what we found in the chest what I held in my hands was a worthy treasure. It was the scabbard of a sword and it was exquisitely decorated. What made the hairs on the back of my neck stand on end was the decoration. It was the same as that on the sword we had found in the land of the Cymri. This was the scabbard for the sword we had found in the cave!

"Replace the stone. I would not have these people know that there may be such treasures here."

Chapter 3

"Someone is coming- at the southern gate!"

Tostig's urgent call meant we would have to wait to open the chest. "Let us move!"

We sped back across the parade ground to the northern gate and fled back to the river. Pausing only to fasten the chest securely to the back of one of the beasts we moved swiftly east. I had no idea if the people hereabouts were friendly or not. I assumed they would be as we would be and '*act first, ask questions second*'.

"Snorri take the rear. Beorn and Arturus take the point."

I was pleased to see that every warrior had a weapon in his hand. I led one of the ponies while Cnut led the other. We had no armour with us and just four shields on the ponies. If this came to fighting then we would have to rely on bows and swords. We made our way back around the settlement. Each step brought us closer to safety and, ironically, closer to the danger. I would not be happy until we saw the hills of our home. This flat land was dangerous.

We reached our camp from the previous night before dark. This time we did not just slump down and relax. Thorkell the Tall and Tostig went back up the Roman Road and laid some traps. They were simple alarms but they would alert us to an enemy. While Haaken prepared some food, albeit cold, the rest of us rigged deadfalls and trips amongst the bushes. Again they would not stop anyone but we would know of their presence.

When I was satisfied we went to the cold camp and ate our wild garlic and dried wolf. It was not very appetising but it filled a hole, as my mother might have said. The nearby stream provided water which was refreshing if a little metallic in taste. The rest of my men all stared at the box while Arturus admired the scabbard.

"This is *wyrd* father. How did the Romans have the scabbard?"

"They may not have done. The man who wrote on the parchment talked of a Lord Lann and that does not sound

Roman. We will have to speak with Deidra and Macha when we return home. They may be able to shed light. I am pleased now that Bjorn Bagsecgson has repaired the blade and I am even more determined now to discover the stones to complete its renovation."

"Are you not going to open the chest, Dragon Heart?"

"No, Haaken. It is secure now and we may have to move quickly. We have waited long enough to find the chest, a couple more days will not hurt." I smiled for Haaken was just desperate to conjure another story from the myth of the sword and the scabbard. He hoped there would be another treasure within the chest which would astound his listeners. He revelled in the gasps of awe when he told his stories and revealed secrets hidden for years.

"We watch tonight. Two men on and eight off. One hour and we change."

It was a tried and trusted method. Aiden had taught us all how to count to four thousand we estimated that to be an hour. It meant we all got some sleep and those awake had something to keep themselves occupied as they counted. It did not matter if we made a mistake so long as we reached four or five thousand.

Arturus and I were woken by Haaken and Cnut. I had said we would take the middle watch. It meant the least sleep but it was my way. I would not shirk a duty and nor would my son. We also had the advantage that Wolf watched with us and his ears were worth two men at least.

Arturus went to speak and I put my finger to my lips. There were two reasons: one I did not want to disturb the sleep of my comrades and secondly it prevented you hearing the night. I listened to the movement of small animals through the undergrowth. The swoop of an owl as it plucked a mouse from the ground. The snuffling of a hedgehog as it ate its way through the slugs and snails. They were all comforting sounds in the night. And then came the most deadly of sounds, silence. It was followed by confirmation; a low almost imperceptible growl from Wolf. There were humans and they were close.

I tapped Arturus on the shoulder and drew my sword silently. I gestured to the ponies. He would secure and then saddle them. I shook Haaken and Cnut. Having just been on duty they would know it was danger. I then walked to the road and listened. The silence was too complete. Someone was out there. I heard the noise of a branch trap being released. There was a slight groan. They were to the east of us.

My Ulfheonar were awake and armed. I glanced around and saw that Arturus had saddled one pony and fitted the chest. He was working on the second. Wolf suddenly darted forward and disappeared. I heard a cry as he sank his teeth into the leg of an intruder.

We remained still. The night visitors realised that they had been spotted and they burst towards us. Our stillness meant that we were invisible. I saw a half naked warrior with spiky hair and a spear charge into the camp. I crouched and swept my sword horizontally. It ripped open his naked middle and he fell dead at my feet. I heard cries from my right as my men killed and wounded others but I kept my eyes to the front. Another warrior, this time with a shield and a small war axe lunged at me. I grabbed the haft of his axe as it plunged towards my head and pulled him off balance. I thrust the tip of my sword under his arm and it emerged at his neck. And then there was silence or almost silence for I could hear the death rattle from some of those who had not gone to the Otherworld straight away.

I spun around and counted my men. "Arturus the pony with the chest. Tostig, the other pony. Snorri, scout. Head south."

With those three away to safety we checked who we had been fighting. They were not Saxons. Their weapons were crudely made and they had no armour. Sigtrygg said, "They are from the north. These are the ones they call Picts or perhaps from Dál Raida. They are savages."

"They are dead savages now."

"I think we have accounted for them all let us go."

We moved quickly until we caught up with the others. Dawn saw us amongst the hills. Cnut was not happy that we were taking the road. "We might as well have drawn a map for them to follow."

Haaken shook his head, "How do you know that we are being followed?"

"We killed too many back there. They will want to avenge their dead."

"Cnut is right and besides we can use this opportunity to see more parts of this land. We will head south west towards those high peaks. Unless I miss my guess it will bring us out close to Lang's Dale."

I was their jarl and they obeyed. We left the road and Snorri disguised our path. The going was no different for a while. We were travelling along the flat lands of a river bottom but then we began to climb. Our journey became more difficult. It was little more than a sheep's track we followed but it wound in the direction we wanted. We saw a huge body of water below us. It was almost as big as Windar's Mere. This land was a land of mountains and water. As we climbed we saw, far behind, the Roman Road and, to my dismay, warriors upon it. There appeared to be twenty or so and they had two horses.

I was not certain if we had been seen and so I ordered the men to drop down from the skyline. Our pace was more urgent now; we needed to hurry. Had we not been Ulfheonar I am not sure that we would have made it. The land became wilder and wilder. There were few trees. If someone could get above us then we would have no place to hide. We ascended a ridge and saw before us the most beautiful mere I have ever seen. The mountains along the side reminded me of the Old Man who watched over Cyninges-tūn but that was not what made me stop and start. The reflection of the mountains in the water and the sun dipping in the west made it look like my step father.

"Look yonder men, it is Butar's Mere."

Strangely that gave us all hope. Butar would watch over us. When we dropped down the next ridge and the mere was hidden from view I stopped. "Enough. We are Ulfheonar. We will wait here and destroy these barbarians. I have run enough."

The smiles on my warrior's faces told me I had made the correct decision. Snorri grinned, "I am the youngest. I will run back and scout them out. They may have given up."

Arturus said, "No, I am the youngest so I will come with you!" I was as proud of my son that day as any day.

They disappeared and Haaken went to the saddle bags. "Then let us eat while we may."

We prepared for battle. I took the whetstone and put an edge on Ragnar's Spirit. It had tasted blood already and would not be as sharp as it had been. I did the same with my dagger.

Haaken brought over some food for us. It was still the cold, dried wolf meat and we all chewed to make our bodies think they were being fed something which was worth eating. It also gave us something to do. Before we fought we each had an energy within which needed an outlet.

"Tostig, take the ponies a little lower down the slope and tether them. I do not want them to run when the fighting begins."

As he did so Cnut pointed to a tumble of rocks close to the top of the ridge. We had passed beneath them when we had crested the rise. "That would make a good place for an ambush."

"Aye it would. Haaken and Tostig can be here with me. The rest hide in the rocks with Cnut. When they reach the top they will see the three of us and think we are easy prey."

I knew they would not like to see me tethered like a goat but I was jarl. Tostig returned and stood with Haaken and me as the rest hid themselves in the rocks. Those with bows and spears readied them.

Snorri and Arturus burst over the ridge. "They are behind us. There are two warriors on horses. They both have helmets, shields and spears. There are twenty warriors with them."

"Good. Go to the rocks with the others. Cnut commands."

Arturus looked as though he would argue. Snorri patted him on the back. "Come, scout, and bring your dog. We obey the jarl."

They disappeared in the rocks. I knew where they were but I could not see them. Our pursuers would have the same problem.

The two horsemen appeared on the ridge which soon filled with the barbarians. The horses were really large ponies and the warrior's feet almost touched the ground. The leader shouted something in a language I had never heard. It did not matter what he said. I knew what he would do. He would charge us hoping that the three of us would flinch at a pair of armed horsemen. His men would follow ready to finish off any survivors.

I had chosen the spot we were on because it was flat. The slope before us was steep. The horses would be going too fast for the riders to control and the warriors would be running down a steep slope too. That worked in our favour.

I saw the leader raise his sword and the warriors roared. They charged. The horses soon outstripped the men and I saw that the two warriors were struggling to slow down their horses. Behind them Cnut and my warriors began to rain death on the unsuspecting half naked men.

One of the horsemen heard the scream of a dying warrior behind him and made the mistake of turning his head. As his horse veered off course he fell to the ground and rolled towards us. Haaken stepped towards him and his sword took his head. The leader dragged his reins so that his horse was aimed at me. I gambled on the horse wishing to avoid me. I saw its head move slightly to my right and so I stepped to the left. Although the leader had a shield I had Ragnar's Spirit. I swung it horizontally. It struck the shield and bit into the wood. The planks of the shield shivered and split and the sword continued along to rip into his arm. As he leaned away from the blow he fell from the horse. Even though he was wearing a helmet, the rock into which he fell was harder and his skull was crushed.

I heard a cheer behind me and saw that the small warband had been slaughtered. Arturus had his sword raised in the air and I saw the blood. My son had killed his first warrior. He was a man and he was now Ulfheonar.

The two horses were a valuable addition to our herd. The weapons were poor quality but we took them for Bjorn our smith could use them to make nails and farm tools. Some might even make bosses for shields. Our detour meant that we struggled to make it back to Cyninges-tūn before dark. As I had anticipated our journey took us through Lang's Dale. His home was no longer cheery. It was an empty and cold house but we stayed there anyway. We had ever been a friend to Lang and his family. Their spirits would protect us.

We reached our home on the morrow. As we trekked the last mile or so from the boggy tarns Haaken reminded me of the animals we had seen on the fells.

"I know, my friend, and I would have you take some men to round them up. The Allfather knows that we will need them."

As we entered the stockade my own words were visible in the thin gaunt faces of those within. Even Erik and Kara looked undernourished. I should have known that my wife would share the little extra we had with those who did not. Apart from the ponies, poor weapons and the chest, we came back empty handed.

The warm greeting from my wife and daughter made me feel even guiltier. I was the leader and it was my duty to provide for my people.

"Well what was this treasure?"

"It is in the warrior hall. I wanted my Ulfheonar to be there when we opened it. Arturus fetch the sword."

We left for the warrior hall and my Ulfheonar stood expectantly around the long table upon which sat the scabbard and the chest. "Send for Bjorn and Aiden. They helped to make the sword that was broken whole again. They should be here to see it complete."

I waited until all were present. Each of them had played their part in the acquisition of the treasure. "Arturus, the sword."

He handed me the weapon. It would never be used for war again but it still looked magnificent. It looked like no other blade I had ever seen and Bjorn Bagsecgson had told me that it was ancient, even beyond the times of the Romans. When I slid it into its scabbard the sound it made seemed like a sigh. My blacksmith touched the hammer amulet he wore around his neck. When metal spoke it was the word of the gods.

"Now the sword is complete!"

I handed it to Arturus who raised it. He passed it to Bjorn and then Aiden. Finally it was passed around all of the Ulfheonar until it returned to me. The circle was complete and I laid it upon the table. I turned the chest around. There was a lock. "Shall we unpick it, Aiden?"

I asked the question of my mystic who grinned and like a magician produced a key from his tunic. The key was new.

"How?"

He said, "Wait, my lord, until we see if it works then I will explain my magic."

He put the key into the lock and began to turn. There was some resistance and he retrieved the key and took out a small file. He rubbed it along the edge and replaced it into the lock. He looked more nervous, "Perhaps I am not the magician I think I am." This time, when he turned the key, there was a reassuring click as the lock was opened. Everyone looked at him. He smiled, with relief this time, "I took the lock of the other chest apart and reasoned that whoever had the original key might have used the same key for two chests. I made a key. It opened the other chest and I prayed that it would open this one. It did."

I clapped him on his back. "You are still a magician!"

Every one held their breath as I slowly opened the lid. Kara and her mother sighed with disappointment when they saw the parchments on the top. The rest of us smiled for we knew its weight and we remembered that the parchment in the previous chest had hidden treasures beneath the dusty documents. I handed the writing to Aiden. Beneath them lay two leather bags. I could see that the leather was of the finest quality and appeared not to have suffered during its burial. I lifted one out and untied the leather thong. I poured a pile of golden coins upon the table.

There was a collective gasp as the gold glittered in the firelight. I picked one up. It had the face of a man upon it and I recognised it as a coin similar to the ones we had earlier found. "These are Roman!"

Erika took it from me. "These will prevent our people starving!"

I had thought to buy better weapons but I supposed that we could compromise. I lifted the second bag. This one felt lighter and not as uniform. When I untied the thong jewels dropped out and spilled across the table. There were rubies and emeralds and white stones I had not seen before.

Bjorn Bagsecgson suddenly grabbed one and held it up triumphantly. "It is the missing stone from the sword! The sword can be complete!" He put the stone in the hole at the crosspiece. It was a perfect fit.

Aiden picked up a small gold coin. "And I can use this coin to make a golden mount; it shall not fall again!"

For the first time in a long time I felt that our luck had changed. We had come through the winter feeling as though we had made a mistake. People had died and we were suffering. Our ships had been eaten and our animals had died. In this one stroke we had reversed that luck. Our lives would get better.

Little did we know of the webs the sisters were spinning and the plans they had for all of us.

Chapter 4

Arturus was now an Ulfheonar. We held the ceremony in the dark of night and he donned his new wolf cloak. Haaken pointed out that it would be better had he allowed it to season but my son was young enough to have no patience at all! He and the rest of my men went to collect the animals we had seen on the fells. He proudly told all who would listen that he was now Wolf Killer, son of Dragon Heart!

Aiden and I trekked down to Ragnar Bollison to see the progress on the ship. It had been six days and, although I knew it would be a skeleton yet I was anxious to examine it. Aiden brought with him the parchments. He had looked at them briefly but we both knew they would need a closer examination. I was proud enough not to want too many of my people seeing how I struggled to read. Aiden would not be critical of me. We had both had lessons from the sisters of the White Christ. I had given up but he had persevered. I also wished to speak with Pasgen. The small trading ship we had given him still floated and had been a winter lifeline for the small settlement. I hoped for news of the outside world.

As I walked with Aiden I saw how much he had grown. Unlike Arturus he had not broadened out. He was still slender of build for he did not spend the hours with a sword and shield as my son did. "Are you happy with us, Aiden?"

He looked at me as though he did not understand the question. "Happy, my lord?"

"We are not of your people. Do you regret your decision to leave Hibernia?"

He laughed, "You are my people now, Lord Dragon Heart. Here I am respected, honoured even. The mighty Bjorn consults me on the art of smithing. I am more than happy. I would never wish to leave your service."

I disliked the word service; it seemed barely a hand span away from slave. "You do not serve me, Aiden. I hope you realise that. You may leave at any time and I pay for the work you do."

He thought he had offended me. "Oh no my lord. I mean no disrespect to you."

That was better. "You are like a son to me Aiden and I hope that you know that. The Lady Erika also values you and your contribution to the life at Cyninges-tūn."

"I know and I would do anything for her."

"Good. Now have you examined those parchments?"

"Briefly. I think, my lord, that they are more valuable than the gold and the jewels we found."

He amazed me and I stopped. "You jest! How can that be?"

"There are maps; not just of Britannia but lands further afield. There is a map of the Empire of Rome, that which is called Byzantium."

"And Miklagård?" He nodded. "I have been told that the streets are paved with gold so you may be right about the value of these writings. What else is there?"

"The others will need more work, my lord. There are many words I do not know and I will need to ask Macha and Deidra what they mean. And there are other writings. It will take me some time to decipher and understand them all. I think, amongst them are plans and instructions for making weapons."

"Truly?"

"Truly."

"Then you may be right and you should guard them well. Keep them about you at all times."

He patted his leather satchel which he had made. It contained all that he needed to work gold and to heal those who were ill. His skills there were improving. "They are with me always."

When we reached the river I was astounded at the progress. "Ragnar, you have worked wonders!" He nodded, obviously proud. "Come and tell me what you have done." I had seen ships built from a distance before but I had never been this close to the actual construction.

He led me down to the hull. "We began with the large piece of oak we felled." He nodded and patted it as though it

was a pet animal. "It is a fine piece of wood. It told me how
to carve its shape. It is one reason we have been so swift.
When a tree talks to you then you know the vessel will be
sound. The stem and the stern were joined and they fitted
well. We had enough straight pieces from the same tree to
make the strakes." He stroked the wooden hull. "That too is
important. All of the hull will come from the same tree. She
will serve you well. We now attach the ribs. It is vital that
we do that carefully for they give the strength to the whole
ship."

He suddenly began to cough and he held a cloth to his
mouth. When it came away I saw that there was blood on it.
"You have worked too hard! Rest! A few days longer will
not hurt the ship."

He shook his head as he drew me away from his son and
the other workers. He said quietly, "You do not understand,
my lord. When I said this would be my last ship it is because
I will soon be in the Otherworld." He nodded to Aiden who
was watching us. "I have seen the volva and Aiden. They
know that my time is coming to an end. I hurry not for you,
my lord, but for me. I must see this ship launched and then I
can die in peace. Do not tell my son. He will worry. His
mother died two seasons ago and I am all that is left. I leave
him my skills. He will build you good ships, my lord." He
suddenly smiled, "But this one will be the best!"

"You are a good man, Ragnar Bollison."

"I have tried to be and to live up to Prince Butar's
standards. We are all merely men and we sometimes fail."
He hesitated, "My son will work for you when I am gone?"

"I promise that he will be my ship builder."

He seemed to cheer up and returned to watch his workers
as the ribs and their cleats were hammered into place. I
joined Aiden at the bow. I ran my hand over the wood which
had been smoothed so that it felt like skin. "Is there no hope
for him?"

Aiden shook his head, "I am learning how to heal but his
cough has become worse. He has become thinner and each

day there is more blood. He is racing death to see if he can finish the ship. If he does then he will have won."

"Is there anything which we can do to make life easier for him?"

"You have done that lord. His spirit will be in this ship and so long as this ship floats then he will live."

I watched my ship builder wander off. There was a little more bounce to his step. He picked up an adze and a breast augur. He stood looking at the piece of oak which had been roughly shaped already. I knew what he was doing, he was carving the most import part of the ship; the dragon prow. As the master builder of this ship, no-one, not even his own son, would be allowed to carve this vital piece of wood. I stood with Aiden; both of us were fascinated by his skill. He already had his chisels there. He used the adze to shape and smooth the wood a little more. The hole into which it would fit was equally smooth. Satisfied he picked up the breast augur. He drilled a hole through the wood he had just shaped. The spirals of oak which emerged looked like brown worms.

He stood back and looked at the wood. It was beautifully shaped but the part which would be the head was just a shapeless blob. He sighed and, taking his mallet and his chisel he began to chip off pieces of wood. He suddenly stopped and looked at us.

"My lord, it will bring bad luck if you see the prow before it is finished. I promise you that you shall be the first to see it."

"I understand, Ragnar. I was just fascinated by the process."

"Then when I am gone you can watch my son. He is a fine craftsman."

We left and walked along the river to the village. The sentries bowed as we entered. Pasgen was in the warrior hall speaking with someone. Aiden and I waited at the door. It would have been rude to interrupt. "No, Lord Dragon Heart. This concerns you. Come."

I was intrigued. As we approached I could see, from his attire, that the man was a seafarer. He nodded as we sat down.

"This is Captain Griffith Ap Llewellyn. His ship is out in the bay. He began to trade with us at the end of last year and he always brings useful news."

"I am Dragon Heart of Cyninges-tūn. I am pleased to speak with a sailor who has travelled the world."

He spoke and I struggled to understand him for he spoke with a thick accent. "There were times when I would have fled from such as you, a wolf of the sea but Pasgen here assures me that you do not prey on ships. I hope that is true else I may be consigning some of my friends to your clutches."

"You have my word that I have never raided a ship at sea in my life." I smiled, "I have, however, raided the land of the Cymri."

He laughed, "Pasgen said that you were honest. Well I have just told the headman of a disease which is sweeping through Northumbria and Mercia. They call if the coughing disease. Those who die from it become very hot. They cough and they sneeze. They are unable to eat and they die. The gods must favour some for there are some people who manage to survive. The followers of the White Christ say it is a punishment from God for their sins." He shook his head, "No offence but I would have thought that he would have inflicted such a curse on your people who do not follow the White Christ."

"As would I. Thank you for that information. We will bear it in mind. Do they have the disease in Cymru and Hibernia?"

He shook his head, "I did not hear of it when I visited those lands."

"Thank you. And Man, what do you hear of Man?"

"They do not have the disease."

"And how do the people fare?"

"We do not trade with them. Some ships were robbed who went there for honest trade. I heard that some crews were killed. I do not risk my ship."

"We have goods we would trade with you. Do you trade with Frankia?"

"We have done in the past but there is much discord in the land now. The Emperor Charlemagne is tightening his grip on the land. We have not visited there for some time."

"Does gold still trade well?"

He looked suddenly interested. "All men are interested in gold. You have some?"

"Let us say we have acquired some wealth and we wish to use it in trade."

"In that case let me know what you need and we can come to an arrangement."

"Food."

He sank back into his seat and shook his head. "Food is more valuable than gold at the moment. The fierce winter and the disease mean that many people are suffering. Those who follow the old ways say it is because many people are converting to the White Christ and the gods do not like it."

It always astounded me that people ascribed such disasters to a change in religion. Did they not know it was just the Norns. The Weird Sisters toyed with men as children sometimes did with spiders and small animals. You could do little about it, it was just wyrd.

"If you could get hold of food or animals then we will pay you a fair price."

He nodded. "Perhaps I should not be telling you this, but the Hibernians were spared the worst of the weather and their flocks look to have increased. But I will do as you ask and seek food. If I can get some…"

"Then deliver it to the headman here and he will pay you."

He suddenly looked at Pasgen, "You have gold too?"

I laughed, "He will when I give him some."

I now had even more to worry about. I had planned a raid on the Northumbrians and the Mercians. Both were short journeys and would have meant we were away for a few days. Hibernia was a poorer country and we would have to travel further inland to achieve what we wanted. It was then I wondered about our change of fortune.

Aiden and I journeyed back to Cyninges-tūn. It would do no good to be looking over Ragnar's shoulder. I knew he was doing the best he could. His news had disturbed me. The older skilled men of the village would all need replacing. What of Bjorn our smith? It was not just warriors who had to be trained. I determined to speak with Erika. She was wise and would know what to do.

It was too late when we returned and I waited until the following morning. It was the first morning that the sun felt a little warm and I led her down to the Water. It was so still and flat that you felt as though you could walk upon it. A male duck quacked his way after a female. It was a sign of spring; the animals were returning.

I told her of Ragnar and his premonition. "He is old but I am sad that he will die. We need men such as him."

"I know. How can we encourage them?"

She gestured behind her with her head. "The gods and your ancestor have put the means in your grasp."

"How?"

"The gold and the jewels; we can pay for skilled men to come to the village and to work. You could visit places where there are such men and encourage them to come here."

I grabbed her and hugged her. "I do not know what I would do without you."

As she pulled away she said, cheekily, "And do not even think of doing so."

She was not surprised when I told her of her brother and what he was doing on Man. She was just disappointed. "I can now see the effect Prince Butar and you had upon him. You brought out the best in him. The shrill harpy he is with brings out the worst."

"And you bring out the best in me."

My men returned two days later. They had done well and Wolf had earned his food. They had over sixty sheep, including twenty lambs. There were four cows and a very young bull. He had been attacked by a wolf and we could see the wound on his leg. Aiden laughed when we showed our concern. "He does not need his leg to be able to make cattle for us. I can heal the wound. He will limp but the cows will not mind that!"

We divided the sheep into three flocks. I sent a message to Windar to come and fetch his flock and we drove the third flock to the western settlement. We kept the cows. When Windar came we would tell him how to increase his own animals. With the horses we had captured we were now more mobile.

I spent some time with Haaken, Cnut and Aiden. We pored over the maps which Aiden had found. He was able to interpret and read them. More importantly he was able to explain them to my two friends who could not read. Haaken became quite excited when he saw the map of the Middle Sea. "There will be real treasure there, Dragon Heart. They would not be the poor Hibernians."

I shook my head, "I would not wish to be away from my family for such a long time."

He looked disappointed, "But we would be away from our families too."

I laughed, "The difference is I do not want to be away and I think that you do. You have an eye for the ladies."

He laughed too and tapped his dead eye, "Thank the Allfather it is not this one then!"

I left it another four days before I returned to Úlfarrston and the new ship. They had worked hard. The keelson and the crossbeams had been fitted. Bolli Ragnarson strode over to me. He looked pleased. "We have done well, my lord. We are about to fit the mast fish. Within a week we will be ready to try her in the water."

I clapped him on the back. "You have worked wonders. Where is your father?"

His face darkened a little. "He looked tired and I told him to take a rest."

"Good. I think he must." His eyes searched my face for the hint that I knew anything more. I owed it to Ragnar to keep a neutral expression. "I will seek his company." Aiden followed me as we went to the far side of the construction site that had been a beach. There was a tree and behind it I could see the crouched back of my shipwright. We heard the sound of a mallet on a chisel and saw the familiar twirls of oak.

I called, "Ragnar, may we approach?"

I heard a chuckle followed by a cough. "You have good timing my lord, I have just finished. Come."

We walked around and saw that he had managed to cover the prow with his cloak. He stood and stretched his back. He looked thinner than he had before. He had a sparkle in his eyes as he turned to face me. "This is the finest prow I have ever made. I need to paint it yet but it is finished otherwise and I would have you see it."

He twirled the cloak and revealed the dragon carving. It was magnificent. There were two teeth protruding from a mouth and a forked tongue darting out. The eyes were enormous and it appeared to have a bosom like a woman. "It is perfect!"

"Not yet, my lord. When I have painted it you will see the effect I have striven for."

"You have made it look like a woman?"

He shook his head. "If so she only has one breast." He began to laugh but it turned into a bloody cough.

Aiden reached into his satchel. He took out a small skin and said, "Drink this. It will ease your pain."

Ragnar did so and he actually smiled when he handed it back to Aiden. Aiden shook his head, "Keep it and take a small amount when you feel the pain but I must warn you, it will make you sleepy."

"Thank you, gladramenn. I will save the remainder for the nights." He patted the chest. "I have not made a woman I have made a heart. I have made a heart for your new ship, '*The Heart of the Dragon*'."

Two days before the ship was due to be tried on the water a rider galloped in. "My lord, Bolli Ragnarson says you must come quickly and bring the gladramenn with you. His father is ill!"

Aiden and I had expected this and we rode as though our lives depended upon it. The sound of work was absent from the shipyard and the warriors and workers were gathered around a shelter thrown up between two trees. Bolli jumped to his feet and ran from his father's side when he saw us.

"Thank the Allfather you came so quickly! My father is ill."

I nodded to Aiden who went to Ragnar's side. "Your father is dying." He looked at me blankly as though I was speaking a foreign language. I nodded. "He told me so. It is why he said this would be his last ship. It is finished is it not?"

He nodded and I could see him welling with emotion. "He is going to the Otherworld and he will find great honour there for your father has skills of which Odin himself would be proud. Let us go to him."

I put my arm around him and we went to the old man. He was smiling. Bolli said, "He is better! You are truly gifted, Aiden."

"No, my friend, I have eased his pain. He will feel nothing but the end is near. Say what you must for there is little time."

He knelt down and Ragnar said, "My son, I am proud of you. You will build great ships and I will watch from the Otherworld. Grieve not for me. I go to join your mother, Prince Butar and Olaf the Toothless. Serve the Jarl well for he is the hope for our people." Bolli nodded. I could see the tears coursing down his cheeks. "Jarl."

I knelt and took his other hand. "I have a boon. After my body has been burned I wish my ashes to be scattered in the bottom of the ship. When '*The Heart of the Dragon*' sails I will be there in the ship."

"I will be honoured to sail with you."

He looked beyond me. "Your magic is strong Hibernian. I feel sleepy now. I will just close my eyes."

We remained silent. Gradually I felt his fingers slacken on my hand. Bolli looked at me, his eyes wide. I nodded. "He has gone, Bolli Ragnarson. Your father is now in the Otherworld." I stood and placed his hand on his chest. I waved my arms for the workers to move away. Bolli needed to say goodbye to his father in his own way.

Chapter 5

The launching ceremony was an emotional experience for all. The finished ship waited for the rising tide and Bolli's workers held the ropes taut. They would pull the blocks securing the ship away and it would float into the river. Bolli and I were the only ones aboard. My family and the Ulfheonar watched, along with Pasgen, from the bank. The ashes of his father had been spread along the hull before the pine deck had been fitted. The ship was complete save that the mast had to be raised. It lay now on the mast fish. Bolli and I stood at the stern watching the rising waters.

"This is good, Lord Dragon Heart. When he first left us I was sad but now that I stand here on the last ship he built I can feel his spirit in the wood." He stroked the steer board. "He made this for *'Wolf'* and that is good too for it will remember how to sail and your touch. It is a good day."

I looked at the shipwright. "And it is sad too, Bolli Ragnarson, for the ship will be leaving the land."

"But you will care for the ship as my father cares for you. I will make another ship and that will have some of me within it."

"Good! Do not let your father's skills die."

We felt a slight movement and Bolli nodded. "It is time my lord."

"This is my ship built by Ragnar Bollison and we name her *'The Heart of the Dragon'*."

Bolli waved his arm and his men pulled and strained as the blocks of wood supporting the side slid away. Suddenly the whole ship slipped alarmingly. We had been prepared and we held the steer board but even so the water of the river seemed too close to the side for comfort.

Bolli smiled at my reaction. "Fear not, Lord Dragon Heart, it is always so. She teases us. She will right herself."

He was correct and we swung the other way. She floated. There was a huge cheer from the shore. I turned and waved to Magnus Larsson my ship man and he ordered the men to haul us back towards the shore. We could prepare the drekar for sea!

It took four days to fit her out completely. She needed some ballast in the bottom and her mast stepping. The sail took half a day to fit. The shrouds, stays and sheets had to be well fitted and Bolli took his time. Magnus, who would watch over the ship when I was ashore, watched every action with the eyes of a mother observing her child's first steps. *'Heart'*, as she became known, was different to *'Wolf'*. She did not use rowlocks but had holes in the strake below the sheerstrake. While the stores were brought on board my Ulfheonar fitted the oars and we practised removing them. It would be something we would have to get used to. Finally the crew brought aboard their chests and placed them next to the oars. They would be their seats for the next month.

As Haaken and Cnut organised the warriors who would be coming with us I returned to the land. Pasgen, Jarl Rolf and Erika waited for me. "We are almost ready."

Rolf looked wistfully at the new ship. "I wish I was going with you, my lord."

"Aye but I am happy that you will be here to watch over my family. I know that they will be safe."

He gave a slight bow. "I will protect your family with my life, Jarl Dagon Heart."

Erika pointed to the carved prow. Now that it was fitted it looked magnificent. Ragnar had painted a red heart upon the dragon's chest and its tongue was bright yellow. He had carved scales into the wood and painted them so that they made the dragon look alive. It was, however, the eyes which drew your attention for they were so realistic that you would swear they followed you. "That is the finest prow I have ever seen. I am happy for Ragnar Bollison and his dragon will guard you while you hunt." She kissed me gently on the cheek. "Come back to us safely."

"I will. Do you return home tonight?"

"No, Pasgen and his people have offered us their hospitality and a feast."

"That is good of you, headman."

"Our women are keen to speak with the Lady Erika; she has travelled and they have not."

That pleased me for I knew that my wife missed the company of other women. She smiled, "And when you return you may have another son."

"Or daughter. It matters not to me."

She laughed, "You lie well, my husband, as do all men!"

Magnus shouted, "My lord, the tide!"

I waved, "Farewell. We will be back in a month at the most."

"Do not worry about us. Now that we have animals the people will eat and we can fish. May the Allfather watch over you!"

As we edged slowly south I felt as happy as I had ever felt. I had a new and well made ship. I had the finest crew a jarl could have and I had a home which was safe. I edged the steer board a little to the west and Arturus and I waved at our family. We heard Wolf barking. He did not like to be left behind. As the men got into the rhythm we picked up speed and our ship fairly flew across the water. I knew that Cnut and the men were showing off for those watching. He had a faster beat than he would normally use. I did not mind. We did not often get the chance to show off.

As soon as we cleared the headland I turned to Magnus. "Get the ship's boys to lower the sail. The wind is from the east."

"Aye, jarl."

I waited until the stays were taut and shouted, "Oars in!" I eased the steer board over a fraction and the wind took us. The dragon prow seemed to rise as though she wanted to fly. There was a rattle as the oars were laid down and then a cheer from the fifty warriors we had brought. '*The Heart of the Dragon*' was truly launched.

We had a bigger boat but there were more of us and, while the rowers and crew worked out the best place to be I let Magnus steer. "We head west." I pointed to the pennant. "The wind is from the north east. It will take us there swiftly."

51

He nodded and held the steer board. I could see the
excitement on his face. Snorri and Arturus had both been
ship's boys but they saw it as a step to becoming warriors.
Magnus just wanted to be a sailor.

I went forward to Aiden who sat on his chest with the
maps laid out. "Do these Roman maps help us, Aiden?"

"The places they show may have changed their names but
I can use what we learn to make them better. I have copied
them all and the originals are in Cyninges-tūn. Once we
return we will have more information. They show where
people lived in the time of the Romans."

"Then that is a good place to start." Hibernia might be a
poor place to raid but they had no disease there. Once we
had secured some more animals and slaves we could travel
to Frankia to buy more weapons.

Haaken and Cnut joined us. Most of the men were
leaning on the side, sheltered from the spray by their shields.
"This is a fine ship, Jarl Dragon Heart. The higher freeboard
makes a great deal of difference. I thought it might have
slowed us but we are faster than any ship I have ever sailed
in."

I patted the sheerstrake. "That is the work of Ragnar. He
shaped and smoothed the hull so that we cut through the
water quicker. But he warned me that we would need to take
her out of the water twice a year to clear the weed and watch
for worms."

Aiden tapped his sea chest. "In those papers it talks of
painting a ship's hull with something to discourage worms. I
have the Latin name for it and when we reach Frankia we
could buy some and see if it works."

"You were right, Aiden, the treasure in the chest was in
the parchment and not the gold."

The coast appeared before dusk. We had made good time.
Rather than risking the east coast, where we knew many
Vikings went raiding, we decided to head around the
northern coast and raid the west. With Aiden's map we knew
where the edge of the world lay and, so long as we kept the
coast to the east, we would be safe. We kept the sail lowered

as we headed north east. The wind had veered a little so that it came a little more from the east. Those ashore, who saw us, would have their bells ringing to warn of our presence. They would know that the wolves from the sea were close by. If we intended raiding them we would have lowered the sail but I saved my warriors' arms. We would need to row in the morning when we closed with the shore.

We had studied the maps and could find no places of interest marked. We would use Aiden's mind. He had pointed out a river marked on the map. "People choose rivers and hills to build their homes. The map here shows a river and a hill."

It had been as good a suggestion as any. We hoped that other Vikings had ignored the northern coast. Pasgen had told us that there was now a Viking kingdom on the east coast of Hibernia. They had fortified the town they called Dyflin. It was another reason to avoid that area. Sihtric Silkbeard was known to haunt the area and he was as slimy a warrior as his famous beard.

We hove to when we felt the current from the river we sought. With sail lowered we edged into the shore. We could see the land and the breakers ahead with a flatter piece of water between them. That would be the river. With Arturus and Snorri at the prow we slowly entered the river. It was a narrow entrance and I wondered if I had made an error. Their arms remained upright and I trusted their judgement. Once we had passed through the narrow entrance the river widened out so much I thought it might be a mere. We moored in the middle while my men prepared for battle.

I would take only forty of my warriors with me. We were in new territory and I wanted my new ship protected. The ten men and four crew could easily row the vessel and moor her away from the shore. Aiden would come with us. He had the language and he had the knowledge which we would need.

We put on our red cochineal first and made our eyes look like those of wolves. Then we began to don our armour and helmets. I was luckier than my men for I had Aiden to help me dress. My Ulfheonar aided each other. Once dressed and before I put my helmet on I went to the prow and sniffed the air. There was a faint whiff of wood smoke from the land to our left. I turned to Magnus. "We will land over there."

The ten warriors who would be guarding the ship rowed slowly across the river to the shore. At the prow Ketil, another of the ship's boys, stared at the water. Suddenly his hand came up and Magnus hissed, "Back water!"

Ketil jumped over the side and there was a small splash. I made my way to the prow. Ketil was waist deep in the water. "It is sand, my lord!"

That was a relief. I did not want the hull damaging with stones and underwater obstacles. Jumping into the river I ruffled his hair as I went past him. "Good boy! Guard her well."

I donned my helmet and went along the beach to find a trail of some kind. My men were soon ashore and I saw my ship as it edged into the middle of the river. It was a pity that we could not hide it but there were no overhanging trees. We had told the people of this land that the Viking wolves were hunting. They would hide if they had any sense.

I waved my arm and Snorri and Beorn Three Fingers trotted off down the river. We followed behind them. If there was danger then they would alert us. The river bent round to a narrow entrance and I saw that we could have sailed further in and moored next to the shore. We reached Beorn.

"Snorri thinks there is a settlement above us. The smell of wood smoke is stronger here and we have heard animals."

"The Allfather smiles on us this day!" I turned to Aiden, "You stay close to me."

The men gathered around us at the foot of the gently rising hill. Snorri reappeared. "It is a monastery. There is a stockade but it is meant to keep animals in and not us out." I saw his teeth flash a grin in the moonlight. "There is but one gate in. The stockade is as high as Ketil."

"Erik Dog Bite, you and Tostig Wolf Hand stay here and guard the path."

The rest of us wound our way up the path. I saw a faint lightening of the sky beyond the hill. Dawn was but a couple of hours away. Suddenly the silence was shattered by the tolling of the bell. We now knew what that meant; the monks were rising. Had we reached the monastery just a little sooner then we would have achieved complete surprise. I waved my arm and Thorkell the Tall took six warriors to cut off the escape of any monks who spied us. When we reached the gate Snorri and Arturus clambered over to open it. I saw a faint glow from the wooden buildings just beyond the animal pens.

"Beorn," I whispered, "take four men and secure the animals."

I left them to collect our valuable animals and led the others towards the building I guessed was the church. The tolling of the bell had stopped but the sound had come from the building which looked to be the largest in the stockade. Just as I reached it the door opened and a monk in a brown kyrtle stood there. He tried to shut the door but Ragnar's Spirit was quicker and he fell backwards, his dying hand opening the door as he did so. Haaken and Cnut leapt through the open door. It was light within; there were candles burning. I saw six monks; four were on their knees and two appeared to be standing at a table with a piece of white linen on it.

Haaken and Cnut raced towards it and the monks picked up the metal candle holders to use as weapons. Two priests ran for the door which I could see at the back. "Sigtrygg, take Arturus and Snorri, round the back!"

Haaken and Cnut slew two of the monks. Haaken picked up one of the monks who were cowering on the floor and struck him in the face with his shield to render him unconscious. When Cnut tried the same to the last monk he drew a knife and jabbed it at Cnut's face. Had he not had a full face helmet on he might have lost an eye. As it was his sword ended the monk's foolish resistance.

"Haaken and Cnut, collect any treasure." I led the men through the rear door. One of the monks who had fled lay dead at the feet of Snorri while the other was being bound by Arturus.

He snarled something at me, I did not understand it. I turned to Aiden, "He called you a wolf devil and cursed you to burn in somewhere called Hades." He pointed at my head, "I think it is the red eyes."

I laughed. The curses of the followers of the White Christ could not hurt me. "Find the other monks. Arturus, take this one back to the ship with the animals and the monk in the church."

The sky was definitely lighter and I wished to be back aboard my ship before the sun rose too high in the sky. "Search the monastery and gather any slaves and treasure."

I saw Thorkell and his men approaching. "There were two men who tried to escape." He pointed at the bound figures. They did not get far."

"Good, send them to the ship." I looked around. I could see my men spreading through the buildings. There were occasional shouts and cries. "Aiden, let us find the place their abbot sleeps. We may find something useful there."

The two of us headed for a dark building towards the rear. As we passed a small hut which had already been searched I picked up the lighted candle I saw glowing within. I handed it to Aiden who shielded it with his hand. The door of the darkened building was open and I went in with my sword drawn. When Aiden entered the soft yellow light flooded the monk's cell. There on a crudely made table was one of the books of the White Christ. We had a valuable treasure! "Put that in your bag." While Aiden did so I looked around the bare cell. There appeared to be little else of value save the bedding, which we gathered. The linen was always useful.

By the time we reached the top of the path the monastery had been looted and my men descended. Sigtrygg and Sven White Hair brought up the rear. When we reached the beach dawn was breaking and Snorri whistled. We saw the oars rise and fall as Magnus brought '*The Heart of the Dragon*' over to us. It had not been our most successful raid. We only had five slaves. The five pigs and eight goats were a valuable addition to our animals but the only treasure we could sell was the book and two candlesticks.

By the time we were aboard the sun had lit the opposite hillside. I could not see any settlements there although it was obvious we were on a large and open body of water. Aiden told me that the locals called them a Lough.

"Magnus take us north."

My Ulfheonar rowed in their armour. They had not exerted themselves. I had Snorri watching in the prow. His sharp eyes would aid us. He suddenly waved left. Ketil ran down the centre of the boat. "My Lord, Snorri says there is an island. It is not far away." He pointed to the north west.

As we edged from the inlet I leaned on the steer board. I could see the dot ahead. "Hoist the sail!"

The wind still held and we were able to store the oars as we sped to the tiny prick of land which rose about four or five miles off shore. I had no doubt that we had been seen. I was not even certain that we had prevented any monks from escaping but we needed rest and we had too little to return home. The island looked like our only choice. As we closed with it I saw that it was literally a small rock erupting from the sea. It looked to be uninhabited but it was also large enough to hide us from prying eyes. After an hour or so of sailing I dropped the sail and we anchored just fifty paces from shore. Our approach meant that we could see that there was not a living creature on the rock save birds. We anchored.

"Magnus, we will sleep. The warriors who were aboard last night can have the first watch. Wake me at noon and watch the prisoners. I do not want them escaping."

We all stripped our armour from our bodies. The relief was wonderful. One or two of my warriors dropped over the side and swam around the ship. Some believed it aided sleep. For me, I needed no aid and I was asleep within moments of removing my armour.

Chapter 6

I was woken by Haaken. He had piece of cooked meat and a horn of ale. "Here Dragon Heart, we need to wake you. Your snoring was disturbing the fish."

I heard the laughter from my Ulfheonar. They were in a good mood. I drank the ale first. I could see the ship's boys and the ten guards asleep as were the monks. "Did they behave?"

"Aye, Aiden spoke with them and discovered that the place was called Doire Calgach. He also discovered, by listening to them that there is another such monastery on the north west coast." He pointed, "Just around that headland."

"I had hoped for a settlement. Female slaves are of more value than monks."

Haaken smacked the side of the ship. "And there is a village there too! The Allfather smiles upon us."

I finished eating the meat and wiped my greasy hand on my beard. "Do we know how far away it is?"

He pointed to Aiden's sleeping form. "The boy is bright and that is the truth. He asked them questions about the land rather than the place and he discovered that the village and the monastery are a short way up a small river."

"Then we shall sail after dark." I looked at the sky and saw that they had allowed me to sleep longer than I wished. It was the middle of the afternoon. There was little point in chastising them I would just have to ensure that Aiden woke me the next time. He would obey my orders.

We sailed just as the sun was setting in the west. We hoped that its dying rays would point the way. We rowed to keep a lower silhouette. It was not far. The Allfather was, indeed, with us. A pinprick of light glittered from the river and the buildings above. Aiden had done well. It would not be a long march from the ship. This time we could moor the ship close to the shore.

As we sailed I was suddenly reminded of the problems of stealing animals; the smell. Our new ship had an earthy aroma. I hoped that Ragnar Bollison approved. We rowed the last mile towards the beach as slowly as we could. Sharp eyed Snorri was at the prow and Arturus had climbed the mast. I would not have us run aground. When Snorri's arms came up we stopped rowing and nudged towards the beach on the incoming tide.

Snorri leapt into the sea and we donned our mail. Haaken detailed ten warriors to watch the ship and we jumped ashore to begin our ascent of the hill. We had more of an idea this time of the location of the monastery. We had seen it, briefly, before the sun had set. The smell from their fires was still in the air as was the smell from their animals. Both boded well as they showed it was a prosperous place.

I divided the men into two groups. We would separate closer to our target. We headed up the track which Snorri had discovered. We were aided this time by the smells and our brief glimpse of it. This one had a wall around the village and another one around the monastery. They were very close but, from the sea, we could not tell if they were joined. Aiden had said, before we left the ship, that he thought they would be joined. Thorkell the Tall led half of the warriors to the right, along the valley. He would approach the walls, which we could see as a dark shadow ahead.

We were Ulfheonar and we could move like ghosts. We used that skill as we padded along the obvious trail. Suddenly Snorri held his hand and we all dropped to the ground and waited. We could hear voices. Aiden was just behind me. "They have heard that there is a Viking ship around."

"Pass the word back that we are expected."

I bellied up towards Arturus and Snorri. I whispered, in their ears, "They have seen the ship. Go carefully."

It would not stop us. It just made life a little more difficult. They would be listening for any sound. The voices we could hear disappeared. I took that to mean that the guards had moved on. We slithered up the bank. I could see a ditch. It was not deep but it was an obstacle and it made the stockade a little higher than it would otherwise have been.

I moved next to Snorri and we peered along the walls. There were at least five guards that we could see patrolling the ramparts. Snorri drew his bow. Since Beorn's encounter with the wolf he had not been able to draw a bow. Arturus had the second such weapon and they aimed at the men furthest from us. The two men fell silently to their deaths. I tapped Haaken and Cnut and we went forward as one. Luckily the ditch was free of obstacles and we descended before rising to the wall. Sigtrygg, Tostig Wolf Hand and Erik Dog Bite joined us.

As the others joined hands with their shields Sigtrygg and I prepared to mount them. We had practised this before. As I stepped on to the shield Haaken and Cnut lifted it in one motion high above their heads. I jumped over the ramparts. Landing before Sigtrygg I stabbed the first surprised sentry before he could shout a warning. I heard the double thump of the two guards who had been struck by arrows before Sigtrygg killed his man. The fifth was close to the ladder and he yelled something. I guess it was the alarm because a bell began to toll.

We ran towards the gate. Sigtrygg was in front of me and he was a fearless warrior. He held Saxon Killer before him and, as the first guard rushed from the gate with a spear held defensively, Sigtrygg knocked the spear away with his shield and swung his blade at the man's head. The warrior behind stepped backwards which was a mistake for it allowed Sigtrygg to charge him and knock him from the walls. I climbed down the ladder towards the gate.

When I reached the bottom I found four fully armed warriors ready to attack me. Behind them I saw more men, this time just armed with a sword or a spear, emerge from the huts. We had to strike quickly.

When the odds are against you the best form of defence is attack and I yelled, "Ragnar's Spirit!" and charged them. I went for the two men to the left of the small line. I held my shield ready to block any blows and I swung my blade horizontally. It cracked and crashed into the first warrior's shield and it split. The blade continued on and sliced into his arm. He screamed in pain and dropped to his knees. Two swords struck my shield but I knew that it was well made and I swung my sword at the man's legs. He was not expecting the blow and I felt it grind against bone. He screamed and fell backwards against the third warrior. Spinning to my right I brought Ragnar's Spirit to chop through the sword arm of the fourth warrior. Pausing only to stab the fallen warrior in the neck I turned and ran to the gate. Haaken and Cnut were just descending while I saw Arturus and Snorri loosing arrows at men behind me.

There were two men at the gate. They stood no chance against the three of us. While Haaken and I guarded him, Cnut opened the gate and my Ulfheonar flooded in. The wolves were amongst the sheep!

There was chaos as the men of the settlement fell. The few warriors with armour had fallen already and the women and children were fleeing. There had to be another gate in the east for they were racing that way. "Secure the gate!"

I ran after those fleeing. A spear suddenly jabbed from a hut as I passed. It struck my mail. I whipped my sword around blindly and felt it sink into unprotected flesh. I saw a young Hibernian clutching at his torn throat. The spear had broken my mail but not pierced my leather byrnie. Haaken and Cnut appeared at my side. "Wait for us, Dragon Heart! You cannot do this alone!"

The east gate I had assumed was there, was open. It led into the monastery. I heard the screams from the refugees as they ran into Thorkell and his warriors. I had been worried that they might have found other warriors but when I saw the monks lying face down with two Ulfheonar standing guard I knew that we had won.

"Secure the gates and bring all the prisoners here. Where is Aiden?"

I looked around and saw him hurrying towards me. "I am sorry my lord, I could not keep up with you."

I remembered the sudden thrust of the spear. "Perhaps it is as well else you might have suffered this." I put my fingers in the holes in my mail. "Come let us find the church."

There was a building with a small stone tower and it was topped by a cross. We headed for it. There were candles burning but the floor was puddled with blood and two monks lay there. I reached down and took the golden pendant from one. This one had to be the abbot or chief monk. "See if there is a hidden chamber." I grabbed the candlesticks and placed them with the pendant. The abbot had two fine rings and I took them from him.

"No, my lord, there is no hidden chamber nor are there any fine books."

"Gather these treasures and we will go back to the ship." As we walked through the deserted monastery, for the prisoners were all gathered close to the gate I said, "There were mailed warriors, Aiden. What do you make of that?"

"Perhaps the monk we questioned knew that this was well defended and hoped that we would die."

"If that is true then he will suffer the blood eagle."

"Or it could be that they discovered what we had done and reinforced the village."

"Find out. Ask one of the prisoners." Haaken and Cnut awaited me. "Did we lose any?"

Cnut nodded, "Two dead: Thorfinn Olafson and Harald Green Eye. Four men were wounded."

It could have been worse. "We will give them a funeral in the warrior hall. Prepare their bodies."

We had a healthy haul of prisoners. Most of the men in the village had died or fled. Some of the women and children had escaped too. We had four priests, two men, eight women and five children. There were two cows and another four pigs. The arms we had captured were adequate.

"Have the weapons, armour and heavy objects stowed beneath the deck. Take the prisoners down to the *'Heart'*, Aiden."

Aiden nodded and went to one of the men. I took off my helmet. Suddenly one of the prisoners, although bound, leapt at me with hatred in his eyes. He yelled something at me as he came. Before I could even react Arturus' sword had whipped across the man's neck and decapitated him.

"Thank you my son. What did he say, Aiden?"

"He shouted, *'Die, Wolf of the Sea!'*"

I nodded, "He was a brave man although foolish."

Haaken and Cnut returned. "The bodies are readied Dragon Heart." Cnut held out the golden wolf charms I had given them. They would be returned to their families. Their swords, armour and wolf cloaks would be burned with them.

They had been laid out on the table in the warrior hall. Their swords were in their hands. The firewood from the hall and the furniture had been laid around them. "Go to Valhalla and await us brothers. It has been an honour to serve with you."

Haaken, Cnut and I thrust our torches into the firewood. It was dry and dead. It flared immediately. We waited until the table caught and then left. When the flames suddenly flared up to the roof the women and children wailed. Their home was being destroyed and they would never return. I knew what they were thinking. I had suffered that too.

"Take them to the ship. We sail!" As we walked down the path I asked Aiden, "Well?"

"The king, he is called Padraigh, was told of our attack and he sent warriors to all of the villages hereabouts." I nodded. "It would have been better had he kept a watch for us then he might have been able to bring his army to meet us."

"He has a big army?"

"At least two hundred warriors. He is a powerful warrior."

As we watched the prisoners and animals being loaded I stored that information. If we returned here then I would remember that.

The ship was well laden and I thanked Ragnar Bollison again. If this had been *'Wolf'* we would have been swamped. The higher freeboard meant we sailed still. However I did not want to risk sailing too far. "We will head for Dál Riata and the land of the Picts."

The Dál Riata was not the kingdom it had been. At one time they had threatened even Northumbria but they were still the closest people who might buy the slaves. We would not sell them the book, we could get a higher price in Frankia or even Wessex but the slaves were an encumbrance and the sooner we were rid of them the better.

The Norns did not wish us to sail to the land of Dál Riata. We sighted a sail to the east. The sea was usually empty. Another sail could mean a wolf such as us or a sheep. The wind or the Norns determined our course. It was blowing from the north west. Our voyage north would have meant rowing and so I put the steer board over to turn us in that direction.

"Ketil, up the mast and see what vessel it is. Are they alone?"

Haaken and the Ulfheonar retrieved their bows from their chests. It was as well to be prepared.

"It is a knarr, my lord and looks to be alone."

I relaxed a little. A knarr meant it might well be our people. The captain saw us and tried to turn to the west to take advantage of the wind. Ragnar had built well and we flew across the water. The knarr was a tubby little thing and broad in the beam. *'The Heart of the Dragon'* was a long ship and meant to cut through the water. The captain wisely lowered his sail in surrender.

"Take in the sail, Magnus."

We slowed as we approached the wallowing ship. I saw that there were warriors on board but also women and children as well as animals. My men had lined the side and we must have looked frightening. The women cowered behind their men.

"I am Jarl Dragon Heart. Who are you and where are you bound?" Their answer would determine their fate.

To my surprise the warrior at the steer board began to smile. "Then thank the Allfather we have found you. I am Trygg Olafson from Orkneyjar and we have been seeking you."

"You have found me. Give me your tale." Our ships bobbed up and down next to each other and he had to shout.

"Our people had lived on Orkneyjar for some years but we had a dispute with the Jarl. Had we stayed there would have been a blood feud and so we left. We had two ships. This one and a small drekar called the '*Serpent*'. We remembered Prince Butar and Jarl Dragon Heart. We had heard that you had a home on Man where you welcomed homeless such as us."

"Prince Butar died."

"We heard. When we reached Man the jarl there attacked us. My father and brother were on '*Serpent*'. It was captured and they were killed. At least I think that they were killed." He looked sadly to the south, "We cursed you for we thought the jarl was you. Now we know that it was not I take back the curse."

I gave a wry smile to Aiden who shook his head, "That is good of you. We no longer live on Man. We live to the east."

"Do you welcome settlers still?"

"We do."

"Then we will swear allegiance to you."

I turned to Haaken and Cnut. "What do we do?"

"We are not destined to sail north, my lord. We sail home and sell the slaves and the book in Frankia. It is *wyrd*."

I nodded. "You are right." I cupped my hands. "Follow us!"

The precious winds meant that we laboured to reach Pasgen's port. When we did so it was after dark. The gates of his town were barred. We spent a cold night on our ships. The only joy we had was that we were able to unload the animals and we penned them close to the ship. It made for a less pungent night.

When dawn broke Pasgen came to speak with us. He was full of apologies. "I am sorry my lord. The sentries just said there were two strange ships on the river. I shall punish them for their foolishness."

"No, my friend. I applaud their caution. There are others out there who look like us."

We left Magnus with ten warriors and the priests of the White Christ. They would clean the ship while we went to Cyninges-tūn. Trygg and his people followed us as we headed north. The construction of the second drekar was well under way and I could see that Bolli had learned well from his father. I was not surprised that there was less urgency. His father had been racing death. Bolli would make the best vessel that he could to honour his father. Driving the animals took time and I sent Snorri and Arturus ahead to warn my wife.

I walked with Trygg. I wanted to know this man. We were flanked by Cnut and Haaken. "Did you see the jarl who attacked your father?"

Trygg shook his head. "All that we saw were his warriors as they swarmed over my father's ship. He had no shields up and went in peace."

Haaken said, "This sounds familiar."

My wife's brother had indeed changed. "Why were you not on board your father's ship? You look like a seasoned warrior to me." I had noticed his warrior bands, fine sword and helmet. He looked as though he could handle himself.

"I was the eldest. I was given the task of sailing the families." He gestured behind us. "There are but four warriors left from our clan. I will have to pay back this jarl."

I nodded, "He is my wife's brother."

He stopped and he stared at me. "Is this a trap? Do you deceive us?"

"I have never been foresworn. He is my wife's brother but we are no longer family. We went our own ways when I came here. Many of his oathsworn followed me."

"I am sorry, Jarl Dragon Heart. Forgive my words."

"They are forgiven but do not make the mistake of questioning me again."

He looked contrite. Cnut patted him on the back, "You will learn that Dragon Heart cannot lie. He is an honest jarl in a dishonest world."

"Tell me, what skills do your people have?"

"We are sailors and our other skill is in the tending of animals." He pointed at the sheep he had brought with him.

"Good then you will be a valuable addition to our home."

As we stepped from beneath the canopy of the trees the expanse of the water and the Old Man appeared before us. I spread my arm, expansively, "Here is Cyninges-tūn."

"This is Valhalla on earth. This is beautiful."

Chapter 7

We sailed south three days later. My wife had made the women welcome and their skills as herders were soon put to good use. "I can see that the Allfather sent you to us for now we can sail to Frankia and use your knarr to transport the cargo."

Trygg was more than happy to be of service. We left the choicest slaves at Cyninges-tūn and the rest were placed on board Trygg's knarr. The holy book of the White Christ I retained on my ship. We sailed south and the same wind which had prevented us from reaching Dál Riata took us, instead, south.

We had to sail a little more slowly than we would have liked but it enabled Magnus and me to learn how to sail the '*Heart*'. Every drekar is different. The way she heels and hoggs varies and the effect of the steer board. Magnus and I discovered that she was very responsive to the slightest touch of the steer board. She could turn as quickly as a fine horse. That first morning as we headed south we learned much. It was just as well.

Ketil was the lookout on the mast; he had the youngest and the sharpest eyes. He suddenly shouted, "Longships astern!"

The Island of Man was to the northwest of us; we knew who they would be. "Arm yourselves!"

Had we not had the knarr as our consort we could have outrun them despite the fact that they had the weather gauge. I had spare rowers. However, I could not leave Trygg to the ships I knew were Jarl Erik's. "Take over, Magnus, while I speak with Trygg." Going to the side closest to the knarr I cupped my hands, "Longships astern of us!"

"We saw them. They are the ones from Man!"

"We will drop behind you. Keep on this course."

"We will."

I walked to the mast. I pointed to the sail. "Reef the sail until they have overtaken us. It is Jarl Erik who is behind us." Ketil and Erik Short Toe raced to obey me.

Haaken was prepared for war and had on his mail already. "Will we fight him?"

I nodded. "Aiden, my mail. We will discourage him. I would not kill my sister's brother."

Cnut snorted, "If I know Erik he will not be on board. He will have others doing his work."

Gradually the knarr passed us. I saw that Trygg had armed his crew. I recognised one of the ships, it was '*Man*' the other one I did not recognise and she was smaller. '*Man*' had thirty oars but did not have the freeboard which we had. It meant we could heel more than they could and sail closer to the wind. Jarl Erik's captain was in for a shock. He would not know that we had extra crew.

"Man the oars. I want those not on the oars ready with their bows. We will see if we can stop them with arrows first."

Sea battles between drekar followed a pattern. They would close with each other and engage in a battle with arrows then warriors would board the weaker vessel. We would disrupt that pattern. I could row and loose arrows.

They were now half a mile or so behind us. "Magnus get the sail down." We used the terms Cnut and Haaken for left and right. As the sails came down I shouted, "Cnut rowers, backwater!"

As Haaken's side continued to row I put the steer board hard over. We heeled so hard that I thought even our high freeboard would not save us but Ragnar had built well and we spun around. I could see that we had taken them by surprise. "I will sail between them. Archers clear their sterns."

I saw the men with bows, including Snorri and Arturus split into two groups. The two drekar were trying to reef their sails. I had the initiative and I would not relinquish it. I recognised the two captains. One was Thrand Red Beard and the other was Tostig Tostigson. Both were fair captains. The fact that they had stayed with Jarl Erik spoke much of their character. If they had had a plan they might have done better but they were both just trying to fight by themselves. The smaller threttanessa was to our right. I nudged the steer board towards it. There was a double whoosh as the arrows were launched. There was chaos at the stern of the threttanessa. The steersman fell to his death with two arrows in him. The drekar veered away from us and my archers sent another wave of arrows towards them. I put our steer board over to take us towards the stern of *'Man'*.

The archers had had less success for they had men with shields protecting those near to the steer board but, as I turned us across their stern the archers were able to rain death on the rowers. She slowed as rowers died and the rhythm was ruined. All of my archers were now loosing as fast as they could notch their arrows. Had we wanted I could have captured her easily but that was not my intention.

"We will go after the threttanessa. "

'Man' was, effectively dead in the water. Tostig Tostigson was ordering his men to arm themselves. We crossed her bows and my archers had one last shower of arrows to deliver. The smaller drekar was now trying to go after the knarr.

"Cnut, up the rate."

'The Heart of the Dragon' began to move like a greyhound. No matter how hard the other drekar rowed she could not escape us. I would teach Jarl Erik a lesson. We approached from their rear. I sent my archers to the dragon prow and, as we closed, they loosed their arrows at the stern. There were sixteen warriors loosing their arrows and the rowers had to stop rowing and protect themselves with their shields. "Up oars!"

As I put our ship next to theirs our hull shattered the steer board side oars. "Make them fast!"

Magnus threw the grapnel hook and it bit into the smaller ship. It was the length of a man's leg below us. "Board!"

As my warriors leapt aboard I said to Aiden, "Watch for the other ship."

I crossed to the stern. Thrand Red Beard hefted his axe as I leapt down on to his deck. He swung his axe at me and I took the blow on my shield. I had fought alongside this warrior and knew that he was impetuous. He was not like my Ulfheonar. He did not try to outthink his opponent. He just rushed at him. He tried that with me. He was a big man and he used his weight and his strength. I used the speed of my feet. As he swung I evaded and slashed at him with Ragnar's Spirit. He was so keen to get to grips with me that he came forward too quickly and my sword ripped a deep gash in his cheek. It infuriated him and he swung his axe from behind his head. It thudded and stuck in to the gunwale. He tugged to free it. I brought my sword down and his head rolled into the dark grey waters.

Seeing their captain dead those men who still lived threw themselves into the sea. Those with armour drowned but some of the others began to swim away.

"Back to the *'Heart'*. Haaken, burn her!"

As we stepped back onboard my ship Haaken used his flint to begin a fire on the deck close to the mast. Their sail was still down and, as he leapt aboard our ship the flames caught the sail and took hold.

"Magnus, lower the sail." We were already drifting away from the stricken drekar and the sail soon moved us away from danger. As I steered towards the knarr I saw *'Man'* as it tried to close with its stricken consort. It would fail.

When we reached Trygg he shouted. "The drekar you sank was *'Serpent'*. You have avenged my family. I thank you."

I nodded to him and then took off my helmet. It had been a savage but a brief encounter. As we continued our journey I was satisfied with the outcome. Tostig Tostigson would return to Duboglassio and lick his wounds. I had not known that the small ship had been Trygg's father but perhaps the Norns had. We were the weird sisters' tools.

Dusk found us off the coast of Cymru. We had given Anglesey a wide berth for it was a Saxon stronghold. We sailed south beyond the mountain where I had found the tomb. We did not like to sail in the dark and I headed for the estuary where we had found the sword which now rested in my hall. We sailed a little way up the river and anchored close to the shore.

Haaken and Snorri led a patrol of Ulfheonar to scout the land and they returned to give us the news that we were alone. Soon we had a fire going and we had the slaves make us some hot food. Aiden supervised. We did not want to be poisoned. Trygg kept looking nervously at the hills which rose precipitously above us.

"We ride a sea anchor at night rather than risk places we do not know."

"We know this place for we found some gold and precious stones in the mines up river but we keep a good guard at night. Four men watch for an hour and then we change."

He finished the horn of ale he was drinking. "I thought you were doomed when you turned to take on two drekar."

"My ship is not as other ships. We carry more men and she is new. They gave us the advantage and I knew the captains of the two ships. I had fought alongside both of them. I knew their weaknesses and my men's strengths."

"Is it true that your sword was touched by the gods?"

"It was. And it has the spirit of the old warrior who trained me within it. It is a special blade."

"We heard of it on Orkneyjar. The tales of you and your wolf men are told in the long nights of winter. Many young men wish to serve with you." He looked wistfully into the flames. "My two younger brothers were two such warriors."

"They will be in Valhalla now."

"Aye, and they are avenged. I can rest easy." He lay back against a tree stump.

"Tomorrow may be more difficult. We have to sail around the savage rocks at the end of the land of the Cymri. If we become separated keep sailing east towards Frankia. Stay close to the coast. We will find you." He did not look happy. I smiled. "We have sailed this coast often. I know Frankia well. Once you have done this once you will find it easier."

I could see that he was far from convinced. He would learn as we had all learned.

When we eventually reached the savage coast filled with rocks, hidden islands and wild winds from the edge of the world I tasked Aiden with watching the knarr behind us. Magnus and the boys were each attending a stay or a sheet ready to adjust should the wind change. The salt had stuck to my beard and my eyes were red raw from constantly looking up at the pennant from the mast head. As we had to sail at the same speed as the knarr the rowers did not have to row. If we lost them they would.

"Reef it!" Magnus and his boys would shorten the sail by the length of Magnus' arm when ordered to reef. I gave the order as we made the turn east. The wind had, remarkably, stayed from the north west on our run south. I dreaded to think of the journey home if the winds were the same. As soon as we turned the troughs became deeper. "Another reef!"

I watched as the sail strained and billowed against the wind. The Allfather was urging us on our way. Night was falling and I was looking for an anchorage when Trygg's knarr disappeared from view.

"It was there one moment, my lord and then gone the next."

"Take in two reefs!"

With the smallest sail possible we slowed dramatically. I dared not turn around for we could easily broach. If Trygg continued at the same speed he would overtake us and if not then I would see his wreckage. It all depended upon Ran. Haaken and Cnut joined me at the stern as we stared west. The light was already fading but we were looking to the west where there was the last vestige of the sun.

. I began to fear that we had lost him when Aiden called, "There she is." He pointed to the north west.

The knarr was inshore of us. He had taken a reef out of his sail too. I saw some of his crew waving at us. I put the steer board over to edge us closer. When we were within hailing distance he shouted, "We lost two of the priests. They panicked when the winds came…"

"It doesn't matter. It is *wyrd*! Follow me and stay close."

I steered towards the land which was hidden in the darkening eastern sky. Aiden had studied the Roman maps. "Well," I asked, "are there any safe anchorages nearby?"

It was a cruel question for I had no idea where we were so how could I expect him to know? "I think, my lord, that there should be two or three not far away. The map shows bays." He shrugged, "I cannot guarantee that they will be uninhabited."

"Just so long as they are somewhere to anchor, I care not." I gambled that we would find somewhere without ships. The sight of a drekar normally made people hide rather than seek contact. We could not sail any further. Those on the knarr would be in a state. Poor Trygg would be out of his depth, quite literally.

"Up forrard then, Aiden, and use those eyes of yours. Take Arturus too."

"Let out a reef!"

We could afford to go a little faster now. The knarr was almost on our beam. The light behind us faded a little more and I wondered if we had strayed too far from the shore. Then Arturus waved us to the left and I put the steer board over. I saw it. There were cliffs but between them was a piece of lower ground which suggested a bay of some kind. I ordered another reef to be taken and watched as Trygg did the same. The closer we came to the cliffs the clearer the anchorage became. It was a beach surrounded by high cliffs. As we approached I saw that the breakers suggested sand rather than rocks. Even so we went in slowly. I had the sail lowered some forty paces from shore and let the waves take us in. We slid gently up the beach. We were still afloat for I could feel the stern bobbing up and down.

Arturus and Snorri were already in the water and Haaken and Cnut had their bows strung in case of danger. The knarr ground softly on to the beach too. Ketil followed Arturus with the rope which he secured to a rock. We waited anxiously. Arturus returned. "It is safe. We can go ashore. The cliffs are high and there are no paths." He flourished something in his hand, "And we have food." They were gulls' eggs.

The slaves were brought ashore but they were tied hand and foot. We did not wish them to be tempted to escape. We risked a fire. It was unlikely that there was anyone around. The cliffs were too high and exposed to make a good site for a home and we needed hot food.

"What happened?"

"The waves were high and one of the priests dropped to his knees and began to pray. One of my men who could understand his words said that the priest swore we were going to die and God was punishing you for taking the priests. He ran to the prow and pleaded with his God for his life. A second priest joined them and then a wave took them overboard. The other priests wanted me to turn around." He shook his head, "Olaf had to hit them with a trenail to calm them." He shook his head. "This White Christ of theirs is a strange god."

"I agree. I know not why they follow him. At least we know which god to plead with. I asked Ran's help before we left Úlfarrston and when we changed direction. If they cause more trouble then throw them overboard."

"But we will lose the trade."

"Better we lose the trade than the ship. I will speak with them." I shouted, "Aiden, I need your words!"

Aiden joined me and I went to the tethered slaves. I addressed the men for the women appeared to have accepted their fate. "The priests who caused the trouble and died nearly got you all killed. I have told my captain that he is to throw overboard any who cause trouble." I nodded to Aiden, "Translate."

Although I had some Hibernian I wanted no misunderstanding. When he had translated they stared at me with hate burning in their eyes. It did not worry me. Had they had courage they would have fought us when we had taken them. They were getting what they deserved. If they did not want to be treated as sheep then they needed a sheepdog!

"When we reach Frankia you will be sold. If you are lucky you will be employed by a lord who will treat you well and use your reading skills. You will live! Cross me and you will die!"

When Aiden had translated I asked, "Do they understand?"

One of them looked at me, sadly and said, "We understand."

I returned to Trygg. The food was now ready. "One of your slaves can understand us. He is the one who is taller than the others. I have told them what you will do to them."

Many people might think me cruel but I am not. This is the way of the world. I had been a slave and now I was the jarl of my own fiefdom. You could change your stars or you could crawl on your belly. The Allfather needed to know what kind of man you were.

Chapter 8

We had no more trouble and we reached the Rinaz without any further losses. It was the middle of the afternoon when we saw the river and I breathed a sigh of relief that we had managed to reach our destination still together.

"Sails!"

Ketil's shrill voice was accompanied by his hand which stretched to the south. There were two small ships approaching us. They were filled with armed men.

"Lower the sail. Let us see what they want. Be ready to repel boarders if this is some sort of trick." Neither ship seemed a danger to us. I had more than four times the number of men I could see on both ships but something was not right.

They lowered their sail and bobbed up and down next to us. They were lower in the water than we were and we were able to see that each boat had twelve men on board. All wore mail and were well armed.

One man stepped forward and spoke to us, haltingly, in our language. "Men of the Norse are not allowed on the Rinaz! Go away, pirates!"

"We are here to trade. We are not pirates."

"It matters not; the Emperor Charlemagne has barred you from this river."

I did not like his attitude and I found his words offensive. "You and your little boats will not take long to sink and then who is to stop us entering your river?"

He actually grinned at me. "You could sink us but then the ships of our Emperor would hunt you down. Even if you reached Aachen you would be arrested and executed. Go home!"

Haaken and Cnut had been listening. They did not like the insults I had been forced to take. Two arrows flew from their bows and the grinning spokesman was hurled overboard. I frowned. I was not certain if anyone else spoke our language. And I did not like the fact that their action had made us enemies of the Emperor Charlemagne, whoever he was. The two ships suddenly hoisted sail and made all speed for the distant river.

"There was no need for that!"

"He was annoying us. If they had any warships here we would have seen them."

"What do we do now? Sail all the way back home?"

Aiden said, "We could go to Frisia. That captain from Cymru said there were trading centres there." He pointed north. "The Roman maps say they are not far away."

Haaken shrugged, "It is worth a try. We have nothing to lose."

Trygg pulled alongside us. I leaned over. "We will sail north and find a Frisian port."

As we headed north I asked Aiden what he knew of this Charlemagne. "I have not heard the name but Emperor sounds Roman."

"I think someone told me he ruled the old Roman Empire but I thought that was further east."

"So did I. I will see what I can discover when we reach a port."

We sailed slowly through new waters. We saw low islands and narrow channels. I wondered which one to pick when Ketil shouted. "Mastheads!"

He pointed to the east and put the steer board over. "Drop the sail and run out the oars. We will enter gently." The channel seemed wide enough and the low lying islands enabled us to see some buildings and the masts of many ships. We later found that we had come across the island of Wierirgen. I saw other long ships tied to the wooden jetties as well as knarrs and even some long low river barges. We were one of the longer ones. We stopped in the middle of a channel. I was not certain what to do next. A small rowing boat came out and we were spoken to by one of our people.

"Captain, tie up to a jetty. There are spare berths at the northern end. You come here to trade?"

The question seemed without ulterior motive but our warlike appearance might have worried the locals. We were the largest ship in the port. "We come to trade."

He seemed relieved. "You have come to the right place."

When we reached the berth I was still a little suspicious. "Keep most of the men on board. I will take Sigtrygg and Arturus with me. Make sure we have sufficient guards along the jetty."

"Are you going mailed?"

I shook my head, "I will just need Ragnar's Spirit." As we had sailed through the port I had noticed that the men were not wearing armour. It would not do to appear to be belligerent. With my son and Sigtrygg I was confident I could deal with any problem I might encounter.

We left the ship and walked along the wooden jetty. Crossing a bridge to the land I saw that there were some substantial looking buildings. All were wooden but they gave the impression of prosperity. The man in the rowing boat strode down to meet me. I could see that he was a warrior, his sword had warrior bands and his face had a long scar running down one cheek.

"I am Rorik of Dorestad! Welcome to the town of trade!"

He was an ebullient and cheerful man but his eyes belied the smile. He was calculating. I later discovered that money and business coursed through his veins instead of blood.

"Come, there is a fine ale wife here and she serves the best wheat beer you have ever drunk. Allow me to buy you one and then you can tell me what you wish to trade."

"Are you the jarl here?"

"Jarl?" He laughed, "No. I am just a trader but I do own a warehouse and I do like to make trades with fellow Vikings."

He pointed up at the sheaf of wheat hanging up outside the hut. "Here it is."

The hut was surprisingly well lit by bowls of seal oil. There were no seats but there were crude tables. I noticed that they all deferred to him and moved back to allow us room. He was important. He strode up to a table where a woman held a jug. "Four of your wheat beers, Agnetha."

She was a tough looking woman and I saw that she had had her nose broken at some time. She held out her palm into which Rorik dropped some coins. I got the impression he did not like her action but after a brief grimace his mouth returned to the smile.

He handed me my horn of ale. Arturus and Sigtrygg were left to pick up their own. Rorik clashed horns with me. We both drank. He was right, it was good ale.

"Now then you know my name but I have not seen you before or your magnificent ship."

"I am Jarl Garth Dragon Heart of Cyninges-tūn." I knew I had surprised him by his face.

"I have heard of you. You fought with Magnus Barelegs and Thorfinn Skull Splitter." I nodded. He pointed at my sword. "Then that must be the sword touched by the gods."

"It is. So tell me when do we trade?"

"That depends what you have to sell. If you have slaves then that would be on Woden's Day. Other items might be traded on any day."

"Swords and sword blanks?"

"Ah," he tapped the side of his nose, "you know that the Emperor Charlemagne had forbidden the sale of swords to the Norse and the Danish?"

"I had heard that the Franks had forbidden their sale to Vikings."

"That doesn't mean to say we cannot arrange the trade but the prices tend to be a little higher than they were."

"We have slaves and we have a holy book of the White Christ."

He suddenly became interested. "That, my friend, calls for another ale." He put two more coins down and Agnetha filled two more horns. "The books of the White Christ are in great demand but I would suggest you do not sell that in public. The Emperor has spies everywhere and if got to hear of it, well, let us just say, his price would be lower and bloodier than others."

"Could you arrange for some interested buyers to meet me then?"

"Of course."

I drank the rest of the ale. "Then as the morrow is Woden's Day I will go back and prepare the slaves so that we can get the best price."

He waved us from the door and we made our way back towards our moored ship. "What did you think to him Sigtrygg?"

"I thought he was as slippery as a freshly caught herring. I would not trust him."

"Nor would I but we will deal with him until we find out a little more about this place."

Once back at the ship I called Trygg aboard *'Heart'* and spoke with my men. "We trade the slaves tomorrow. I would be rid of them. They are mouths to feed and require guarding. When that is done I would have some of you circulate amongst the other ships and businesses. Listen and find out as much as you can."

Beorn Three Fingers asked, "About what?"

I shrugged, "About anything. I have been told that we cannot trade for Frankish blades and that Holy Books have a special market. I have spoken to one man. He is one of our people but we do not trust him. Before I judge him I would have as much information as we can. Until we know more we assume that we are in danger. Haaken, arrange the watches."

I went to the stern to look at the busy little port. Aiden came with me. "You are troubled, my lord?"

"I am troubled. Why does this Charlemagne blockade his own river and allow this free port just a few miles away? It makes no sense to me. I would return after selling the slaves save that we need swords and other supplies. We need seeds and the means to grow our own crops."

"I have been studying those parchments we found. There is a mention of the sword we found." I looked up, suddenly interested. "It was named 'Saxon Slayer'. It came from the land of the Franks before the time of the Romans."

"And we are here, in the land of the Franks."

"Aye my lord, but they discovered this by travelling to Miklagård where they studied the writings of Rome and," he paused dramatically and lowered his voice, "there they bought fine weapons. I believe the armour we saw on Anglesey came from Byzantium."

"You have done well! That is interesting news. We have much to ponder on and all is not as dark as I had first thought."

When I woke the next morning I discovered that our precautions had been wise. Small boats had sailed close to our hulls during the night. Had we not had guards there who were able to chase them away who knew what might have resulted? Of course it might have had little to do with Rorik. Ports always attracted criminals. That was how Rolf and his oathsworn had come into my service.

I had the slaves prepared. We made sure they were washed and most of the vermin chased from their clothes. The women and children had their hair combed. The monks were, generally, clean anyway. Rorik appeared, flanked by two tough looking warriors.

"I came to show you where the sale will be."

"That is kind of you. Haaken!"

Haaken had twelve of the Ulfheonar ready. We did not want to appear to be too belligerent but I wanted a show of force. He lined the men up on either side of the slaves. Cnut and Trygg nodded as we walked towards the centre. They would watch the boat while small groups of my warriors circulated to discover the layout of the port.

Rorik waved an expansive hand around the buildings we passed. He implied ownership. "The Frisians are a fine people but this was a collection of huts until we came."

"You raided?"

He flashed a sharp look at me, "You have a quick mind, Jarl Dragon Heart. Yes we did but it was poor returns and so we stayed. We found that the restrictions on the Rinaz forced many ships, such as yours, to come here instead of Frankia. It has grown."

"And you take a cut."

He laughed, "You are indeed clever and quick! Why not stay and join us. You have the finest drekar I have ever seen and your Ulfheonar have an untarnished reputation."

"I am afraid that I am wary of any new ventures." I inclined my head. "I had an unfortunate alliance with Ragnar Hairy Breeches and besides I have a family waiting for me in my home."

"And where is this Cyninges-tūn? On the island of Man?"

I waved a vague hand, "It is in the north of the land they call Britannia."

"You are cautious; that is wise."

We had reached the centre of the port. There was a square flanked by large buildings. A small dais had been built in the middle and the auctioneer stood there.

Rorik pointed to some animal pens off to the side. "Your men can hold the slaves there and we will call them. I must go and begin the sale."

"Haaken put them in the pens over there. They will be summoned."

He began to move off, "You will be safe?"

"I have Arturus and Aiden here. I think so." Turning to Aiden I said, "You have an ear for languages. Listen and pick up all that you can."

"And me, father?"

"Today you are my bodyguard; keep me safe."

I did not think for one moment that I needed protection in such a public place but it made Arturus feel better.

Rorik stood on the dais. "Welcome to the sale of slaves." He waved a hand towards the pens. "We have a large number today including a consignment of monks from Hibernia." I heard mumbling from a group of well dressed merchants and warriors. They would be the ones I would need to watch. Those who bid for the monks might be interested in the holy book of the White Christ. "On with the sale and remember it is cash only." Although said with a smile there was a threat in his voice and in the attitude of the well armed men who flanked him.

I saw a hooded man who showed the most interest when the monks came for sale. He had soft hands, I was close enough to see that clearly and his fingers were adorned with rings. The two mailed men close by him were obviously his bodyguards. He purchased all of the monks despite competition from three other well dressed men. It suited us for our profits rose. One of the monks went for more than all of the rest of the slaves put together.

When the sale ended I followed him as he went to pay for and collect his acquisitions. I waited while he handed over the coins and watched them counted. Rorik took on that task himself. As he turned I gave a slight bow. "I am Jarl Dragon Heart and you have just bought my slaves. I hope they serve you well."

I saw that he was a younger man than I had expected. He had a neatly trimmed beard and hawk like eyes. His men's hands went to their swords when I spoke. He muttered something to them and they relaxed.

"I am Count Pepin of Colona. They will serve." His eyes searched my face. "You wanted something else?"

"I have a holy book of the White Christ in my possession. I wondered if you might be interested."

He smiled and proffered the cross from around his neck. "We prefer to call ourselves Christians. And you wish to sell this book?"

I saw Rorik watching us keenly and I gestured for us to move away out of earshot. "I have been told that such books have a specialised market and…"

"And knowing that I wanted the monks you sought me out." He laughed, "And some of my people call you barbarians. Yes I am interested. My ship is the '*Sword of Charles Martel*'. It is the one in the centre of the port. Bring it this afternoon." He put his hand on my arm. "Bring two men only." He shrugged apologetically, "You are Norsemen are you not?"

I smiled, "Yes we are. I will bring just two."

The ship in question had three masts as well as ports for ten oars on each side. It had a fighting castle at the stern.

'Heart' could sail rings around it but it would be a hard ship to capture. Much to Arturus' annoyance when I went for the meeting I took Haaken and Aiden with me. Aiden carried the precious book wrapped in a sheepskin.

"Cnut, you and Trygg try to buy some seeds and grain. Use the coin we were just paid for the slaves." I had decided not to use the gold we had found in the Roman fort. That was our reserve and I did not wish to advertise the fact that we had gold. Let them think we only had the money we had received for the slaves.

The Count had many guards aboard his ship. As we approached we were viewed suspiciously. One of them disappeared into the stern castle and the Count emerged. He smiled and waved us on board.

"Come, I have some mulled wine waiting for us. I have been eagerly anticipating the holy book."

He had a cabin. There was a bed and a table with two chairs. He gestured, "Please sit."

I nodded to Aiden who placed the wrapped book on the table. The Count poured me a goblet of the warm wine. "Your good health, Jarl."

The warm and honeyed wine had a sweet and not unpleasant taste. It warmed as it went down. "And yours, Count Pepin."

He licked his lips. I know not if it was from the wine or the anticipation of the book. "May I?"

"Of course."

He unwrapped it with the greatest of care and then he wiped his hands on a piece of clean linen which had been placed on the table. The cover of the book was decorated exquisitely and made of the softest calfskin.

"Beautiful. Was it made by those monks you sold me?"

"We took it from their church so I suppose they did."

"This shows great craftsmanship." He opened it and actually sighed with delight. He moved his fingers across the painted words. "It is a pity you cannot read, Viking."

"I can read a little." I stood behind him and read, " *'In principio creavit Deus caelum et terram.'* " He nodded, "I

85

think it means '*In the beginning God created heaven, and earth*'."

"I am impressed, Norseman! Then you know that this book is valuable?"

"I know that the men of the White Christ, you Christians think so. But as it does not tell me where to buy swords or where the edge of the world is to be found it is of little use to me."

"But it is beautiful."

"As is a sunset and I can watch one of those any time I like."

He laughed, "You are unusual. You are a poet!"

"No, my friend Haaken here is a singer of songs and a teller of tales while Aiden is the poet."

"I like you. Here."

He handed me a leather purse. I opened it and saw gold pieces within. I looked at him suspiciously. "You do not wish to haggle?"

"That is a fair price. More than fair to be truthful but I hope that you will bring any such books you... er ... find, to me."

"Of course." I handed the purse to Aiden. "You will free the monks and have them make more such books for you."

"A mind reader too. Yes, for I love beautiful things."

"I will bring the holy books to you if you can give me some information."

"If I can."

"We need fine weapons and Frankia is closed to us. Where should we go?"

"You are blunt too. You do know that I am related to the Emperor?"

"I guessed as much."

"Then why should I help you?"

"Because you want more books and I can get them for you."

He laughed. "Let me see your sword please. I was told that it is special."

"It is."

He weighed it and balanced it in his hand. "This is an old sword but it is well made. Do you see this?" He pointed to the shallow groove which ran along both sides. I nodded. "Do you know what this is for?"

I had not given it much thought. "I assume to let the blood run away."

He laughed, "I am not certain that Norse warriors worry about such things do you? No it is the sign of a good sword maker. It lightens the sword without compromising its strength. You need swords like this one. There are many swords like this in the Empire. I believe that the blank for this one came from Frankia. There are, however, other swords just as good and in some cases better than Imperial swords. The best can be found in Byzantium; the city of Constantinopolis. I believe you call it Miklagård. It produces the best but it is a long journey. South of here, around Toledo, is a place where they make good weapons. The Arabs have conquered much of that land. We have retaken some in the north, the Marcia Hispanica, and there are free peoples in Navarra, on the north east. They have good weapons and they hold off the Arabs." He sipped his wine and studied me. "I should warn you that it is a wild coast and they are a wild people. We discovered that at Roncesvalles." He shrugged, "But I have seen your ship and your men. You look as though you can look after yourselves." He stood, "And now we must take our leave of you." Leaning in he said, "This place can be a little dangerous at night; especially after a sale. We will sale on the next tide." He held his hand out. "My people have a custom of touching palms when we say farewell." I touched his hand and it was softer than Erika's.

"Farewell."

We headed back to '*The Heart of the Dragon*'. Aiden weighed the bag in his hand. "The purse feels heavy, lord."

"It is, Aiden. we have done well. Now if Trygg and Cnut have done as well we can sail away from here. I trust it not."

Chapter 9

They had indeed been successful. Trygg's knarr was filled with sacks of grain and seed. They had also bought ducks and chickens too as well as cured hams which we split between the two vessels. Cnut beamed. "Perhaps I should be a trader. I only spent half of the coin you gave me."

I was suspicious. "That does not sound right. I want Sven White Beard and ten warriors on board the knarr. We sail on the morning tide."

Haaken asked, "What is amiss?"

"The Count seemed a little eager to leave. He implied that this might be a dangerous place after a sale. Perhaps he too is worried about Rorik and his greedy fingers."

"But he took a share of the auction costs he should be happy."

"Aye but he knows how much gold we have and I would have expected him to charge as much as possible. I think he has an eye for our ships. We are the last ships in the port and we can be cut out easily. Have half of the men sleep now and they can guard tonight."

Haaken nodded, "And then we sail home?"

"No, we will escort Trygg to the coast of Britannia and then we will go to the land of Navarre and see what weapons we can get."

"But they are a wild people!"

I laughed, "And we are not Haaken?"

Arturus did not like being cooped up on the boat. He wanted to explore the town. "You will learn, my son, that life is not all an adventure. Sometimes we have to let our minds rule our hearts."

He went to the prow to sulk. Aiden smiled, "He is still young, Jarl Dragon Heart. He has seen but thirteen summers. You are deceived by his size and his prowess as a warrior. His mind has yet to catch up with his body. Do not worry I will speak with him."

Aiden was more like a big brother to Arturus. Thinking of my duties as a father I wondered how Erika was. She had promised me a new son by the time I returned. I would now be delayed. I wondered if she had given birth yet. I could not rush back, much as I might wish to. We had secured the food but we still needed weapons and while we had the money to do so then we had to act.

He woke me when all was dark. "Haaken sent me. There are men approaching the ships from the land and the sea."

I took no satisfaction from being right. "Are the men ready?"

"Aye my lord, the ships boys are ready with bows and they guard the mast."

My worry was Trygg's vessel. It was smaller with fewer men. Moored close to the prow I made my way there. Aiden woke Arturus as I donned my helmet, picked up my shield and slid Ragnar's Spirit from its scabbard. I saw that my men were crouched beneath the gunwale. The wharf rats would get a surprise.

Haaken and Cnut slid next to me. "We have placed men on both sides."

"Good. I want the two of you to choose eight men and go to the aid of the knarr should they need it."

I reached the prow and peered over. I could see shadows moving across the bridges from the land and the water, too, was filled with moving patches of dark. They were counting on us being asleep.

When they came they came suddenly and silently. One moment they were shadows and the next their hands were on the gunwale as they pulled themselves up. My men were ready and blades leapt to sever arms and slice into necks. A face appeared before me and I stabbed him in the chest. He screamed back into the water. The sound was like an alarm. Two more came from the river side and I swung Ragnar's Spirit at their heads. The blade sliced across the nose and cheeks of one and ripped into the neck of his companion. I had cleared the prow. I heard shouts from the knarr. "Haaken! Cnut!"

The ten warriors hacked their way across the gangplank and headed towards the knarr. I could see that my ship was

secure. I stood next to the carved dragon and leapt towards
the stern of the knarr. I landed on one man and heard
something crack beneath my feet. A second warrior was
about to stab Trygg's unguarded back. He screamed in pain
and surprise when my blade emerged through his chest.

The sudden reinforcements had worked and the survivors
threw themselves into the water to grab a waiting boat and
escape. Magnus and the boys loosed arrow after arrow.
Rorik had learned a valuable lesson that night. Do not take
liberties with the Ulfheonar.

"Take any weapons from the dead and then throw the
bodies overboard."

I heard a groan from close by my feet. The man I had
landed upon moaned, "You have broken my back. End it
now, I beg of you."

He was a Dane and his fingers still gripped his sword.
"Go to the Allfather."

I slid the edge across his throat and he sighed as he died.

When the bodies had been removed I ordered the
weapons into the hull of the knarr. We had four wounded
warriors. I put them on board the knarr with Sven. Taking
Sven and Trygg to one side I said, "When we leave I will go
with you as far as the coast. You will sail home. Sven knows
the route and our people need what you have."

Sven White Hair had served me long enough not to argue.
"And what will I tell your lady, Jarl?"

"Tell her we sail south for weapons."

As soon as the tide was right we cast off. We saw no-one
as we headed south but I knew that eyes were watching us.
We might return again but I would not trust those who lived
on the island. They might be of Norse descent but they were
thieves.

Dawn saw us heading north west. The wind was still from
the north but had drifted to a more north easterly direction. I
hoped that it would change soon else my men would have a
long voyage home as they tacked back and forth. When we
saw the dark smudge of the coast we waved our farewells
and turned south. The slow moving knarr would take longer

to reach home than it would us. We were free from the shackles of sailing with a consort. With the wind behind us we flew. We had sea room and I stood well off the coast. I did not wish to risk either Rorik's pirates or Charlemagne's Imperial ships.

We sailed until late afternoon and then I risked closing with the coast. Aiden had his maps out and was trying to guess where we might be. We saw the coast appear to the east as well as ahead of us. "There are many islands around here. We could find one for shelter. And there is a river, the Sequana, which flows from a large place the parchment calls Parisius."

"Mark them down when we reach the river. We will not use it yet, we have no need of supplies but when we make our way north we may need to."

Ketil shouted down when he saw the first of the islands. There looked to be a string of them heading along the coast. "Oars out, Magnus, get the sail down."

I did to want us silhouetted against the setting sun and we would sail slowly until we found an uninhabited island. "Arturus, climb up the mast and find us a deserted island."

My son was happy for that meant he would not be rowing and he always preferred to do exciting things. I was confident he would know what we needed. It had to be small yet large enough to hide our shape and it should have a beach. We passed two before he whistled and pointed at one which looked like a whale.

Once we moored Snorri and Beorn climbed the small rise to spy out the mainland. They returned with good news. They could not see any settlements on the mainland. It meant we could risk a fire. We ate well and we drank well. I had bought a barrel of wheat beer from Agnetha. It made up for the fact that my men had not enjoyed some time ashore.

Aiden took us through the parchments after we had eaten. It did not mention the people of Navarre but it did mention one or two places where there were old Roman forts. It would be a start.

"Who are these Arabs the Count spoke of?"

I shrugged, "Warriors I suppose."

Aiden ventured, "I believe they are brown skinned warriors who come from Africa which is as hot as Norway and Denmark are cold. They are fierce."

Cnut and Haaken exchanged a glance which told me that neither was happy. "You do not approve of our voyage?"

"It seems to me," said Cnut, "that we are risking much and there is little to be gained."

"Give me your sword, Cnut."

He handed it over, puzzled. "Aiden, close your eyes and put out your arms." He did so. I laid Cnut's sword across them. "Feel that weight. Can you remember it?"

"Aye my lord."

I took the sword and handed it back to Cnut. Aiden would not open his eyes until I told him to. I laid Ragnar's Spirit on them. "Now this weight. Do you have it?"

"Aye my lord."

I sheathed my sword. "Open your eyes." He did so. "Now which was heavier the first or the second."

"That is easy it was the first one."

I saw Haaken nodding his understanding. When the Count had examined my sword he had not heard the words as I had. "You see Cnut, it is all in the design. We can have lighter, better weapons but we need to get them from somewhere other than Frankia and the Holy Roman Empire. For myself I would travel to Miklagård, but we would be away for too long. Even now I will reach home after my son has been born but we need the weapons."

Cnut looked at his own blade, "You are right, as ever. We will find out for ourselves if these men of Navarre are as wild as the Count said."

We left before dawn so that any watchers would not see us. I risked sailing closer to the coast as we journeyed south. I was anxious that Aiden make the map as accurate as possible. I knew that we could use such maps to our advantage. If we knew which places were undefended then we could all become richer.

Viking Wolf

We passed many fortified towns as we headed south and a river as big as the Rinaz. We also saw undefended monasteries. They were tempting but I knew we would have the journey north to pick up some easy treasure. We also passed manned towers. They were simple structures which were round and rose like a finger. I guessed they were simple watch towers to search for warriors and ships such as us.

We found no island and had to beach the ship just after a small coastal sea. It was almost dark and we would have risked the sea save that we smelled wood smoke. It was inhabited. The beach we found was surrounded on three sides by marshes and our hunters managed to net fifteen good size birds. We ate well.

Aiden had told us that we would see the land of Navarre the next day. For that reason I had fifteen of our men don their armour and weapons. We would need to be able to respond to any threat.

The coast began to turn west and we watched as the cliffs grew. This was more like the land of the Norse! We were far enough out to sea so that we could run if threatened. Ketil spotted the river and a walled fishing port in the early afternoon. We had seen a larger fortified town earlier in the morning. We needed something smaller. The walled fishing port seemed perfect. We saw no tower close by although we were some way out to sea. I risked heading inshore. Landing at a small beach a mile or so to the west of the port we secured the ship. The *'Heart of the Dragon'* was hidden by two small headlands. It was not perfect but we needed to discover if there were fine weapons in this land as we had been told. I was not certain that the fishing port would yield high quality arms but we would try it.

I left ten men on board and the rest of us donned armour and headed up the track which zigzagged up the cliffs. We had been at sea for over a week and it showed. Only Snorri and Arturus were not out of breath when we reached the top. Leaving Thorir as a sentry we set off north east towards the fishing village. We would be approaching from the landward side. The sun was dipping in the west and we would have an hour or so of daylight left. I intended to scout out the area before we attacked the next day.

Suddenly Snorri waved us to the ground. We fell like shadows beneath our wolf cloaks. We heard the sound of hooves in the distance. There were horses galloping nearby and the sound was growing closer. I realised that we had been walking along a trail. If horses were coming they would use it. "Roll to the side."

My urgent call made everyone roll from the path. I was not certain if we would remain hidden but had we stayed on the path then we would have been seen for sure. I risked a look and I saw ten horsemen in the distance. They had helmets and shields but my eye was drawn to the long spears they held. They would see us easily and the spears could keep us at bay.

"When they close rise and ambush them."

The Norns had decided that we would not have an easy journey. The horsemen had been sent to test us. I would have to rise and draw my sword in one motion. Tostig, Snorri and Arturus were in front of me. They would be at the most risk. Miraculously the first two riders passed me without incident but the fifth rider must have seen Tostig. I saw his spear rise and fall and Tostig screamed.

"To your feet!" I unsheathed Ragnar's Spirit and punched at the nearest horse with my shield. As the rider struggled to control his mount I stabbed underneath his shield. My blade entered his heart and came out through his shoulder. He fell to the ground and the horse veered away. I saw a spear as it was jabbed towards me I spun my shield and took the blow. It knocked me to the ground. The horse reared and I saw the spear as it was raised ready to strike me. I felt like a stranded fish. I grabbed the end of the spear as the head closed with me. I pulled. The rider forgot to let go and I watched as he fell on the blade of my outstretched sword. His lifeless head lolled on my chest. Pushing him away I rose to my feet.

I saw, to my horror and dismay, two riders fleeing back towards the fishing village but when I looked I saw that they were not heading for the coast, they were heading for a hill.

A flash of light from the setting sun showed, for an instant, a castle!

"Grab any spare horses and all the arms we can carry." I pointed. "There is a castle there."

We put Tostig's inert body and the arms of the dead on the two horses we managed to capture and then we set off at a fast pace back towards the ship. The sun was setting rapidly now and the Norns must have been cackling to themselves when Einar tripped. We heard the crack as a bone broke and we had to carry him too.

"Thorkell, keep them going. Sigtrygg, Haaken and Cnut with me." They joined me swords drawn. The blood on their blades told me that they had fought. "We will keep to the rear in case we have to slow them down."

We went a little slower not wishing to suffer Einar's fate. The journey seemed much longer than the one we had made earlier. Perhaps it was the dark which now enveloped us. I realised that the trail we had followed gave our pursuers a clear idea of where we were going. I wondered if they had ships they would send after us. There was little point in speculating.

When we reached the top of the cliff Thorir was waiting. He suddenly shouted, "Horsemen!"

We turned and there was a column of horsemen hurtling towards us. We were saved, not by our weapons, but the land. The horses had to slow down because of the steep cliff. The five of us raced at them and we all swung our swords to make a wall of death before the horses. My blade bit into the shoulder of one of the horses sending the unfortunate beast and rider over the cliff. I felt a spear crack into the side of my helmet. It made my head ring. I swung my shield around, just in time to meet the same spear trying to pierce my mail. I swung Ragnar's Spirit and chopped the shaft in two. I pushed my shield against the horse and the horse and rider also tumbled over the cliff to their death on the rocks below.

The riders dismounted and they approached us. I took in that some of them had armour but their shields were smaller than ours. "At them!" Even though outnumbered we charged them. My sword cracked through the shield of the first horseman and I butted his surprised face. As he fell I stabbed him. To my left I heard a scream as Thorir was speared. In death he pulled his killer to the rocks below. I could see, in the distance more horsemen.

"Back to the ship!"

We began to edge back down the cliff. The horses would struggle to follow us. It was our only chance. Suddenly Sigtrygg raced forward and with three rapid blows killed one and wounded two of the horsemen. The others fell back and we moved a little quicker down the cliff. We had a lead and I intended to keep it.

Aiden and Marcus had turned our ship around so that we were already facing out to sea. As we ran down the last fifty paces I saw that Thorkell had our archers ready and they began to loose arrows at our pursuers. The arms and the bodies were on board and the horses we had used were just standing there. I smacked them on the rump and chased them back towards the cliff. The two frightened animals ran at the men of Navarre who were trying to reach us.

Sigtrygg was the last man to be pulled aboard and I shouted, "Loose sail and row!"

We were lucky that they had no bows but I saw, as we pulled away, that there were forty of them on the beach. We had had a fortunate escape. The Allfather watched out for us.

I did not head east, I headed north. I wanted to avoid the fishing port. "Keep a lookout for ships!"

Aiden was tending to the wounded. Einar had a broken leg but he could still row. Tostig was dead and Ragnar Siggison had a sword wound to the arm. It could have been worse.

"Ships to the steer board!"

I looked to see where Ketil pointed. There were three long low ships pulling towards us. Had we sailed along the coast we would have been caught. "Double bank the rowers!"

Every warrior save Ragnar took an oar. There were just the ship's boys, Aiden and myself not rowing. "Keep at this pace Cnut, I will tell you when to up the rate."

We were heading towards the open sea. Somewhere ahead was the edge of the world. I hoped that we could frighten those pursuing us into giving up.

"Magnus, come here!"

Magnus came and I gave him the steer board. I turned to get a better look at the three ships. They were smaller than we were with just ten oars on each side. We had more sail but, at the moment, it was not helping us for we were sailing into the wind. If we turned the ship to get more wind we would be heading back to the coast. We would suffer the vagaries of the wind. It was now too dark to make out the men on board. If I had had any idea how many men there were I might have risked a fight at sea. There were too many things I didn't know. There might be heavier crews and more ships. I had plotted my course, now I would sail it.

I took the steer board. "Arm the boys with bows. If they close we will discourage them."

"Aye my lord."

The ships behind were definitely gaining. I estimated that, at this speed, they would be upon us before midnight. I had a plan but it involved perfect timing.

I felt something whizz past my ear and I saw an arrow strike the sail. It did not tear it but fell at the feet of a surprised Thorkell. He grinned.

"I am going to turn us north west and then bring her round to north east."

Haaken looked up at the pennant, "But that will take us into the wind."

"I know and as soon as we do, Cnut, I want full speed. I want them to turn too. Once they are committed then we will head north west again until we lose them."

Ketil said fearfully, "To the edge of the world and the wild seas?"

I laughed, "You are my oathsworn! Let us enjoy the journey!"

My men all cheered and I wondered what the men of
Navarre thought of the noise which would carry over the
water to them. I put the steer board over and we moved a
little faster. We opened a slight gap as we caught the three
ships by surprise. "Magnus when we slow have your archers
ready to shower the leading ship." I was pleased to see Aiden
join them with an arrow notched. Five arrows or more would
wend their way to their targets.

The three ships worked hard and began to catch us again.
"Ready, archers!"

I put the steer board over and the ship slowed
dramatically as the wind struck our sail head on. I had caught
the three ships by surprise. They ploughed on and were just
forty paces from us. "Now Magnus! Cnut, double speed!"
Magnus and his boys managed three flights before the speed
of our rowers took us away from the three confused ships.
As they turned to follow us they too slowed and a sizeable
gap opened. Their smaller crews could not manage the
power of my men. My crew rowed at double speed and we
fairly flew through the black night. "Aiden where are they?"

"I can barely see them."

I counted to five hundred in my head and then put the
steer board over. We moved much faster now as the wind
and the rowers took us towards the edge of the world.

"I can't see them."

We rowed for another count of five hundred at double
speed and then I said, "Normal speed." The wind more than
made up for the loss of oar power and we moved quickly
through the water.

When Aiden reported that he could no longer see them I
ordered half of the rowers to rest. We kept pulling north
west. I changed the rowers when Aiden had counted three
thousand. After four changes I ordered the oars to be stowed.
If they were still close to us then they were worthy
adversaries. With thick cloud cover I had no idea of our
position. The wind still came from the steer board side and I
assumed we were still heading north west but I had no real
idea. The edge of the world was somewhere ahead of us. I

prayed for dawn. I did not want to sail over the edge in the dark.

When dawn eventually broke I knew where the east was and we turned due north. We were barely making headway but at least we would not sail off the edge of the world. When the sun finally rose Ketil scampered up the mast and reported not a sail in sight. We had out run our pursuers.

Chapter 10

I let the men sleep as we drifted north. With the wind still coming from the north east I had to keep tacking. Aiden opened the maps and all that we could see was empty space. We could strike Hibernia, or Wessex or we could keep sailing north until we struck the top of the world and the ice wall. We had no idea of our position. I hoped that the weapons had been worth the sacrifice. By noon I was feeling sleepy but the wind veered around a little to come more from the east. When Haaken woke he took over the steering and I drifted off into a troubled sleep. Losing my Ulfheonar always haunted me. I awoke and discovered Aiden dressing the wound on my hand. I had forgotten the blow.

"When were you going to tell us about this Jarl Dragon Heart? It could have become poisoned and you would have been Jarl One Hand!"

I smiled. He was like Erika the way he nagged me. He dressed the wound and I watched as night fell. The seas, whilst not wild were rougher than we would have liked. We had little choice. We had to keep sailing north.

I rotated the ship's boys in the prow. The mast head was too dangerous. What worried me was that the easterly wind would continue to push us west towards the edge of the world. The clouds hid the stars, as they had for the last two nights. The sudden squall which thudded into us seemed to whirl from the south. It was a relief in two ways. It moved us northwards faster and the rainwater washed the salt from our faces and beards. We used a piece of canvas to collect some water. Fresh rain water was a good sign; it was sent from the gods. They smiled on us yet.

Dawn was a thin grey light from the east. The wind had turned so that it now came from the south east. I risked more sail and relied upon the sharp eyes of my boys. Magnus shouted, "Land ahead!"

Aiden needed no urging. He ran between the sleeping rowers to the prow and peered northward. The crew began to wake. His footsteps on the deck and the shout had awoken them. Above us I heard the gulls as they mobbed a different bird I had never seen before. That in itself was a good sign.

Haaken joined me, "Is it the edge of the world?"

I smiled. The poet in Haaken both feared and was drawn to the idea of sailing to the edge of the world. If we survived then he would have tales to tell until his dying day. "I hope not but Aiden will tell us."

He came back and his expression gave me hope. "I think these are the isles at the end of On Corn Walum." He pointed east where the sky was lightening. "They are to the north and there is the land to the east. The Romans called them Scillonia Insula."

I nodded, "Syllingar! I know where we are. Full sail, Magnus."

I put the steer board over to take us west. The wind caught the sail and as the boys trimmed the stays and the sheets, we flew once more. The islands were a deadly set of teeth which guarded the end of the mainland. I had heard that there were people who lived there but we just wanted to pass them on the last leg of our journey home.

We had the tricky part to come for we had to turn north and sail between Hibernia and Cymru. Once we had passed them we would just have to negotiate Anglesey and the island of Man and then we would be home and I would see my new son.

Once we had cleared the rocks I handed over to Cnut and slept again. My nightmares did not return. We were heading home. Perhaps my dead Ulfheonar had already reached Valhalla and interceded with the gods. Certainly our voyage was becoming easier. The winds and my rowers had made us fly across the seas. The danger of death had given us extra strength and, perhaps, saved us.

When I awoke it was because Aiden had tapped me on the shoulder. "My lord, we are approaching Anglesey. We thought you would wish to be awake."

"I do. Have you slept?"

He shook his head, "I do nothing save look at the land and the maps. I will sleep when we reach Cyninges-tūn."

I nodded. Aiden was special. He was a gladramenn. "Wake the men and have them prepare for trouble."

Aiden looked at me. "Have you the second sight now?"

"Let us just say that the attack when we came south worried me."

The wind had now veered completely and was coming from the west. It was a cold and a wet wind. We were not travelling as quickly as we had been but we were less than half a day from home. I looked at the sky. It was late afternoon. We would reach Úlfarrston after dark.

"Sails ahead!"

We had just passed Anglesey safely when the shout came from Ketil. "Where away?"

"North west!"

I put the steer board over a little to take us more north and west than north. We would investigate. The westerly wind gave us the wind gauge. If this was danger then we could avoid it. I wondered if it might be our knarr.

"It is *'Man'* and she is attacking a smaller ship!"

Sometimes voices speak to me and I know not where they come from. This one told me that the small ship was Trygg's. "Oars!"

Cnut organised the rowers and soon we cut through the water like a hot knife through cold butter. Our speed took us closer to them and I could see that Erik's drekar was closing with the knarr. It was Trygg's. Even as I watched the sail came down as grappling hooks snaked across the water. "Full speed, Cnut! Let's hit this bastard!"

We covered the last couple of hundred paces so quickly that I almost forgot to order oars in. As it happened I timed it perfectly. "Oars in! Sail down! Prepare to board!" I aimed the dragon prow for the steer board of *'Man'*. It would also put us between the two ships. "Aiden! My helmet and shield."

He proffered them. "They are here!"

Those at the stern of the drekar saw us. A flurry of arrows came towards us and Aiden held the shield to protect us both. They could not save themselves. Ragnar's well made ship struck the steer board hard and shattered it. The man holding it was thrown from the deck and crushed between the two giants of the sea. Our speed and weight pushed aside the two ships. Our higher freeboard meant that we could just jump on board their ship.

"Grappling hooks away!"

As the boys threw the hooks, my men, led by Haaken and Cnut, leapt on board.

"Aiden keep the archers clearing their decks. Magnus take the steer board."

"My lord! Another drekar!" Aiden pointed to the south west where a strange drekar was taking advantage of the wind and coming to the aid of *'Man'*.

I shouted down to the knarr. "Sven White Hair, get your men aboard us and defend the ship."

I had no idea if they heard me but any that did would obey my orders. I jumped to the deck of the drekar. Tostig Tostigson knew that he was both outclassed and outnumbered by my warriors. He had retreated to the prow with those that had survived the initial onslaught. He was relying on delaying us until his consort arrived. It would be a bloody battle to take them.

"Sigtrygg, Haaken and Cnut shield wall. Snorri and Arturus, take axes and hole her!" My men looked at me. We were deliberately sinking a drekar with us on board. "Just do it!"

With my oathsworn either side of me I moved forward. I had no mail upon me but I wore my leather byrnie and my wolf cloak. I would rely on those for protection. I heard the hacking of axes behind me as Snorri and Arturus obeyed my orders. Tostig and his men did not wait for us to advance but rushed down the deck to us. Fighting on a moving ship involved great balance as well as quick reactions. We had both. As Sven and my men climbed aboard my drekar the deck of *'Man'* dipped alarmingly.

Olaf No-Nose held his arms out for balance and Sigtrygg darted in to stab him in the throat. With a gap in their ranks Sigtrygg and Saxon Killer stepped forward flanked by Cnut and Haaken. My mailed men were protecting their jarl. I am a taller man than most and Thorkell the Tall was next to me. We reached over our front rank to stab our longer swords, blindly, at those behind their front rank. I felt my blade sink into flesh and there was a scream. I pushed into Cnut's back and we heard a splash as one of those at the rear fell overboard.

Sven White Hair's voice came to me from the stern of my ship. "Jarl Dragon Heart, pull back. The other drekar is close."

I risked a look over my shoulder and saw that the drekar's dragon prow was abeam of the mast. I also took in that we were lower in the water. My men had sprung the keel.

"Snorri and Arturus back aboard the *'Heart'*!"

Just then Haaken brought his sword down with a mighty blow and split the helmet and skull of Tostig Tostigson. Sigtrygg and Cnut killed two more and I swung my blade at a warrior who had climbed the gunwale to attack us along the side. My blade sliced completely through one leg and into the other. He tumbled over the side. Tostig's men were now jumping from the stricken ship.

"Back!"

My men turned as the crew of the other drekar jumped down to *'Man's'* deck. I did not recognise the mailed jarl with a dragon painted shield but he came directly for me. This would not be easy. He was mailed and I was not. My Ulfheonar were fighting for their own lives as the new crew flooded on to the deck of the stricken drekar.

The jarl had an axe and he swung it horizontally at my shield. It made my arm shiver and I felt a trickle of blood as the wound in my hand began to bleed again. I could not swing easily for Haaken was next to me. I stabbed forwards in the hope that I might catch him. My sword slid along the links of his mail. He took advantage and swung at me with a back hand blow. I twisted my body and took the blow on my shield. The movement caused a gap to appear between Haaken and me. I brought Ragnar's Spirit over and caught him on his right shoulder. This time the mail did split and the edge ripped into his mail byrnie. He said nothing but I saw him wince. I had hurt him.

"Jarl Dragon Heart, the ship is sinking come back!"

I realised that my back was touching the sheerstrake and my ship was above us. There were just five of us left on board the sinking drekar. If I tried to turn I would die. I saw what he intended as he raised his shield slightly. He was going to punch me in the face with it. There was but one counter, I dropped to my knees as the shield came towards me. The water was around my middle. I held Ragnar's Spirit in both hands and I thrust upwards underneath his mail byrnie. I felt it sink into the soft under flesh of his unprotected groin and he screamed. I pushed harder and felt it grind off bone. When my hands touched his torso I twisted and pulled. His shield dropped and his lifeless body fell backwards. As I pulled out my sword I saw that it was coated in his entrails.

I stood and hands pushed me upwards. As I tumbled to the deck of my ship my last four warriors joined me. I stood and watched the ship I had sailed as a young warrior, slip silently beneath the sea, its deck covered in the dead and the dying.

The drekar which survived was drifting away. Their attack was spent and their Jarl dead. We had won!

The boys were still loosing arrows at the departing drekar to encourage them to leave but I knew they were beaten. Jarl Erik had lost many fine warriors. As I looked around my ship I could see that there would be empty chests on the way home. My longest serving brothers lived still. I saw Aiden binding their wounds but they would fight again. Arturus and Snorri were busy reliving their moments of glory.

I walked to the steer board side and shouted down to the knarr. "Trygg, have you any damage?"

He shook his head. "You came in time. We lost but one of my crew and one of Sven's men. Any longer and…" he shrugged.

"*Wyrd*! Head on back to Úlfarrston. We will watch your stern." His small square sail was lowered and he began to pull, slowly away. "Magnus, lower the sail. Tell your boys they did well."

The knarr was forty paces from us when the sail was tautened and we moved slowly north. I looked over the stern and saw the bodies and the debris from the battle. I hoped that I had curbed Erika's brother. I did not want to have to escort every ship sailing south from Úlfarrston. I looked at the sky. We would not reach Úlfarrston before dark. Indeed, we would be lucky to reach it before morning. The reunion with my wife would have to wait another day. It would be all the sweeter for the wait.

As we neared the coast I shouted to Trygg. "We will anchor in the estuary. If the tide is on the turn we may be grounded. Better to wait until the morning."

"Aye, Jarl Dragon Heart."

I had another troubled sleep. Perhaps it was the warriors who had died in the battle who haunted me. Was I changing? I used to sleep the sleep of a child but lately...

As dawn broke we headed inshore. The tide was on its way in. As we approached the bank closest to Úlfarrston we saw another knarr drawn up on the beach. It looked forlorn and lonely.

"Take her up to the trail and unload our trade goods."

Haaken nodded, "Right boys just another short row and then we march!"

Trygg hailed me. "That is my cousin's knarr. What is it doing here?"

"I know not. Follow Haaken and unload her. I will discover all."

I was as intrigued as any. I strode over to the gate. The sentry recognised me and it was opened. Pasgen had barely risen. He bowed. "Did you have a good voyage Jarl Dragon Heart?"

"It was successful but I have to tell you that the men of Man are pirates. We were attacked leaving and returning."

His face fell, "My ship is overdue. She left before you did. I thought there must have been storms."

106

I nodded. "I fear foul play. When we have recovered I will take my men and we will pay the island of Man a visit."

He smiled, "We thank you Jarl Dragon Heart. I would hate to see the prosperity you brought taken away by thieves."

I pointed to the river. "Who does the knarr belong to?"

"It arrived seven days ago, in the morning. At first we thought it was the one you had taken away. They said they had followed the other from Orkneyjar." He shook his head. "It was pitiful, four of the women were ill. One died on the first afternoon. I sent a message to your lady. Rolf and your daughter came the next day to escort them to Cyninges-tūn. We have not heard from them since."

"Has my wife given birth yet?"

He shrugged, "She had not when your daughter came but who knows."

I suddenly remembered the land of Navarre and the towers. "I would suggest you build a tall stone tower at the point closest to the sea. If you man that you can see further out to sea and spy any dangers which approach."

He nodded, "That is a good idea but where would we get the stone?"

I pointed to the mountains and hills rising to the north. "The earth has many rocks and stones. I will get my men to mine some and we will bring them down to you."

When I reached my men the goods had been unloaded and they were ready to carry them. Although I was anxious to see both the progress on the new drekar and the weapons from Navarre, I was more anxious to see my family and our new refugees. All of us were laden down as we headed north. We even had to leave some seed with Pasgen and the ships' boys for we could not carry it all. I helped Haaken, Cnut and Sigtrygg to carry our newly acquired weapons. For some reason my burden seemed to get heavier the further north we went. Haaken put it down to the black heavy clouds we could see ahead. They were the thunder clouds which showed that the Allfather was angry about something. The omens were not good.

The watchers in the villages would see us as soon as we began to walk up the Water. We were a mile or so along when I saw a rider in the distance and he was galloping hard. I frowned. I feared it was ill news. Had the wolves returned? Then I remembered those men from the north we had slain; had others come for revenge? I knew that I had too much imagination; it was my curse but I could not help the pictures of raiders in the valley slaughtering my people.

When I saw it was Rolf I felt relieved. My people would be safe. Rolf would have died rather than let anything happen to them.

He reined up and threw himself from his saddle and dropped at my feet. I knew his wounds still troubled him and I went to raise him up.

"Jarl Dragon Heart, I have failed you."

My Ulfheonar had laid down their burdens and were looking, in concern at Rolf. "You could never fail me. Rise and tell me your news. The anticipation of bad news is often worse than the bad news itself."

He rose slowly and when I looked on his face I had never seen him so distressed. "The Lady Erika and your new born son, Jarl Dragon Heart, they are dead."

Chapter 11

Arturus ran up to Rolf and began to shake him. "You lie! You lie! It cannot be true!"

Rolf shook his head. "I would give my life for it to be a lie but I speak the truth."

I nodded at Aiden and he put his arm around Arturus and led him away. "Let us sit on the stones while you tell your tale. I am anxious to get home but I wish to know all before I do so."

"It began seven days or so ago. Pasgen sent news that a knarr full of Trygg's sick relatives had arrived on the river. Your wife sent me and Kara to bring them to Cyninges-tūn. She was ever kind that way and she said it was our duty. She housed the sick women, for it was the women who were ill, in your hall. Two of them recovered thanks to your daughter and your wife. Then three days ago the birth pains came and your son was delivered by Kara. We were all overjoyed. But your wife began to cough as did Kara and your son. Over the next day no matter what the women of the village could do she worsened. The Lady Erica sent all from the hall save the sick women and child."

He suddenly began to cry. Men never cried. Rolf had been a fine warrior and the most dependable of jarls and yet now tears coursed down his beard.

"I should have disobeyed her, my lord and stayed with them."

I smiled, remembering my strong willed wife. "It would have taken the Allfather himself to cross my wife. If she told you that then it would be for a good reason."

He nodded and gathered himself, "When we went to the hall the next day, all were dead, save Kara. She came to the door of the hall and she seemed almost happy. She was certainly at peace and she was healed. The coughing had gone."

His words seemed to echo across the Water. I looked up and saw birds circling above. It seemed almost dream like.

Perhaps I was dreaming and this would end when I awoke. I closed my eyes and opened them again. This was no dream.

"Have the dead been buried?"

Rolf shook his head, "No, Jarl Dragon Heart, that is the most remarkable thing. Your daughter told us that you would return today and we should wait for you. She knew that you would return!"

I saw my Ulfheonar clutch their amulets. This bordered on witchcraft. Only Aiden seemed unconcerned. Trygg looked as though he was trying to find somewhere to hide. They were his family; what had they brought into our life?

"Let us go and pay our respects to my wife and see my daughter."

We marched the last few miles in a stunned silence. When we reached my hall I saw that the people were looking fearfully at us. They seemed afraid of my reaction. I kept a straight face and I held in the emotion I was feeling. I needed to speak with Kara. She was the only one who could tell me what had happened. She stood at the door of the hall and she was smiling. That was not what amazed me; she looked older. It was as though I had left a child and found a woman. She put her arms around me and said, "Welcome home, father."

She embraced Arturus. "Come, brother and say farewell to our mother."

We went into the hall and I saw Aiden close it and stand outside. Along with Haaken and Cnut he would ensure our privacy in this moment of grief.

Erika was laid out on the bed and dressed in a simple white shift. In her arms she held our dead son. That was the moment when my resolve nearly failed me. I felt my eyes begin to fill as my heart sank. It was Kara who got me through the moment.

"Mother is happy. You should know that."

I nodded. Had I spoken then the grief might have been too much. Behind me I heard Arturus' sobs and that too made me determined to be strong. I leaned over the two bodies and kissed them both. They were cold, like marble. I murmured, "Farewell." When I stood I felt that I could speak.

"Tell me all, my daughter."

She led me to the table and poured Arturus and me a horn of ale each. She waited until we had drunk before she began. "When the women came we knew how serious it was. I have been studying with the other volva and we decided that my mother and I would look after them. She sent away Seara, Scanlan and Maewe. She did not wish them to be ill too. Deidra and Macha felt it was their duty to help but Mother was insistent. She wanted but the two of us in the hall. It seemed to me that she knew what was to come. The two of us looked after the sick," She smiled, "I learned much and mother was a tower of strength but no matter what we did nothing seemed to work. After the first death we knew that we were just waiting for them to die." She hung her head a little. "I confess that I wanted to flee but mother was strong. She told me this was how women fought. She said you would not give up in battle because of difficulties and neither should we. We did all that we could. When Butar, for that was the name mother gave him, began to come I had to help. He was a healthy and a happy child. He came out not crying but he seemed to be almost laughing and we took that to be a good sign."

She sat on the bed next to Arturus and stroked his hair much as Erika had done when he had been a child. He had left the table and was holding his dead mother's hand. "She saw her death coming, brother. When we knew that we had the same condition mother told me that she would die but I would live. She would ensure that I lived. The other women died and there were just the three of us left alive in the hall. She made me light candles while I still could for she was weak from the child birth. The hall glowed with a beautiful golden light and then, as I returned, my new brother Butar, died. He coughed and a single tear rolled from one eye and then he died. The only sound he had made had been the laugh when he had been born."

111

"That was the moment when I thought that I would break down but mother told me that he had gone to the Otherworld and she would join him. She told me to get into bed and be ready to welcome you back. She told me to enter the dream world of the volva."

So this was witchcraft. I looked at my child whom I had lost. I had gained a volva but the child was gone forever. That hurt.

"When I slept I left my body and went with my mother high into the sky. We saw you sailing towards the edge of the world and she told me that you would be safe. You would not fall over the edge. We flew down to our Water and, as we flew over it she told me that she would die but she would live on through me. She told me I would be a volva and I would have the second sight." She sighed, "Then I woke and she was dead. I had lost my cough and I was a woman. I know what I shall be, father. I will be the volva for Cyninges-tūn. I shall find cures for the ills that hurt our people. I will keep home for you and watch over our folk when you and Arturus are away."

"Until you marry."

Her eyes and her face were deadly serious as she said, "I shall never marry. If I marry then I will lose my powers."

I was stunned. "What of your children, my grandchildren."

She smiled, "I have seen the future and Arturus will give you many grandchildren. As for me, I shall be the mother of our people. And now we must lay my mother and Butar in the ground. I have had the men prepare her barrow."

She stood and laid a white linen sheet over Erika. I noticed then that she and my son had been laid on a wooden bier which lay on top of the bed. She left the room and I stood with Arturus. He shook his head. "She has grown father. She has changed."

"She is still your sister."

He shook his head, "I am not sure. We left her as a child and she has changed overnight into a woman. How can that be?"

"Just as you went on the wolf hunt a boy and came back a warrior, my son. It is a change we all go through."

Kara returned with Haaken, Cnut, Sigtrygg and Thorkell. "These will bear our mother to her grave."

I almost smiled for my Ulfheonar were completely under her spell. She led them out of the hall. The whole of the village lined a route down to the water. It had been Erika's favourite place. There was a huge mound of earth already and a flat space with a wooden bier. The bodies were carried to the shore. Kara held up her hand. The warriors stopped and there was absolute silence. She stepped aside and waved her arm. The four warriors laid the linen covered bier in the centre of the cleared ground on top of the wooden slats.

When they had stepped back Kara pointed to the body and the women of the village came and laid grave goods next to my wife. They were the objects she would need in the Otherworld. There were her combs, her needles, her cooking pot and her necklaces. Finally Kara laid the blue stones I had given them both around my wife's neck. She looked at me and I knew what I had to do. I took the wolf amulet from around my own neck and placed it on my dead son's body. Kara nodded her approval. Stepping back she said, "Our lady goes to the Otherworld where she will watch over us." She bowed her head and everyone from the village trooped around the body placing handfuls of earth upon it. I joined in along with Arturus. I know not what my son thought but I felt as though I was in a dream. We continued until the body was covered and no soil remained. When the mound was finished she ordered the slaves to lay turf upon it. When they had done so, she took flower seeds from a small leather bag and scattered them over the top of the turf. I knew what they were; they were the small blue flowers which my wife loved. They were hardy and, when the spring came, the mound would be covered in a sea of blue.

As we walked back to the hall I asked, "How did you know what to do?"

"My mother told me in a dream." She smiled. "Since she died I have spoken with her each night."

This was truly *wyrd*.

After the funeral I returned to the hall. I just wanted to be alone. Arturus and the Ulfheonar tried to follow me.

"Needs must I have to be alone with my thoughts now. I will see you all when I have made sense of all of this. Be patient with me. Aiden, organise the distribution of the seed and give Bjorn the new weapons to examine."

My gladramenn stared into my face as though trying to determine what I would do. He appeared satisfied. "I will, Jarl Dragon Heart." Leaving his precious satchel on the table he ushered the Ulfheonar out. "Let us leave Jarl Dragon Heart to grieve."

I knew not if it was grief I was feeling or anger. How could I fight *wyrd*? I sat on the bed and tried to take it in. I had known something was amiss. The dreams and nightmares I had endured had not been because I had lost men it was Erika speaking with me and warning me. Could I have prevented this? I lay back on the bed and closed my eyes. Had I been here in my home would it have been any different? The voice came into my head, *'You and Arturus would have died too. You are Dragon Heart and you are the heart of the people. This is as it was meant to be.'* I knew that the voice was right.

I suddenly sat up and opened my eyes. Kara was standing at the door with a smile on her face. "I told you, father, mother is happy now and watches over us. You rest and leave all to me and Rolf. When you wake you will feel better and your new life can begin."

Just as suddenly she was gone. I undressed and slept. She was right I was exhausted and, if truth be told, I wanted the chance to dream for if Erika inhabited the dream world then I would see her again. I did dream and I saw Erika again but this was the young Erika. This was before the Midsummer festival on Man and was when I first came to know her. Ragnar, Butar and my mother appeared in the dreams too but I heard not their words. I did see their smiles and watched the three of them as they laughed and played with the baby Butar. When I woke I felt both refreshed and at one with the world. It had been *wyrd*. I could do nothing about the events which took place. The Norns had woven and I was part of their plans and schemes. It was like trying to tell a storm to abate or the tide to retreat; you could do nothing about either save live with the consequences.

It was the middle of the night when I emerged from my hall. The clouds which had plagued our voyage home had now scudded away and a bright moon peered optimistically above the hills. I could see old Olaf reflected in the waters. The waters were still, save for the occasional ripple where a fish rose close to the surface to devour an insect. It seemed as bright as day. I wandered down to the mound. As I did so I heard the sounds of the woods: the owl swooping on its prey, the snuffle of a hedgehog. I could hear them all clearly. When I reached the mound I touched the freshly laid turf. It was just Erika's body which lay there and her spirit was in the Otherworld but it was a comfort to know that she was close. I walked around the mound and stood on the shore.

I picked up a stone and skimmed it across the water much as I had on the river when I was growing up. What would I do now? Kara would not marry and that meant that Arturus must for he had to have children. My ancestors had sent the sword called Saxon Slayer to me. I was part of a line which stretched back beyond memory. My blood was in the rocks of this land. I was not Norse. I had been born in this land from those who had lived here. I was part of this land the Romans called Britannia. Until I had found the sword and the tomb I had not known that. The sword had changed me from a Viking to something else. I had a past and that past would determine our future. I had been sent the sword for a purpose. Bjorn had told me the sword could never be used in battle and I knew that it was a symbol. Just as the wolf was my symbol so the sword was the symbol of the land. The wolf would fight and the sword would defend. I stood, as the moon dipped below the hills. I knew what we must do; we had to make my home and my land stronger. We had to provide a haven for those who wished to live like us. Erika had shown me that when she had taken in the sick.

I returned to the hall. Save for the two guards on the walls I was the only one who moved. There was silence. There was peace. I lit a candle and sat at the table. Aiden's satchel lay upon it. It had been laid there before we had buried my wife. I took out the parchments and the maps. I could see the additions Aiden had made. These were the copies. I looked carefully at the place we had found the scabbard. It was marked by the original map maker as Luguvalium. I could see the Roman Wall began there and the river flowed through it. I had been sent there by the past. There was more reason than the treasure. That was the bait with which the past had caught me. The treasure was the land and Luguvalium was the key.

I followed the red trail Aiden had marked on the map. It was our journey north. I saw the place where we had fought the barbarians; it was marked by a cross. As I moved my finger west I found a small symbol. I recognised it as a fort for there was one on Windar's Mere. I looked east and saw where Ulf and Ulla had built their farmstead on Ulf's Water. I hoped that he had survived the winter for there was a pattern. The heart of my land was Cyninges-tūn. The body which protected that lay all around and just as I protected my body with armour so we needed to protect the land. I would spend the year making my land secure and then, when it was safe I would go to Miklagård. Part of my destiny lay there. I knew that. I was not a king but I had a kingdom.

Chapter 12

I was still seated at the table when the hall awoke. One of the slaves, Anya, peered fearfully at me as though she expected to be chastised. I smiled, "Fear not, Anya, and I am hungry enough to eat the leather from my boots. Some food would be most welcome." She smiled and scurried off. The sound of my voice woke both Kara and Arturus. The contrast in their faces was startling. Kara looked calm and at peace. Arturus had a red and angry face as though he had been weeping all night.

Kara nodded as she sat down. "You have understood father. I see the change in you." She put her arm around Arturus. He flinched a little. "You may be my big brother but I will heal you." She rose and kissed him on the top of the head, "I will go and make you a yarrow and sage brew. It will bring peace to you and your troubled mind."

After she had gone he said quietly, "She has changed father and it frightens me."

"All things change my son and change itself should not be a threat. Besides she is still Kara, your sister. She has just become a woman." He still looked confused. "Is Wolf, your dog, still the same beast as when he was a pup?"

"Of course not. He plays less and sleeps more."

"And he has changed; as you have changed and Kara has too. As a father I might yearn for the days when the two of you played with me and bounced on my knee but we all grow. Embrace it." I hesitated, "You are now a man my son. You have killed other men. You will soon be a man grown and need to think about fathering children. Your sister has shunned men and that, for her, is a good thing. You will rule this land when I am gone and you need sons."

He looked terrified. "You will not die too, will you?"

"We both know that could happen but I do not think my death is imminent. Just heed my words. This death, which is sad, will change all of us. Let us change for the better."

He seemed happier and after he had drunk Kara's potion he seemed more relaxed. Scanlan came to see me. He had been a slave whom I had freed and he now ran the day to day business of my house.

"I am sorry I could not save the lady, my lord but she sent us hence. We were forced to wait outside while the two of them fought the sickness."

"I know Scanlan and do not reproach yourself. My daughter has told me all. She will now be the lady of the hall. You and the others will heed her commands. I know that she is young but she has an old mind."

He smiled, "I know, Jarl Dragon Heart. Fear not the women of the house all dote on her anyway."

"Good. I shall be away for a while but we need to use the seeds we brought and make sure we have plenty of food. I would not have more of our people die in the winter."

"We have cleared more land by the water and it will yield good crops. The sheep our men brought are growing well and their wool is of a high quality. We will have much to trade before the snows come."

I went first to my blacksmith. I was anxious to see the new weapons we had found. The journey back and the events since we had arrived meant I had never even looked on them.

Bjorn was at his forge already and his boy was heating it up. "I am sorry for your loss, Jarl."

I nodded. I would have to get used to this. "Have you studied the weapons we brought back?"

His demeanour changed. He was like an excited child. He went to a chest and brought out a sword. "I have. They are a wonder, jarl." He pointed to the depression in the middle which was also on my sword. "Haaken and Cnut told me the purpose of this. I feel so foolish. I should have realised that before now. The blade is so much lighter and you use less metal."

I took the sword from him. It was longer than most swords, mine included and yet it felt lighter. "Frankia is closed to us. We could go to the land which made this sword but that would take a long time. Could you make swords like this?"

It was as though he had not thought of the question until that moment. "Not if we have to use the poor quality iron from captured weapons."

It was a good answer, "Suppose we could get you better iron; how then?"

He looked at the blade and I could see his mind working. He looked down the Water and then up at the hills. "We would need more men and a bigger building if we are to smelt our own iron but, yes, we could. I could use these blades as models."

I nodded, "I would use Aiden and his sharp mind."

He grinned, "He would have been the first person with whom I spoke." He frowned, "Where will you go for the iron?"

"I know not yet but I suspect that Aiden can help there too."

"Yes my lord?"

Aiden appeared from behind me. "We need to make our own iron rather than Bjorn here just reworking old iron."

He beamed. "In the parchments it tells how the Romans built kilns for their iron and I have ideas how to make the blades stronger yet lighter."

I could see Bjorn was intrigued. "How? It is not like gold you know. You cannot melt it and make it run."

Aiden looked at him, "Why not? If the rock is hot enough it will melt."

"But you would need it in something which would not melt. Have you such a vessel?"

"Not yet but I have yet to read all." He looked at me. "They would have many such books in Constantinopolis."

I saw Bjorn's puzzled look, "Miklagård," I said. Realisation dawned. "That is for the future. Tell Bjorn how you would make them stronger."

He looked around and then looked in his satchel. There were some pieces of yarn he used to tie up his parchments. He handed one to Bjorn. "Break it."

He did so easily and laughed, "Give me a challenge."

Aiden laughed and bound together many of the pieces. He twisted them and tied them together. The he dipped it into the water. "Now try."

No matter how much he strained he could not. "That is unfair. This is more like rope."

"Exactly. You do the same with the iron. Make thin bars and twist them together. When they are twisted you flatten them, fold them in two and keep repeating until you have a thin blade which is made from many layers."

"That is similar to what we do."

"Aye but then you take four smaller pieces and join them along the two sides. You will have a gap in the middle to make it lighter and yet you will have more strength. The tang will just have the core of iron. With the higher quality iron which we can produce ourselves we will have no need for Frankish blades."

"It will take much longer."

It was my turn to contribute. "Not if we employ more men. We have strong warriors who can no longer fight. Men like Rolf. They can beat iron. You would make the final sword but they could do the repetitive work. I have decided. We make the kiln and make our own swords. We have enough for now. You have until next spring to make us the finest swords in Britannia."

"Come then, Aiden, show me how to make this iron kiln!"

When I reached the warrior hall I found myself feeling hopeful and that should not be. I had lost my wife and yet, deep in my heart and my head, I knew that I had not. She and my mother had much in common and just as I spoke with my mother in my dreams so I would speak with Erika. I would never touch her again but she would be with me wherever I travelled.

The Ulfheonar looked at me warily. Trygg, in particular, looked apprehensive. The man next to him was almost shaking with fear. I knew who it was. "Trygg what is the name of your relative?"

He spoke quietly and gestured towards the fearful man. "This is my cousin, Siggi Olafson."

I went over to him and clasped his arm. He looked surprised. "I am sorry for your loss, Siggi."

"I thought you would be angry and cast me out."

"Why?"

"We brought the sickness into your home and your family died."

"As your family died. It was meant to be and we can do nothing about it. Will you join us here? We need hard working families. If you are half the sailor your cousin is then we will do well."

"Aye my lord, I am your man."

"Good. Then Trygg, I want you and your cousin to go to Úlfarrston. Help Bolli to finish the drekar. When it is finished the two of you can be escorted to Frisia and we will trade."

Haaken looked surprised. "You will trade with those murderers?"

"Of course. They will be cautious next time and we know what to expect. We received good prices did we not? And there are many priests. If the Count wishes to buy and then free slaves, who are we to argue?"

"And what of us. What do we do until the ship is finished?"

I pointed north. "We make our land secure. We raid and conquer Luguvalium."

Kara and Arturus were the only ones who understood my energy. I knew that many of the women disapproved of my actions. They thought it showed disrespect to my wife. They wanted me to mourn. I was doing this just to honour her. It was for her that I was making our land safe. She had given her life for the people and the land so that she could become part of the land.

We called at Windar's Mere on our way north so that I could explain to Windar my new ideas. "I want you to make your kinsman, Ulf, secure the eastern approach. He should make a wall strong enough to prevent anyone, Saxon or other, from invading and raiding from the north west. Even if you have to garrison his farm yourself it will be worth it. We go to make the north safe and when I have been to the west it will be winter and we will sleep easier this year."

Windar shook his head, "You are changed Jarl Dragon Heart. Your eyes burn fiercely. We will do this. I have men who would travel north with you."

I shook my head, "No but I will need them when we sail in the autumn for I need two drekar filled with warriors. I intended to show the other Vikings that we are now powerful. I want them to fear us here in our home."

In truth I needed no more men. I led a warband of sixty warriors. Half of them were Ulfheonar. With our new weapons I feared no-one. Once we had taken Luguvalium I would travel the valley of the Itouna to subjugate the people. If they accepted my rule I would let them live but opposition would result in slavery or death. It was a harsh world and my loyalty was to my own and not strangers.

With Aiden still building his kiln I would have to rely on my own reading skills should we come across any books. As well as my warriors we also brought ten of the older boys. I was keen to gather any animals we might find and it would also be an opportunity to see how they fared when there was adversity and combat.

Reaching the col close to the Grassy Mere was a momentous occasion for many of the warriors and boys with me. Some had ventured this far north in search of game but it was a new world beyond the narrow pass.

We had time, this time, to investigate smoke. I wanted to know who lived in this land. Snorri spotted a number of huts up a side valley just after the col. The land was flatter here and looked as though it might support farms. I took just ten Ulfheonar to investigate. We would not need more. Dressed for war we would intimidate most people. I sent Thorkell and four warriors around to the north and we headed up the valley. The trees had hidden the fertile little dale and I spotted sheep and goats on the slopes. They had animals. I heard a dog barking ahead and knew that we were spotted.

As the trees thinned I could see that they had cleared the land
and were growing vegetables and what looked like either
barley or rye.

There was a stockade but it was barely high enough to
stop their fowl escaping. Three men stood there with an axe,
an old spear and a Roman sword.

They spoke to me in the language of the Cymri. I
understood their words. I could speak a little.

"Who are you? We have nothing worth stealing."

Our weapons were sheathed and I spread my arms. "We
mean you no harm but we now live just down the valley
close to the large lakes. I am Jarl Dragon Heart. And who are
you?"

The one with the sword spoke, "I am Osric of Thirl and
this is my family." He seemed to see our shields and
weapons for the first time. "You are the men of the north, the
Norsemen."

"We are."

"What do you wish of us?"

"Nothing… at the moment. We are heading north to the
place where the Itouna passes the Roman fort."

His face became angry, "Then you will need to be careful
for there are animals that live there. The men of the
Hibernians and Saxons dwell close by and they are a cruel
people."

We heard shouts from the north and the men turned
around. Thorkell and his men were walking towards us and a
gaggle of women and children ran before them."

"So you trick us too!"

"No, your families will not be harmed I gave my word.
You were saying about the Hibernians and the Saxons. I
have not heard of them before."

"The Saxons came many years ago and they were bad
enough masters. They would take our young sheep and our
crops. But then the Hibernians came and joined them and
then they began to take our children and our women as
slaves." He pointed to the north east. "We lived close to
those hills and there were many of us. We were forced to

flee here to this hidden valley." He spat on the ground. "It is hidden no more."

"If I get rid of this menace will your swear fealty to me."

He looked at me suspiciously. "What would you wish us to do?"

I shook my head, "Warn me of any danger from the north. Share any surplus you might have." I looked at the family. They all had similar looks. "And I have young men and young women who might wish to settle close by. I would have you make them welcome."

He looked at the other men. They looked to be his sons. "Can you do as you say? I count only ten men. Dál Uí Néill has over a hundred."

"And are they as well armed as we are?"

"Are you the ones who killed his brother?"

"I know not of his brother."

"Some time ago his brother led a band chasing some cattle thieves south. They never returned."

"How do you know this?"

"We hide from his men but there are others who live close to him and suffer his privations, they speak with us."

"Then, yes, we did."

"If you return, Jarl Dragon Heart, then we will swear fealty to you."

By the time we reached the river we had spoken with six such headmen. All of them wished to throw off the cruelty of their present masters. Haaken was sceptical. "Will we not become the masters they hate once we have rid them of these warriors?"

"Do we do as they say?"

"We have."

"Aye, when we raided the Saxons or the Hibernians. We are changing."

Cnut had more practicalities on his mind. "Word will get back to this Dál Uí Néill. Some of those we spoke with will try to ingratiate themselves with him by selling us out."

"I know. I want to draw him out."

"And how will we do that?"

"We have done it already. We only ever sent ten men into the settlements. If he hears of us he will think we are but ten. Despite the stories he spread about the loss of his brother and his men the fact that none returned will tell him that we are dangerous. He will not sit behind his walls; he will come to look for us. That suits us. We have the best scouts in the land and we will know when he comes. Were you afraid of his brother and his poor weapons?"

"Of course not."

"Then why fear this one? He may outnumber us but that is always the case. We are Ulfheonar!"

Another advantage of bringing the boys with us was that they could spread out with Beorn, Arturus and Snorri, acting as extra scouts. It increased the warning we would have. We travelled along the river. It was flat land but the bank was lined with marshes and high grass. It made it poor land for farming but perfect for hiding us.

We lay up close to the river. The midges and the biting insects feasted well but we managed to avoid the attentions of any warriors. That night I sent out my three scouts to close with the fortress and the settlement.

Snorri brought news of the enemy. He had seen columns of warriors and they were scouring the land for us. They had reinvested the fort and he had twenty men guarding its walls. That was foolish for it lessened the men he had to find and kill us.

Arturus and Beorn reported much the same although they were able to tell us that there were three horsemen with each column and they looked to be searching south, west and east. It is strange the way ideas come to you. Instead of ambushing the columns one by one I saw a way to bring this Dál Uí Néill to us.

"We will take the fort."

Even Haaken was surprised and he knew me best of all. "But that is madness! They will return to the fort and we will never take it."

"Suppose we go now. How many men will there be within the fortress?"

Snorri grinned, "Twenty only."

"If Aiden were here he would tell you that such a number means one, two or three sentries at the most on the walls. We watch until their attention is elsewhere and, one by one we close with the walls." I almost had them convinced. "When we saw the gates Cnut, were they in good order?"

He laughed, "The boys with slings could bring them down." I remembered that the last time we had seen the gates they had been lying in the ditch. I doubted that they had been repaired well.

"And it is the boys with slings and our archers who will ensure victory. They will watch the walls and at the first sign of alarm they will clear them."

It was a bold though risky strategy. I was normally cautious. Something had changed in me.

We made our way along the river bank. We remembered the fort from our earlier visit. With wolf skins over our armour I sent the Ulfheonar around the four sides of the fort. Each had four boys with them. The remainder I left at the river. I took the southern gate. Arturus and Snorri were amongst my warriors. The other three parties were led by Haaken, Cnut and Thorkell. All could be relied upon.

The gate was, as I had expected, closed but it looked both worn and damaged. It had been attacked and breached before being repaired. The original builders had cleared the ground around the ditch. Since that time bushes and weeds had sprung up. The boys could easily lie hidden whilst our cloaks would make us dark shadows.

We watched the three men who were atop the wall. They moved up and down the wall a few times until we saw a pattern emerge. They would walk the walls and then stop in the tower where they would talk. Once they entered the doorway we were hidden could move and when they emerged we would stop. As soon as they entered the door we sprinted forward. We managed forty paces before we had to stop. Snorri dropped first and then we all joined him on the ground. Once in the gate house they would talk and occasionally peer out. They would see what they expected to see. When they moved again we sprinted, just twenty paces this time. We were now less than fifty paces from the ditch. Their eyes would be more likely to be viewing further away to watch for distant enemies.

They remained on the wall a little longer this time and I wondered if we had been seen. Snorri again saw them move and he ran, with Arturus, as fast as he could. They both reached the ditch before the sentries returned. The young boys and four other Ulfheonar then made it safely. There were just three of us left with a twenty pace run. As soon as they left the tower we ran as quickly as we could. Snorri and the others had not been idle. They had cleared a path of the accumulated rubbish and were now crouched beneath the Roman wall.

By keeping close to the wall we were safe. I waved Snorri and two boys to the other side of the gate where they could pick off the solitary guard who was there. I sent Arturus and two boys to deal with the sentry on the gate and I remained with Einar and one of the boys. We had to wait until all three had split up. I dropped my hand. Three arrows and four stones flew.

Even while they were in the air I had my Ulfheonar boost Sigtrygg and me up to the top of the wall. Sigtrygg was a strong young man and he hauled himself over. I was struggling until his ham like hand came over to pull me up. He grinned, "You are getting old, Jarl Dragon Heart!"

I could see that only two sentries had survived and they were quickly despatched by Thorkell and Haaken. "Get the gates open and the men inside."

It took a very short time for us to take over the fort. I turned from the southern gate. The town was not far away but there was neither noise nor reaction. They had not seen what had gone on and they assumed that we were the guards. All soldiers look the same to farmers.

"Get the men without armour on to the gates. I want this leader to see his men on the walls." My plan was simple. I would let this Dál Uí Néill enter the fortress and then we would attack him from the ramparts.

127

A cursory examination of the interior showed that they had done little save to move their belongings into the old barracks. They had neither repaired nor improved the defences. The gates had only been crudely repaired.

"Snorri, take off your mail. You have good eyes. Become the captain of the guard."

While he did that the rest of us took the opportunity to drink and to take off our helmets and cloaks. Haaken laughed, "Your adventures make for wonderful, if unlikely sagas, Dragon Heart. To take such a place with slingers is... well it beggars belief!"

"Perhaps we should do the unexpected more but do not forget, one of my ancestors lived and fought here. The spirits of the dead watch over the living!"

It was dusk when the first of the columns appeared. They trudged as though they had marched all day. That was good; they would be tired. As soon as Snorri saw them we were called to arms and I sent all of my men to the walls except for Haaken, Cnut and Sigtrygg. When the gates were open, by Snorri and Beorn they would just see us. I wanted them to be angry and charge us. My men and slingers would do the rest. We knew that there were twenty in each column. That was a reasonable number for us to handle.

I do not think it was their leader who entered first. He was not completely mailed and his sword was not well kept. However, when he saw me and my companions he charged at us. There were three of them who were mounted. Their charge took them from the security of their men who were suddenly struck by lead balls and arrows. Snorri and Beorn raced to finish off any who still stood.

The four of us faced the horsemen. We held our shields out before us and our swords were ready to strike. Sigtrygg and I swung at the same time. His blade took the horse in the neck while mine severed the warrior's arm. He flew from his dying mount and his life blood spurted across the old Roman parade ground. Haaken and Cnut killed the two others without hurting the horses.

I wondered if they would all be this simple.

Unfortunately, the next two columns arrived together and the last one was but a hundred paces behind. This would be a harder fight. "Einar, Sven and Ragnar Siggison, join us here."

We waited, the seven of us, and we could not disguise the slaughter which had happened. We did not move the bodies and they would see them as soon as the gates were opened. I stood in the middle of the wedge. With Sigtrygg to my right and Haaken to my left I felt as safe as in my own hall.

This time, when the gate was opened and the men rode in, they halted. Dál Uí Néill himself was at their head and he was wary. I knew it was him from his armour and his weapons. He saw me and reached down for something hanging from his saddle. He held it up and I saw it was the head of the son of Osric of Thirl. He hurled it towards me, shouting, "You must be Jarl Dragon Heart. This worm told me your name. You are the one who killed my brother."

"I am!"

"Then I will try out your blood eagle upon you. As for the rest of your men, their heads will adorn my walls before evening."

I did not mind his words but I wished that he would fully enter. My men were unable to use their weapons from above until he and his men had all entered.

"Why not try me now, spawn of a Saxon whore!"

I could see that I had angered him. He drew his war axe. "I will Lochlannach but why should I deign to dismount when we have you outnumbered?" He turned to his men. "Forward, but move slowly. I do not want these rats fleeing!"

He was far too over confident. I knew not why he had a long handled axe whilst on a horse. He had as much chance of hitting his mount as me. He came with his eight horsemen in the middle. His other men spread out on either side like a huge wedge. I could count only ten shields between them. Their weapons were dull and, from where I stood, badly maintained. These were not warriors, these were bandits. When the last ones were in, Snorri and Beorn slammed shut the doors and the killing began. My men emerged from the towers and rained death on to the men milling below. Some turned and tried to get at them. The arrows and lead balls slew them.

Dál Uí Néill spurred his horse on and the eight charged at us. There were three spears held by those attacking and they would be the most dangerous of the weapons until we were face to face. I had my shield before me and those of Haaken and Sigtrygg locked alongside. As the spears struck the shields we leaned forward. I saw Haaken reach over and hack at the head of the spear; the wood was sliced cleanly in two. I saw the long axe swinging overhand towards my head. With the spears now useless I raised and angled my shield. I jabbed blindly with my sword as the axe came down. Dál Uí Néill's mount turned its head to avoid the blade and the axe bit into the leather of my shield and snagged on an iron nail. Dál Uí Néill tried to hang on to the axe and the reins as his horse tumbled to the ground.

It was now every man for himself. Our small wall was broken. Dál Uí Néill rolled away from his horse and held his axe in two hands. He swung it around his head in a double loop and advanced towards me. Had I not faced one before I would have been worried. The whirling axe was at head height and it seemed impossible to avoid. I waited until it had swung over and then I stepped forwards and hacked at his head with Ragnar's Spirit. The move took him by surprise. He tried to step back but the edge tore across his face and his chest. Blood spurted. He had a diagonal cut from one cheek across a ruined mouth and the mail on his byrnie was torn. He stepped back and spat out a ruined tooth.

He feigned flight and spun around. The axe head had tremendous speed. I raised my shield to take the blow. My arm was numb from the force of the strike. As he tugged the head free I darted forward to stab him. The blade ripped through the mail and into his side. It came away bloody and he roared his pain as he finally freed his axe.

I lowered my shield to gauge his next move. I would not be able to take too many more blows. He was moving a little more slowly now and his breathing was laboured. The loss of blood was weakening him. I took in that we were the only ones left fighting. I could see my warriors despatching the dying or watching us. They would not interfere.

Instead of a swing he pulled the axe back over his head. He would be able to generate tremendous power from such a strike. I took a step forward and swung Ragnar's Spirit horizontally. It tore open his throat. The axe fell from his hands and his body slumped to the ground. He died in a widening pool of his own blood.

My men cheered. We had won!

Chapter 13

The horses which had not been killed were captured. "Get to the settlement and capture the villagers before they flee."

The six who had fought alongside me grabbed the horses and galloped off through the southern gate. Arturus ran to me. "I thought he had you with the axe!"

"They look more dangerous than they are. He was a fierce warrior."

Suddenly one of the boys from the north tower shouted, "Jarl Dragon Heart! A ship is sailing towards the sea."

I ran to the north wall and ascended to the ramparts. Someone must have escaped and warned the villagers. I saw a small ship, a little bigger than our knarr heading west along the river. My men would find poor pickings in the village. I took the opportunity of walking along the wall to view the land we had now taken.

Dál Uí Néill had held this land with just a hundred poorly armed men. He had oppressed and abused the people. We could do it with fewer men and a more enlightened approach. Arturus joined me as we walked. "It was a great victory, father. You outwitted him!"

I shook my head, "In the battle of wits my opponent was unarmed. These were not true warriors my son. Those men of Navarre, they were warriors. When you fight warriors who are true warriors then you will be lucky to escape a battle unscathed. You either win or your bones bleach on the battlefield. Remember that. You choose your battles wisely. I never had any doubt about the outcome of this one. Once we gained entry then victory was assured."

There were a few prisoners. Most were old women and men. None of them would fetch much at auction. They were bound until I could decide what to do with them. The metal was gathered together and stacked near a cart we recovered. Bjorn would be able to use those. After we had bathed in the river and a meal was cooked we sat in the old Roman barracks. I knew my men now and understood their dreams and desires.

"Thorkell, Sven and Einar, do you miss the mountain of Wyddfa?"

Thorkell grabbed his amulet as though I had read his mind. He knew me well enough to tell me the truth. "I do my lord. I like being my own man."

"What think you to this land?"

"It is good and the mountains, while not so high, are solid."

"Would you be jarl here and hold this land for me?"

His face answered before his voice. "Aye my lord."

I stood and waved towards Thorkell. "If there are others who wish to fight here with Jarl Thorkell the Tall then they can do so." I knew that they would talk with each other, as men do and I would not get a real number until the morning. There was a hubbub of noise as they began to discuss the choices. I turned to Thorkell. "When I return to Úlfarrston I will have a threttanessa built for here. This will be our rock of the north!"

He nodded, "Thank you, Jarl Dragon Heart and this will not be like Cymru. I will make sure that this time my men will be vigilant. We will not lose this stad."

"That was not your fault; that was *wyrd*."

Twenty men wished to stay. Ragnar Siggison, Einar, Sven White Hair and Harald Green Eye asked to follow Thorkell. I was happy for the five Ulfheonar would hold together the others. I was happy that many boys wished to stay but I told them they would have to prove themselves as warriors first. When my new ship was finished we would return with their women and their belongings. The captured slaves would tend for them until then.

"Do we repair the fort?"

I shook my head. "We do not have enough men for that. Destroy the doors. We can use the buildings for protection in the winter but build wooden walls yonder." I pointed to a small hill which rose above the river. "It we prosper then we can always build new gates. I do not think that the enemies who come will be in great numbers."

We left Thorkell the Tall to view his land. We gave him two of the captured horses. He would have the whole summer to establish himself and build his halls. The turf on his roofs would be well established by winter and they would be warm. I did not think that they would suffer as we had for the river was close by. I felt happier as I led my men south.

When we reached the flatter ground I sent Haaken with most of the men to sweep west and along the coast. "We need the people to accept our rule. Be gentle with them but firm. I would know what there is along the coast."

"And you, Jarl Dragon Heart?"

"I will take Arturus and Snorri. I will visit with Osric of Thirl. I shall tell him that the man who killed his son is now dead."

We took three of the small horses we had captured and headed down the valley. Osric and his family, as I had expected, hid from us. We dismounted close to their cluster of round huts. We watered the horses and waited. Eventually Osric and his son, Osgar, emerged from the trees.

"We were not sure if you were the others or not."

I nodded, "They will come no more. We killed them all. My men now control the land to the north. You can farm in peace."

He nodded, "Thank you."

"I am sorry for your son."

"Osric is dead?"

"He is."

"He should not have died at that man's hands."

There was little I could say to that. "Remember, Osric, that you now have friends to the south of the Grassy Mere. If you wish to trade then you will be safe there. If the winters are too harsh then you can go to the fort in the north or to my home." He looked dubious. "The offer remains whether your trust us or not. I think that time might show you my good intentions but I would not have you and your family suffer because you are suspicious."

"My people have suffered at the hands of warriors for generations. It will take time."

The thought came to me that Osric and his family might be descended from the same people as Pasgen. "If you do come to Cyninges-tūn you can view the sword of your people." He frowned, "The sword that was called Saxon Slayer in times past."

His eyes widened. "It exists? It is not just a story?" He suddenly seemed to see my cloak and those of my two companions. "You are the wolf warriors told of in the tales of Lann the Saxon killer?"

"We are wolf warriors but we are not those men reborn."

"It was foretold that one day someone would return and take up the sword to free this land. Are you that warrior?"

"I do not know Osric of Thirl. The Norns have brought me here and led me to find the sword that was lost but my journey is not yet complete. We all play our parts. Mine, I think, is to make this land safe."

He looked happier. "We will come to your home Jarl Dragon Heart and we will trade. I would see the sword that was lost for we tell those tales in the long winter nights and it warms us."

We left Osric and I took Snorri and Arturus towards Ulf's Water. If Windar had done as I asked then our eastern border might also be secure.

We took the shortest route, although not the easiest route. We headed up the mountain which dominated this land. We wound our way up the steep slope. By noon we had reached the top and we looked down upon the small mere just below the summit. We watered the horses while I viewed Ulf's Water. It twisted away to the north east. From this high vantage point I could see how narrow the valley was. I just hoped that Ulf and his brother Ulla had obeyed Windar's commands.

The sheep trail twisted eastwards. I saw, as at Cyninges-tūn, the plentiful rocks. I wondered if there was any iron to be found below the ground. That would, truly, be a boon for us. As we descended I saw that Ulf and his family had done as I had asked. There was a stone wall which defended the cluster of halls and huts. The warriors stopped their work and came over to us as we headed towards the wall and the gate.

Ulf and his older brother Ulla were good warriors but both preferred farming and fishing. Ulla was the fisherman and I saw his boat drawn up on the beach. He had been repairing his nets. Ulf and his sons laid down their axes and wiped their hands as they approached.

"Jarl Dragon Heart it is good to see you." Ulf bowed his head a little, "We were sorry to hear about your wife." Windar had obviously sent a message to tell Ulf the news.

"*Wyrd*." He nodded. "You have done well here Ulf and you too Ulla. Thorkell the Tall is now jarl of the land to the north. He is building a home on the Itouna."

"Good. Then this is truly our land now."

"It is but you have a great responsibility here Ulf. If the Saxons come then your home will be in their path. Can you defend it?"

He spread his arms. Ulla and I have six sons and we have other kin working to gather stone. This will be well defended."

"And weapons? Do you all have blades?"

"We have enough."

"Good. To recompense you for your efforts we will send you some new swords when Bjorn has made them." I looked at the buildings. "Do you have a horse or a pony?"

"We have one pony which we use for hauling stone."

"Then I will send you two more. Have one of your sons learn to ride then you can let Windar know if the Saxons come."

"Aye, my lord we will."

As we began the last part of our journey towards Windar's Mere, I was happy about the new defences. They would not stop an enemy but they would slow him down and allow us to react.

Two days later I reached my home. Kara had been busy and she had reorganised the hall. Macha and Deidra had been two of the priests of the White Christ. They had been amongst the first slaves we had captured. Thanks to Erika they had become less like slaves and more like servants. They never relinquished their beliefs but they had begun to see that we were not the savages we were portrayed. Along with Seara and Maewe the women ran the settlement. All four of them were devoted to Kara, as they had been to her mother. They now obeyed her commands and seemed happy in the new arrangements.

All five women were busy in the hall. I could see that they now had a curtain which separated off part of the main hall. Kara peered from behind it when she heard my steps.

She hugged me and said, as she opened the curtain, "This is where I shall heal the people!"

I could see that she had had someone, probably Scanlan and Aiden, build her a table and chairs. There were also shelves with the small pots we had recently traded.

"Here I can keep all that I need." She stared intently at my face. "You do not mind the changes I have made?"

I shook my head, "I only need a space to sleep and store my weapons. I told you that you could make changes here."

She looked beyond me to Arturus. "And you brother?"

He grinned, "No sister, for it now gives me the excuse to sleep in the warrior hall with the other warriors. We can be less tidy there!"

Aiden and Bjorn had finished building the iron kiln. They were keen to show me how it worked.

"Here are four holes around the base and I have been making bellows from pigskin. Bjorn here can have four boys working them. The hotter we can make it then the better the metal. We had plenty of rocks from Old Olaf and it is well made. We estimated that we can make enough iron for two swords each day."

I was pleased. That was a good target. "And axes?"

"The same."

Aiden looked pleased but Bjorn added a word of caution. "We can do all of that, my lord, only if we have iron."

Therein lay the problem. We had taken some from the Dunum but that was across the country and it was too risky to take it by land. By sea would take too long.

"We need another source then?"

"Aye my lord. We have enough from our stores and the newly captured weapons to make a start but within a month we will have run out."

"And Bjorn has many orders for ploughs. Now that we have cleared so many trees then our farmers wish to plough. The rocks in the soil break our old ploughs. Bjorn needs to make them with the newer, stronger iron."

Being Jarl of Cyninges-tūn and the other stad was never an easy task. No sooner had one problem been solved than another reared its head.

"I will be visiting with Bolli soon. When our other ship is ready we will give thought to how to get more iron."

Aiden and Arturus accompanied me down to Úlfarrston. I hoped that my new drekar would be ready. Aiden spoke of his reading while we travelled. The newly acquired horses made the journey far quicker and we could talk as we rode.

"I have found that there were many iron mines in the southern half of Britannia."

"That means Saxons."

"Not necessarily. There are many deposits in the land of the southern Cymri on the northern banks of the Sabrina. We could trade."

"Would they trade with us?"

"We have two knarr now Jarl Dragon Heart. It is worth trying. We have treasure and gold aplenty. They may need the gold for the Mercians have been expanding west. We might not be the threat that the Saxons are."

It gave me much to ponder as we headed for the busy river.

As soon as I saw the mast above the trees I knew that she was finished. She was not launched yet but Bolli was making sure that all working parts of the ship functioned. I kicked my horse on as I was eager to see the finished drekar.

When we emerged from the trees the ship was upright and the men watched Bolli as he walked around it. It was magnificent. I had anticipated much and my expectations had been met. My eye was drawn to the dragon prow. He carved in a different manner to his father. The head was carved so that it appeared to have a bend in it. He had carved scales into it and it was painted green and blue. As I approached I counted the holes for the oars. There were fifteen of them; that made it slightly smaller than mine.

Bolli saw me and ran up to me, his face showing his excitement too. "This is the work of the Gods, Jarl Dragon Heart. We just finished fitting the mast and you arrive. She is ready to launch!"

"She is a beauty. Have you a name for her?"

"She is yours, Jarl Dragon Heart. It is for you to choose."

I shook my head, "Your father created not only my first ship but the manner in which things will go. You built her and you know what is in her heart. It is for you to name her." I smiled. "You have a name in your head do you not?"

"I do and I forget that you have the second sight Jarl Dragon Heart. I would name her '*Great Serpent*'."

"And I like that name. We will launch her when I get a crew." He beamed and I approached closer. "Would you wish gold in payment for her or a share in the profits from the voyages?"

He gave me a look of surprise for the new owner normally just paid as little as possible for it. I had decided that if I was to have good workmen who would stay with me then I ought to pay them appropriately. "A share my lord! I know that she will make me a rich man!"

"Good. And I have another commission for you. However I will pay gold for the new drekar. It will not be a raider. I wish a threttanessa for Thorkell the Tall. It need not be large. It will just patrol the Itouna."

He rubbed his hands. "Good for I have just the oak in mind. This will be my last ship of the summer. Then my men and I will scour the forests for wood for new boats. I prefer using seasoned wood when I can." He hesitated, "Headman

Pasgen wishes me to build a ship for him and his people. His ship failed to return. Could I build him one?"

"Of course, my friend. You are not in thrall to me. I will see him now and then I will return to Cyninges-tūn."

The only disturbing thoughts in my mind were the last words of Pasgen. He had told me that his ships had not returned. They had had a few trade goods aboard but it was the loss of crew which disturbed him the most. Aiden and I discussed it as we rode along the side of the Water. "I believe it was Jarl Erik, my lord. The seas further south are not as dangerous and we were attacked twice close to his land."

"I believe you are right. We will crew both ships and pay him a visit and then we shall escort the knarr to the Sabrina and do as you suggest. We will trade. If that fails then there is always the sword!"

Haaken and the Ulfheonar arrived two days later. They had had a long journey but a productive one. "The people of the west are keen to be under your protection. Your name is known to them. They believe that it strikes fear into the Hibernians. They are eager to trade for they had little contact with traders."

"Good. Aiden, Scanlan and Rolf can work out the best times for us to trade."

Midsummer had gone and time was of the essence. I sent word to Windar's Mere that I sought a crew for my new ship. It was Haaken who suggested a captain for her. He and I were walking by the Water having had a quiet moment at Erika's grave as the sun went down over the Old Man. "There are many men you could choose Jarl Dragon Heart but I believe that Sigtrygg, although a young warrior he has an old head upon his shoulders. The men like him and he is Ulfheonar."

"I agree but our numbers diminish. We cannot crew even one drekar with the ones who remain."

"That is true but we have fought alongside the other warriors and they are good men. It is your decision Jarl Dragon Heart."

"And I would be a fool to ignore the advice of my oldest friend."

We had more than enough men who volunteered for my two drekar. They knew that their share of the profits would make them rich men. We took Trygg and Siggi with us for we would soon need their knarr and I wanted them to prepare their ships for a long voyage.

The omens were good when we launched '*Great Serpent*'. She barely made a ripple as she slid into the river. The cheers which resounded were greater than when '*Heart*' had been launched. There was less sadness. Bolli's beaming face told the whole world of his pride in his work.

It took two days to fit her out and then we were ready. We would sail to Jarl Erik's stronghold and discover if he had captured Pasgen's ships. Sigtrygg nursed his new drekar as carefully as possible when we left the safety of the shore and headed south. We left on the afternoon tide so that we would arrive after dark. We knew the island as well as any place in the world. We were returning home.

Chapter 14

Knowing the island as well as we did we landed between Hrams-a and Duboglassio. In the old days we had kept a tower manned to watch for raiders such as us. We had taken our time when making the short crossing for Sigtrygg needed time to get to know his ship and its peculiarities. The land and the dark hid us from prying eyes. Just to be safe I sent Snorri and Beorn to the tower we had once used to make sure that we had arrived unnoticed. Once we had landed, the six men we had left on each boat rowed them out a hundred paces or so. They were both too valuable to risk.

When my two scouts returned the disgust on their faces was apparent. "The tower is falling apart. No one has been there since we left."

Jarl Erik would pay the price for his indolence. I wondered if he still lived on the western side of the isle or if he had moved over to Prince Butar's former hall. We would soon find out.

Snorri, Beorn and Arturus ran ahead of us and the rest followed. Our aim was to find those sailors from Pasgen's ships and rescue them. I was also anxious to discover the fate of Trygg's relatives who had been captured aboard the drekar. I was not as hopeful about them. They might well have been sold. We would teach Jarl Erik a lesson and make him find easier victims than us.

Duboglassio had been built by Prince Butar and me. It had well made defences and would be difficult to take. It all depended upon Jarl Erik. Had he maintained the defences? At Cyninges-tūn, despite the fact there were few enemies close by, we still maintained a nightly watch and had the gates closed before dusk each day. Had Erika's brother done the same?

We approached the north eastern side of the town carefully. Although a moonless night with clouds we did not want to be silhouetted against the skyline. As we dropped down the gentle slope we crawled. The smell of smoke and the dark shape of the wooden walls told us when we were less than a mile away. We hunkered down to await our scouts. That was the time when warriors checked the strapping on their shields to ensure it was tight. We adjusted our helmets by removing and replacing them. We slid our blades from our scabbards and we touched our amulets to ask the Allfather for his help. I closed my eyes and asked Ragnar, my wife and my mother to watch over me. When I went to war I knew that I had the spirits behind me as well as within me.

Beorn Three Fingers ghosted next to us. "I left Snorri and Arturus Wolf Killer watching the town. There are no guards." I heard the snort of disgust from Haaken and Cnut. Although our task would be easier it appalled them to think that the standards of our old comrades had fallen so far.

"Good. Have you found the ships?"

"There is one of Pasgen's ships there. We have not found the thrall pens yet. There is one drekar moored in the bay."

"Sigtrygg, take your men and recapture Pasgen's ship. If you can take the drekar then do so."

I heard him in the dark. "It will be a pleasure."

"The rest of you, we will enter and find the slaves first. We will all be Ulfheonar this night." I knew I had said the right thing. All warriors wished to be part of my oathsworn. They would follow my orders. We spread towards the sleeping stad like a dark shadow over the land. We were the wolves that night. Like the pack which we had destroyed we moved as one. Each one of us would give his life for the others. That was why we were dangerous.

Beorn and Arturus rose from the ferns. They used no words. We were close enough now to be heard. I led my twenty five warriors towards the gate. As they had said there were no sentries but the gate was barred. My two scouts slipped over and we heard the slight creak as the heavy wooden bar was lifted. It was their lack of maintenance which came to their aid. The two gates groaned mournfully as they were opened. Time was now of the essence. I signalled for four warriors to watch the gate and I led the rest through the familiar narrow ways between the houses. The thrall pens were towards the rear of the stad.

I thought we had made it without being noticed when a warrior, obviously disturbed by the noise, emerged from the warrior hall. Although Erik Dog Bite led two warriors to silence him it was too late.

"To arms!"

"Snorri, Arturus and Beorn rescue the thralls." The three scouts ran off. "The rest of you, follow me into the warrior hall before they can arm!"

I knew that there would be warriors in Erik's hall but there would be more in the warrior hall and they would have to arm themselves. As I stepped through the door I had to cross the bodies of one of my warriors, Oleg and the warrior who had raised the alarm. Six warriors could be seen, in the glow from the fire, surrounding Erik Dog Bite and the wounded Harald the Clumsy who had followed him.

I recognised Thorfinn Olafson and I swung my sword at his shield. He halted the blow which would have skewered Erik Dog Bite and turned to face me. He roared his challenge at me and hacked at my head with his axe. I fended it with my shield and stabbed with Ragnar's Spirit. He had not donned mail and his turn had opened his stance. The sword went through him and out of his back. He was a big man and he did not die at once. He weakly tried to bring his axe down but it slid from his dying grasp. I twisted it and turned to see where the danger lay.

There had been many warriors in the hall but they had risen, half asleep and without armour. The warriors I had brought were the best we had. Even as I turned the last threat was snuffed out.

"Erik, take the wounded back to the sea."

"Aye my lord."

"Take any treasure that you see!"

I saw that there were some mail byrnies and fine helmets. They were taken as we left. Once we left the hall I heard shouts from the northern end. Jarl Erik's oathsworn had awoken. They would arm first. We had moments only. I saw my son, along with Snorri and Beorn. They were escorting the thralls. There were twenty of them.

"Take them back to our ships."

They hurried them along. I saw that at least four of Pasgen's people were with them. "Shield wall and let us move back carefully."

There were now ten of us. The rest were either at the gate or hurrying down to the ship. As we walked backwards I heard the clash of metal on metal and saw Haaken stab a warrior who had emerged from his hut. Before me I saw a wall of metal approaching. I did not recognise all of the warriors. These must be Jarl Erik's new men. All of them had mail byrnies on. There were fifteen of them. Behind them I saw archers. They were the immediate danger.

"Watch out for the archers."

As we reached the gate we were reinforced by the four men I had left there. We now had four hundred paces to go to reach the sea where we would be reinforced by Sigtrygg and his men. Haaken only had one eye but it worked! "Arrows!"

We turned as one and held our shields up above us. It was like a shower of hail as they rattled into them. I heard a cry and saw one of the warriors I had left at the gate clutching his arm.

"Watch for the charge!"

Sure enough as soon as the arrows had flown the mailed warriors rushed at us. Had my men not been Ulfheonar I might have worried but each man lowered his shield and held his sword above. They came at us without order. Just wishing to get to grips with us every man had run as fast as he could. One younger, fitter warrior reached me and sliced his sword down as he threw himself at our shield wall. His sword cracked into the shield but he was thrown back for my wall did not break. As he struggled to regain his balance Ragnar's Spirit darted out and pierced his throat. He gurgled his life away at my feet.

We stepped back as one. I almost laughed as the next warrior to attack fell over the dead body and was despatched by an exultant Cnut. Their leader saw the chaos and I heard a voice with a strange accent shout, "Stop and form a wedge! On me!"

I glanced over my shoulder and saw that the jetty was empty. Sigtrygg had done as I asked and sought the drekar. There were just Erik Dog Bite and the wounded.

"Arrows!"

Once again they tried to shower us with missiles and, once again we protected ourselves. This time, however, their attack had more purpose. Their leader who had a design with three red radiating legs came directly for me. I did not wait for the blow but instead punched with my shield. There were five arrows sticking from it and when I punched one of the arrows sticking from my shield scored a savage cut across his cheek while a second sank into his hand.

I stepped back as he screamed his anger. "No prisoners!"

I laughed. He assumed they might win. He did not know who he was fighting. As I swung my sword at his head I shouted, "Ulfheonar!"

My men all roared, "Ulfheonar!", as they swung their weapons. It took the mailed men by surprise. We were outnumbered and they expected us to retreat.

The leader took my blow and slightly turned his body to allow him a good swing with his sword. I mirrored his move and I found myself in his wedge with Haaken on one side of me. I was close enough to the warrior to smell what he had eaten the previous night. I hooked my foot behind his and, unable to use my sword effectively I punched and head butted at the same time. He fell over my foot. I stamped on his sword hand and stabbed down with Ragnar's Spirit. His fellows all stepped back.

Cnut shouted, "We had best get to the ship, Sigtrygg has returned!"

I could see more warriors rushing from Duboglassio. "Back to the ship; bring the wounded!"

The arrows showered down upon us as we slowly marched back. The line of dead and wounded warriors slowed down those trying to reach us. When I felt the wood beneath my feet I halted. Those of us in the front rank would need to defend the wounded while they boarded. I felt a movement next to me and Sigtrygg was there. "Sorry Jarl Dragon Heart. They had a crew aboard and they moved her away."

"It matters not you are here now."

Erik Dog Bite's voice sounded. "The wounded are aboard!"

We turned and ran holding our shields behind us. The overcrowded ship was just twenty paces away and we threw ourselves aboard. The sail was down almost as soon as Cnut, the last warrior, fell on board. Haaken and Erik sliced down at the lines which held us to the shore and we began to move away from the shore. We had enough warriors on board to give us a wooden wall of protection and the arrows thudded into wood and leather.

When we were out of range I looked to the shore. Jarl Erik had appeared. I saw the warrior I had fought. He was being supported by two men. He was alive still. He would bear the wound I had given him for the rest of his life.

I saw that the ship was being steered by one of Pasgen's men. I could see that he had a patch over one eye. He nodded at me and shouted, "Thank you Jarl Dragon Heart. I owe you a life." He pointed to the patch, "And I owe them an eye."

I waved my arm in acknowledgment. "Our ships are around the next bay."

We were dangerously overcrowded. The Hibernian built ship had a very low freeboard and there was a danger of us capsizing. I was pleased that it was Pasgen's captain who was steering. He would know his vessel better than any. When we rounded the headland I was relieved to see our ships close to the beach. Arturus and the thralls had made it safely.

When we grounded on the sand Snorri said. "One of the thralls did not come with us. The one with the patch ran to the sea."

I pointed behind me. "He was the captain and he wanted his ship. It is a good thing that he did else we might have sunk. Are any of Trygg's relatives here?"

A youth with a wicked looking scar on his face stepped forward. "Yes, Jarl I am Trygg's brother Eystein and my cousin Olaf."

"Good. Your brother will be relieved." I looked at the others. There were women there too. They were obviously neither Trygg's relatives nor Pasgen's sailors. "You women will be freed when we reach my land." We might be wolves but had gone to the island of Man for vengeance and not treasure. I hoped that Jarl Erik and his men had learned their lesson. We were not to be touched!

We sailed back to our home into the morning sun. The world felt more hopeful. We had lost warriors; we had been fighting our own people. They might be badly led but they were still warriors who trained and fought as we did. The only cloud on the horizon was the drekar which had escaped. It meant Jarl Erik could still raid although his drekar would be smaller than any of mine.

"The new warriors fought well. We will have to see if any could be Ulfheonar."

Haaken shook his head. "You do not choose Ulfheonar, Dragon Heart, you should know that. They are chosen by the wolf as your son was. He may be the youngest Ulfheonar but he is a wolf through and through."

He was right, of course. The fact that men wanted to join us made them fight harder. Sometimes that meant they died young. *Wyrd*. The three mail shirts we had taken would be given to those warriors who had excelled in the battle. That would be reward enough. There would be little else for my men. We would have to raid and trade now to recompense them for their service. We would do as Aiden had suggested and trade with the men of Gwent. His reading and his talks with Deidra and Macha had identified the area where we would trade for iron. We knew little of the people there save that they were at war with the Mercians. Therein lay our hope for we had fought the Mercians.

Pasgen was grateful for our intervention and upset by our losses. "Pasgen, we are warriors. We fight and we die. Those who died will be in Valhalla now. They will be telling those who went before of our glorious victory."

He shook his head. "We have the same bodies, Jarl Dragon Heart but there is a different beast within us. You are the wolf and we are the sheep."

"No, my friend, you do yourself a disservice. You may not be wolves but you fight for what you have." I pointed to the half finished stone tower. "There is a sign that you will not be attacked again."

We spent a few days fitting out for the voyage. We needed water and supplies. The winter was now past and we had managed to produce enough to keep us during the voyage.

Trygg was also grateful and his family joined him on the knarr. They were as well armed as any of my warriors and he and Siggi were determined that they would defend themselves if attacked. It was a fine fleet which set sail south. With two knarr and two drekar there were few who would attack us. Aiden was on my ship whilst the trade goods were split between the knarr. I had the first of the swords made by Bjorn Bagsecgson. It was finely finished but lacked the decoration he would put on the later blades. I had decided to use it as a gift for the ruler of Gwent. It would not hurt and might cement an alliance.

As we sailed south we kept close to the coast. This was not for safety; we feared no man. We were seeking targets for our return. We wanted monasteries so that we could make beneficial trades in Frisia. Each one we identified was marked on the map by Aiden. The maps were now worth their weight in gold.

The rowers had an easy time as we had to sail at the speed of the slow moving knarr. Each night we pulled ashore to camp and to forage. The isolated farms and homes were our food store and we ate well. We were a day's journey from Anglesey and we were using a small island just off the coast for our base when Arturus asked me the question which had been on his mind since Aiden had come aboard.

"When can I have a blade like yours or one such as that made by Bjorn Bagsecgson?"

Although he had grown much, sometimes he was like a child still. "You have treasure of your own do you not?"

He looked at me as though I was speaking a strange tongue. "But you gave the other Ulfheonar the wolf amulets. Aiden made them. I will have a sword instead of a wolf amulet."

I laughed at his request. "And when there is time he will make them for the new Ulfheonar but I give no sword to any warrior. The blade must fight for you. I could have Bjorn Bagsecgson make you one but it would neither feel right nor fight well. You need to give something of yourself for the blade." I shrugged, "Or capture a fine one in battle. That is why men always throw themselves at my blade. They desire to own it. Your sword will be part of you when you fight. Choose it carefully or let it choose you."

He looked at Snorri for help. Snorri nodded, "Your father is right my friend. I took my sword from a Saxon. It is a fine blade but I will buy a better one from Bjorn Bagsecgson this winter. I will have him make one which I choose. I will then have two swords."

Arturus had much to learn and much to take in. He might be the son of the jarl but he was just one of the Ulfheonar. I think that voyage helped him to grow up and know who he was. He would now go to war with a different purpose. He would seek his sword and his fortune. He was on the way to becoming a man and the heir to my land.

Chapter 15

The Sabrina was the biggest river I had seen, so far, in Britannia. The Rinaz was bigger but the power of this river meant we had to employ the rowers and the two knarr had to tack back and forth to make it towards the northern bank. Eventually we found a secluded beach where we landed. We knew that we were close to the iron but we had to be careful. We did not wish to upset the local leaders. We knew not if they were kings or jarls such as I was. We sent our three scouts to find the nearest town. I hoped that there was a port close by which would make loading of any iron easier but we had no idea of the land around this mighty river.

We had picked an isolated part of the river and estuary for no one seemed to be close to us. It was three days before our scouts returned.

"The king of this land is Selfyn Ap Cynan. He is close to Offa's Dyke at the moment fighting the Mercians. There is a port some ten miles west of us. I know not how we missed it and the iron workings are in the hills to the north."

"The three of you have done well." They would each gain a greater share of any reward we might have. I had a dilemma. Did we just go and take their iron? If the king was away and fighting then we would be able to easily. However we had enough enemies at the moment. The Northumbrians and Hibernians were not well disposed towards us and now we had alienated our nearest allies, the men of Man. I walked to the river to let the spirits speak with me.

Strangely they were silent. Perhaps I was not near a holy place and that was why I had silence in my head and I wondered what we ought to do. Arturus appeared next to me. "The people here are poor, father. The ones we spoke with had no weapons and looked hungry."

"You were not threatened?"

"If we chose to I believe that we could conquer this land with just our warriors from our ships."

"But should we do that?"

151

My question was honest for I knew not what the Norns wished me to do.

"No. We have a fine land and we should not be greedy."

"Then we should trade?"

He looked at the river and then nodded. "Aye, and perhaps help this king for the Saxons are no friends of ours."

It was at that moment that I made my decision. "We will sail to this dyke and offer our help, if he will have it, to this king."

My men were quite happy to follow my lead and we sailed further up the river. We passed more settlements closer to the river and many had wooden walls. The river narrowed and steep cliffs rose on both sides. When we were beyond them we saw more signs of war. In the distance were plumes of black smoke. When we found a reasonable anchorage we stopped. Once my men were ashore I left Trygg to guard the four ships with his men and ten extra warriors.

"At the first sign of danger anchor in the river. The ships should be safe there."

"Is this not dangerous, Jarl Dragon Heart?"

"Getting up in the morning can be dangerous. I am gambling. I hope that we gain iron and not just blood but we are in the hands of the Norns and this Selfyn Ap Cynan."

Although we armed I had my men sling their shields on their backs and keep their swords sheathed. We marched towards the cloud of smoke.

Snorri and Beorn ranged far ahead. I had Arturus watching our rear for we could be attacked as intruders and I wished to have some warning.

The warning came from our fore. Snorri and Beorn raced towards us. "The men of Gwent march towards us. They look as though they have been defeated."

I removed my helmet and strode to the head of my column. "Keep your hands from your weapons. We have retreated ourselves and know what it is like."

One of my men shouted from the rear, "Aye but that was when Ragnar Hairy Breeches led us!" The men all laughed and I knew that they were in good spirits.

The road we marched on was an old Roman one with few bends. We saw the retreating Army of Gwent some five hundred paces up the road. They halted. "Haaken and Cnut come with me. Sigtrygg, take command."

As we walked towards the waiting warriors Haaken said, "Life is always lively near you, Dragon Heart. It is never dull!"

"That way we know we are alive my friend."

I could see that they had been in battle. There were twenty warriors on horses. They looked to be the nobles while the rest were a ragged band of men with shields and spears forlornly following. The shields were not the best I had ever seen. Three of the riders rode up to us and held their spears before them.

Their leader spoke to me and I understood him, just. "Who are you and why do you come armed to the land of Gwent?"

I could see that he had fought for there was blood on both him and his mount. "We come in peace. We are from a land far to the north. We would speak with your king." I had no idea if they had a king or not but it would do no harm to assume so.

He looked at his two companions. I knew their dilemma. They had fought in a battle which I assumed they had lost. A fresh band of warriors was a problem they could do without.

"Take us to your king. I swear I will not use my weapons. We come in peace."

"But you are Norsemen!"

I laughed, "We do not always kill. Sometimes we talk."

It may have been the laughter for a smile touched his face. "Come. Three of you cannot do much harm."

He rode behind us and I knew that their spears were close to our backs. I did not mind. We had our shields there and it would take a mighty blow to get through a shield, a mail byrnie and a leather one.

I saw their leader. His mail was torn and I saw blood too. He had not done well. I bowed, "I am Jarl Dragon Heart and I come in peace."

He too took off his helmet and I saw blood where he had been struck. He was a younger man than I was and he looked tired. "You bring armed men in peace then! I am King Selfyn ap Cynan. What would you have of us?"

"We came to trade for we have find goods and we need iron ore but we would fight for you against your enemies in return for iron and we will trade also."

The man I had first spoken with laughed, "I did not expect that from the one who wields the sword touched by the gods."

"You have heard of me."

"I have." He looked seriously at his king, "This man may be many things but a liar is not one of them. If he says he will fight for us then I believe he will. I would take him up on his offer, your majesty. The Mercians will be coming soon. His Norsemen could make all the difference."

"I value your advice Iago ap Griffith but are we in any condition to fight?"

"The Mercians have had a bloody nose and they will seek to finish us off. If we meet them now then we might just turn the tide."

The king dismounted and strode up to me. "Will you give me your hand and swear that you will not betray me?"

I held out my hand, "I so swear."

"Then we should make camp and prepare to meet with Cynhelm of Mercia. He is not far behind us."

We had seen a small rise above the river some half a Roman mile to the west of us. "There is a small hill we could fortify. The river would guard one flank."

"Good. Let us go. March with me so that I may speak with you."

As we marched I examined their weapons. They were not the best that I had ever seen. I was surprised for they had iron. What they needed were the skills to make fine weapons.

"Had we ships then we might be able to make our river flank more secure."

"I have ships. I can send for them."

"You are resourceful. I believe Iago but we have heard that all Norsemen are like the wolves from the sea and the cloaks of your men seem to confirm this."

"Aye, we are the warriors of the wolf, the Ulfheonar but we are no animals. I look after my people much the same as you do with yours." I turned to Haaken. "Go to our men and have them fortify the hill and send some for the ships." As they trotted off I turned to the king. "How many Mercians are there?"

"More than four hundred."

"And how many men do you have?"

"Less than two hundred?" he shrugged, "There are more but they fled the field. They will not return." He smiled at me. "Do you wish to reconsider your offer of help?"

"I gave my word and the odds do not frighten me. I have fought greater numbers. They are Saxons and we know how to fight Saxons."

Iago nodded, "I have heard that they fear you. The mothers of Northumbria tell their children to behave or the Viking wolf will come for them in the dark of night."

"I cannot help the stories fools tell. How many archers do you have?"

"No more than thirty remain."

"If we put them on the hill then they can keep up a rain of arrows over our men's heads. I have slingers who will annoy them."

"You want to annoy them?"

I laughed, "A warrior who is annoyed will do foolish things and forget that he fights with his head and not his heart. The Saxons believe that their shield wall cannot be broken. Believe me they can."

Iago dismounted to walk next to me. We were nearing my men. "You are very confident for one who appears so young."

I shrugged, "I killed my first man when I was little more than a boy. I have been doing this for a long time."

"And it helps to have a sword touched by the gods."

My men had cut down branches from the nearby trees and were making a rampart at the foot of the hill.

"Your men are making a fort?"

"No King Selfyn. It is to break up their attack. They see it as flimsy, which it is but they cannot come across it in a solid wall. We will kill them as they cross it."

The ships reached us and '*The Heart of the Dragon*' touched the beach and Aiden jumped ashore. I waved him to my side. "This is my healer, King Selfyn. Let him look at you."

"I will be fine, Norseman."

"If he looks at you then you will."

Aiden knelt, "I promise that I will heal your wounds." He was a bright boy and he had had already seen the wounds. They were not dangerous but if unattended then they would be.

Iago nodded, "I would be happier your majesty."

"Very well."

Aiden took out his satchel and his water skin. He poured some water in a bowl and added some of the spirit he made. He bathed the wound on the king's arm and his head. The king winced. "Do not worry your majesty, that is all the pain that there will be." He took out his mortar and pestle and ground up some yarrow seeds, some sage and some garlic. When it was smooth he put into another bowl with some honey.

Iago was fascinated. "Honey?"

Aiden shrugged, "It helps wounds heal quicker." He smeared the ointment on the wounds. The wound on the face was left open but the arm was bandaged. "There your majesty. I will see it again in the morning. How does it feel?"

"It feels warm and there is no pain. Are you a wizard?"

I laughed, "We call him one but he prefers to be called a healer."

Just then a man ran in to the camp. "The Saxons are just down the road!"

Iago took charge. "Stand to!"

"Haaken, have the men in two lines from the river to the shore. Have the slingers before us."

I did not think the Mercians would fight. They would see us and expect us to flee. When we did not they would camp and attack us when they were fresh. Men in a defeated army had a tendency to sneak away during the night. I was counting on that.

The Mercians approached us in a wedge. I assumed that their king was the figure on the horse at the rear. Our extra numbers appeared to confuse them. I saw mailed men who looked like leaders rushing to the man on the horse to speak with him. We were not moving. We stood facing each other until the sun began to dip in the west. The Mercians moved back up the river and soon we saw their camp fires.

I made sure that my men had food and we knew who was on duty before I went to speak with the king and Iago. I had a plan. I hoped that they would follow it. If that proved to be true then we had a chance of winning this one sided battle. They both agreed with my ideas, mainly, I think because it would be my men who would be taking all of the risks.

"And you are happy to be paid in iron ore?"

"Yes King Selfyn. I have two ships to transport it back."

"I had thought that all Norsemen took what they wanted."

I laughed, "Oft times we do but this is one occasion where we will trade for we wish the trade to continue for many years hence."

I wandered my camp after dark to make sure that all of my warriors knew what we intended. Haaken and Cnut were not surprised by my plan. "You have a strange mind, Dragon Heart. You do not think as we do. Cnut and I would just walk up to the Mercians and fight them man to man but you are far more subtle. Is this your Saxon blood or the blood of the Romans?"

"I know not. I feel as one of you when I fight alongside you but when I retreat inside my mind I know that I am different." I pointed to Haaken. "Just as inside your mind you are making stories and songs about our battles I am planning. It is what makes us who we are."

Cnut nodded, "And perhaps that is the secret of our success. We are all different. Jarl Erik and his warriors always appeared to be of the same mind as did Ragnar Hairy Breeches and the other Norse leaders."

"And they will not endure. The people of Cyninges-tūn and Windar's Mere will live on."

The next day there was a thin line of thirty warriors running from the bottom of the hill to the river. They were my Ulfheonar. Only Sigtrygg was missing from the Ulfheonar. There were some volunteers from my other warriors too. The archers of the men of Gwent were on the hill top and the spearmen arrayed before them. Only four men of Gwent had deserted during the night. The king sat alone on his horse at the top of the hill while Iago and his oathsworn waited out of sight behind it. *'The Heart of the Dragon'* was moored next to the river.

King Cynhelm and his men marched towards us. Their scouts had been out early. Two had been a little keen and had paid for that with their lives. The others had been more cautious. The Mercians knew our dispositions. They advanced in two warbands. Each had their famous wedge formation. The larger band came at my small group of warriors. Their plan was obvious. They would destroy my handful of men and then sweep around the hill and surround the men of Gwent while the other wedge pinned the men of Gwent against the hill. It was a good plan.

When they were two hundred paces away we closed up a little and my men began to bang their shields with their swords. They chanted, "Ulfheonar! Ulfheonar! Ulfheonar!" It was hypnotic and I noticed that the Saxons slowed. They must have wondered why we did not flee. We were outnumbered and the men on the hill showed no sign of coming to our aid.

We had five slingers before us and the same number before the army of Gwent. They began to hurl their lead and stone balls at the advancing Mercians. Perhaps they thought that they were not a threat. They came on. When the first four warriors fell to the stones of the boys they changed their minds and their shields came up to protect them. It was what I wanted. I waited until they were just fifty paces from us and then yelled, "Charge!"

It was the last thing that the Mercians expected. We raced forward, not as a line but as warriors eager to die! They would think we were going berserk. The Mercian shields protected them from stones but they did not give them a view of their front. I jumped as I approached the warrior at the point of the wedge and brought my sword down on the top of his helmet. The weight of my sword, the height of my jump and the power of my arm smashed through his helmet and he fell dead. My men had done the same all along the line. I turned and ran back to our start position. My men all joined me and they began to laugh. The wedge was in complete disarray. Dead and wounded men lay before them.

The second wedge was already in action against the king but it was a smaller wedge. They had intended that to hold the men of Gwent. The one facing us was the one which would have delivered the hammer blow of victory! Another warrior stood at the front and reorganised his wedge. My slingers kept up a steady rain of missiles. I knew that the Mercians would become angrier. An angry warrior rushes when he should wait. My plan was succeeding.

As we waited Haaken said, "I will put that jump in my next saga. The leap of the wolf it shall be called."

"Good for that means we will survive this battle."

"Of course we will. They are only Saxons, after all!"

This time once they were ready they prepared to charge. This would be the tricky part of the plan. "Boys! Fall back!" My slingers raced behind us. As soon as the wedge lumbered towards us we turned and ran back fifty paces. I had fought in a wedge. A run is not really a run, it is a fast walk but once it is started then it has to be continued until a halt is called. They charged and there was nothing before them. They passed my ship and I saw, as they did so, that two men tripped. We had left obstacles along the ground. The wedge began to break up.

"Now Aiden!" My voice carried over the field and Aiden, his slingers and his archers stood and loosed from the safety of *'The Heart of the Dragon'*. This time there were no shields to protect them. Aiden's fifteen archers and slingers had the unprotected backs of the warriors. They turned to face the new threat.

"Charge!"

We had them so that we charged a wedge which had no shields facing us. They were warding off stones and shot. I stabbed one warrior while I punched a second with my shield. This time we were one solid band of iron and wood and we carved a trail of death through the side of the wedge. We were still heavily outnumbered but the Mercians were confused.

Timing in a battle is all and when Sigtrygg and the rest of my men, who had landed from *'Great Serpent'* behind the Mercian lines, fell upon the rear of the wedge, then the battle was all but won. The final decisive part came when Iago led his horsemen around the rear of the other wedge. The weakest warriors in a wedge are those at the rear. The brave and those who seek glory are at the fore. Soon the Saxons of Mercia were fleeing up the river. Iago and his men pursued them as King Selfyn led his warriors down the hill to fall upon the Mercians. Many of those fighting us threw themselves into the river for we were cutting a swathe through their heart.

There was one warrior, in mail and with more courage than the rest, who tried to halt us by facing me. He had an axe and a red painted shield. He rushed at me and swung his axe overhand. It was similar to my blow which had killed their leader. I held up my shield and, as the axe struck it, allowed the shield to drop and deflect the axe head to the side. The move opened him up and I made a backhand slash with my sword. It tore across his open face. Blood spurted and he stepped back. I swung forehand. His reactions were good and the shield came up. I stepped forward and pushed my shield towards his damaged, bleeding face. He jerked his head back and I thrust Ragnar's Spirit through his open, screaming mouth. He became still and slumped to the floor, his body sliding from my blade.

All order had now gone from the Mercians and they ran in every direction. Those who jumped in the river were either dragged down by the weight of the arms or my archers slew them. The day was ours!

My men knew the value of being the ones to strip the bodies, especially Saxons, of arms. Saxons liked to keep their treasures about them and soon we had a pile of weapons and armour. The treasures the warriors found they would keep. It was their reward for fighting. It was why they sailed with me. Many Viking leaders wanted all the treasure so that they could share it out. My way kept my warriors loyal. Many became rich men that day.

The men of Gwent pursued the Mercians for miles up the river. I did not blame them. The Mercians had chased them and revenge is sweet. It meant that we had the field to ourselves and the weapons and armour were loaded on the boats in a short time. After we had disposed of the Saxon dead in the river we dug a barrow for our dead. Erik the Tall and Eystein Foul Fart had both perished. Erik had been one of the first Ulfheonar and his loss was hard to bear. The others who had fallen were given as much honour. We built the barrow at the foot of the hill where we had made our line. The men of Gwent returned as we were placing the last sods on the top. They watched as we bowed our heads in silence. Each warrior said his own goodbyes.

The king and Iago waited for me as my men went to the ships to remove their armour. Iago nodded approvingly, "You are efficient Norseman. The dead buried, the enemy moved and your men preparing for their next task. You have done this before."

"We have done this before."

The king clasped my arm. "Thank you for your service today. Why not continue to serve me? We can pay you well."

I had seen little evidence of wealth amongst the King's elite. That was always a good measure of the riches of a land. Each one of my men had more gold and silver than all of the horsemen put together. "No, your majesty, for some day you would tire of us or you would not wish to pay us longer. Besides, I like to be my own master."

Iago looked at me and his eyes examined me closely. "This is why you wanted your plan."

I shrugged, "I knew that it would work."

"Well then, if you would come to my capital, Casnewydd, I will send for the iron you want although I thought you would have wanted gold and silver. The fortress is a few miles down the river. It is close to the old Roman fort."

"Do not worry, your majesty, we can get more gold and silver when we want. We need the iron; the gold is a luxury. We also have other trade goods. You may wish to barter. When we have washed and cleaned our weapons we will sail down the river to your capital."

We watched the army as it trudged west. They looked to be in better heart than when we had first seen them but the battles of the past two days and their marching had made them tired. Our journey down the fast flowing Sabrina would be much easier and quicker. I had no doubt that we would arrive before the king.

My warriors, especially those for whom this was their first raid, were in high spirits. Trygg and Siggi, in particular were impressed with my small band of elite warriors. They plagued them with questions about their weapons and armour.

After I had bathed in the river and dressed in clean clothes I supped some ale with them. I decided to suggest a way in which they could become part of my army. "Perhaps you could train your men to be archers."

Trygg looked a little put out. He said, hesitantly, "We would be warriors first."

"Those with bows are warriors. They fight the enemy. Had we not had them today then we might have lost." He did

162

not look convinced and I had to be blunt. "You and Siggi were brought up to be sailors. That is a good trade. Your brother had some training as a warrior." I waved a hand at the men around me. "These were brought up from being babes to fight. Arturus, my son, has killed more than ten men in battle. He is good at what he does. Do not change your nature. I suggest being archers so that you can aid us and defend yourselves. All of us have a part to play in our people."

They seemed happy with my explanation. And I had not lied. They were good sailors and they knew how to get the best from their knarr. My son and I could not sail them as well but we could kill.

Chapter 16

We stayed three days with the men of Gwent. They were keen to trade but they also wished to learn about our skills as warriors. Iago, in particular, was keen to improve his own warriors' skills. "Your weapons are superior to ours. Where did you acquire them?"

"Most in Frankia but we will be making some. The one we gave your king was one we made."

That interested both Iago and the king. He had been quite touched by the gift. We did not tell him that it was a trial weapon. It was stronger and sharper than the ones they had. He had been delighted by the gift. "We will trade more of the iron ore when next you come." The king had almost pleaded, "You will return, will you not?"

"My ships will return." We had exhausted their supplies of iron and I knew it would take them some time to mine more.

As we headed west I felt satisfied with the venture. It had been highly profitable for us. We had had to spend none of the gold or the jewels and we had a hold full of iron ore. The heavily laden knarr meant it was a slow voyage along the south coast of Cymru. It was almost night time when we turned north. A sudden squall blew up from the west and we had to reef our sails. Aiden scanned his map. "My lord, there is a sheltered anchorage not far from here."

"Where away?"

"We should see it soon!"

"We had better or Trygg will capsize and our iron will end up in the hands of Ran!"

The wide fiord loomed up to the east and I signalled the others to follow us. We soon found shelter from the wind and we anchored as soon as it was practicable. The small bay was on the south side of the fiord and we barely bobbed up and down it was so sheltered. Unfortunately it was not a sandy beach and we could not go ashore. We ate cold rations that night. The squall grew into a storm and we were forced to spend most of the day in the bay. The wind turned around during the day as the eye of the storm passed and as soon as it became a milder wind from the east we set sail. I led and **'Great Serpent'** guarded the rear.

We sailed between the northern shore and an island into another bay. It made our motion less violent and we headed north aiming to get as far as we could before dark fell. As we followed the coast west I suddenly saw lights on the hillside and, above the crack of the sails in the wind, I heard the tolling of a bell. That could only mean one thing; a holy place of the White Christ.

"Keep your eyes peeled for a beach. There is treasure in the hills."

The hidden church was well placed for it was surrounded by cliffs and rocks. We would not land. As dark began to fall we passed between another small island and the headland. Then sharp eyed Ketil shouted, "Beach ahead, my lord; on the steer board side."

I saw it. It was less than a mile away and the white sand would enable us to find it, even in the dark. I signalled to the others to follow us and we edged our way north. Night had fallen by the time we dragged the boats ashore.

Sigtrygg sought me out. "What have you found, Jarl Dragon Heart?"

"What makes you think I have found anything?"

"You would have used the island we passed if you had not."

I nodded, "You are right. I think there is a church above us. We will camp here and you and I will take thirty men and investigate."

I took the Ulfheonar and made up the rest from volunteers. Aiden came with us. His eye for treasure was worth ten warriors. There was a path from the beach. I think it must have been used to collect shellfish. Snorri headed up the slope with Arturus. Beorn had suffered a wound to his leg and we had left him in the camp.

The wind was from the west and it brought us the sounds of the holy place before we saw it. Alarmingly it was not the sound of people. We could hear animals. There were sheep, ducks and chickens that appeared to be ahead.

I waved Sigtrygg and his men to the left. They would be able to stop anyone leaving. The gaping gate told the story before we had even entered. They had fled. The sound of the tolling bell had not been a call to prayers but an alarm. We had been seen. I looked to the south and although it was dark I could see the breakers on the other side of the fiord. This was a well chosen site.

Sigtrygg came through the other open gate. He held up a metal candlestick. "They have fled, Jarl Dragon Heart. We found this."

I shrugged, "*Wyrd*. No matter. Gather the animals and anything else which looks as though it might be useful." I was a little disappointed but we had had much luck before. It was only right that we suffer a little too. The bed linens they had left were far better than the ones poorer people used and we took them. Their pots and the cooking vessels were also welcome. Even better were the jars of wine. This had been a rich church of the White Christ. I wondered what treasures they had taken with them. We had to work quickly. There might be warriors nearby and we had suffered enough lately.

"Get everything down to the ships as fast as you can. We will follow." Haaken came with me and Aiden as we took lighted torches to search the church. We had learned, long ago that these places often had hidden treasure.

When we went in Aiden became excited. "This is ancient. The Romans built it. Look!" He pointed to a stone in the wall.

There was a stone inscription in Latin:

MATRIB TEMPL CVM ARA VEX COH I VARD
INSTANTE P D V VSLM

"What does it mean Aiden?"

"I can only understand a little but I think TEMPL means a Roman church."

We all dropped to our hands and knees and took out our daggers. The Romans liked to have secret places where they could hide precious objects. It was sharp eyed Aiden who found it.

"Here, Jarl Dragon Heart. I have found it."

He ran his blade around the edge of the stone which had a Roman number on it, IX. He dug out the dirt of years. It took a longer time than I wanted. Eventually he was happy. We put our three blades in the cracks and all raised them at the same time. I was not sure it would work but gradually the flagstone began to rise. It was slow work but we knew that patience would bring the reward.

The stone popped up and we moved it. There was a damp musty smell rising from the hole. Aiden thrust the lighted torch down but could see nothing. He handed me the torch and then lay down with his arm inside the hole. He suddenly shouted, "I have something!"

He pulled out a metal eagle. It was the size of two outstretched hands. There were the letters SPQR held between the eagle's claws. He handed it to me and went back to his search. The bird looked to be gold and Haaken put the torch closer."It is gold! This is a rich prize indeed!"

It did not feel heavy enough to be gold and I took my knife and rubbed at it. The gold came off revealing base metal beneath. "Gold paint or gilding I think."

Aiden shouted, excitedly, "Haaken, take these." He deposited handfuls of coins on the floor. "They must have been in a bag but it has rotted."

Haaken took off his helmet and scooped the Roman coins into it. By the time Aiden had finished the helmet was full.

"We have spent long enough here. Let us go." I handed the eagle to Aiden. "Carry this."

We left the building and headed for the open gate. We were the last to leave. The rest had obeyed my orders and descended to the ships almost a mile away. Suddenly I heard hooves. It meant only one thing. Horsemen! "Run, take the treasure to the ship and I will watch the rear." We could do nothing else for Haaken's hands were filled with the gold. They ran and I took out my sword. The hooves were still in the distance but they would soon reach the church.

167

The path went steadily down but it was dark and we could not afford to hurry. I stopped and turned. I had heard something. It was voices from the church. I moved down the trail but kept looking back. My helmet covered my face and my hands had mail upon them. With my wolf cloak I was invisible. The trail turned a little and I saw the beach and the ships. The knarrs had been refloated and the men were launching the two drekar. That gave me hope.

I looked to the church and saw horsemen appear. I knew that they could not see the ships yet. They might waste time looking around the church. Then Aiden slipped and the eagle hit a rock. The noise sounded like a bell. The horseman gave a shout and began galloping down the trail. I had to buy some time for my warriors. I held my sword in two hands and waited on the trail. I saw the horse and its rider. The white blaze on the horse and the warrior's face showed me where they were. I swung Ragnar's Spirit across the horse's head. It had sensed me but the rider had not. The dying horse crashed off the trail and rolled down the slope, taking the rider with it. I swung at the other warrior and my sword bit into his leg. He tumbled to the ground screaming. I turned and ran.

Haaken had given the alarm and my archers were already notching arrows as I reached the sand. I saw them release and then Sigtrygg and Arturus raced towards me with swords drawn. When my feet touched the water I turned and saw the line of horsemen. They had stopped near the two men who had been wounded. The Allfather had been watching over me and we boarded our ships.

"I think we have enough treasure. Let us head home."

We used reefed sails to hug the coast until dawn. As dawn broke we took out the eagle. Haaken and Cnut were disappointed with it. "Perhaps Bjorn can melt it down and make a sword from it!"

Aiden shook his head, "This is as valuable as the books of the White Christ."

"Who would buy it?"

"It is Roman and they have an Emperor still. He lives in Miklagård."

"That is a long way to go in the hopes of payment."

Aiden shrugged, "Perhaps in Frisia…"

My mind was already working. We would need to trade in Frisia anyway but I was curious about these Romans. I knew that I had Roman blood in me. When I had visited the cave and seen the painting it had stirred something within me. Perhaps in the land of the Romans I might see something there. I kept my counsel. There was nothing urgent to be decided.

"Look after the eagle, Aiden. We have plenty of treasure from this voyage. We will all profit."

Two days later we saw the familiar mountains ahead and knew that we were almost home. The last time we had done this we had returned to disaster. Would the Norns play the same tricks again?

This time Pasgen had no dire news to impart. Some of the weapons we had taken from the Saxons were good ones and I gave a number to Pasgen. It was important that our allies and neighbours were well protected. We borrowed carts to transport the vast amount of booty we had gained. The animals provided a noisy accompaniment. The new ship being built for Thorkell was coming along well but I would send '*Great Serpent*' with supplies and men for my northern Jarl. Like Pasgen he had to be supported. I would wait until the new threttanessa was built first. Autumn was still some days away.

Cyninges-tūn looked reassuringly secure. The smiling faces and warm reception bespoke a peaceful time since we had been away. Soon it would be autumn and we would need to prepare for winter. The faces of the people told me that they were not worried.

As we travelled up the Water I examined our defences and our homes. We had more settlers arriving and we needed more homes for them. I would have my men clear more of the forest on the western shore. It would make a good place for homes. I knew that some would like to farm on the fells.

Old Ragnar had always liked the high places. There was always much to think about. The life of a jarl was full.

I had two whole days of peace when I arrived back. I was able to taste the cheese made from the milk of the new goats. Deidra and Macha watched my face keenly. It was delicious. Bjorn eulogised about the iron we had brought back and he showed me his new weapons. He was getting better. We even had some fish from the Water for we now had fishermen who had perfected a technique of trapping larger numbers. We could salt and preserve them. All was going well. I commissioned Aiden to make wolf amulets for my new Ulfheonar and we distributed the extra wealth to those who toiled at home. We all shared in the bounty although it was my warriors who gained the most. Both Aiden and Bjorn were inundated with requests for jewellery.

The ill news came with an east wind and Windar himself. He arrived with two of his sons and they rode; a sure sign that it was not good news.

"It is the Northumbrians my lord. They were seen coming west. By now they will be at Ulf's Water. I have my men preparing for war."

"Reinforce Ulf and I will bring my warriors. But make sure your home is defended."

He nodded, "I am sorry, Jarl Dragon Heart."

"Why? This was not your doing and we knew the day would come."

Before he had even mounted his horse I had Scanlan sound the horn. Every warrior knew that we never used it unless it was an emergency.

"The Northumbrians are here. Rolf, I will leave you twenty men and the rest I take with me."

"You think they will come here?"

"I know not but they are cunning. This may be a diversion to draw us hence."

Haaken said, "We have beaten them before and we will beat them again. Will we follow Windar?"

"No we will go by the Rye Dale and over Úlfarrberg. It is shorter and we can fall on the flanks of our enemies."

"It is a risk."

"It is not, for if they defeat Ulf and Windar we shall be able to attack their rear. It is my decision. I need all the slingers and every man who has a bow to bring it."

We can run if needs be, even in armour. Even though it was almost twenty miles we kept up a steady pace. We picked up five more men at the Rye Dale and then we started up the long slope to the top of the mountain. I knew we took a risk and I knew that we would be tired but it would be the one place that they would not look. I pictured it as the Northumbrians would see it. They would attack the ditch and the wooden wall and then we would descend from above them. They would have nowhere left to run. It was why I wanted so many slingers and archers. They would be able to occupy the Northumbrian's attention long enough for us to close with them before they fled.

Snorri and Arturus were our scouts. We had had to leave Beorn with Rolf. I could not risk the wounded. Snorri waited for us. He pointed down the slope. "We are losing men!"

I turned and saw little huddles of men who could not keep up with us. "It doesn't matter. The Ulfheonar will be there and some of the other warriors who are fit. Just find out where the Northumbrians are. Go, the two of you. We will be right behind you."

The sky was darkening as evening approached. I knew that the dark would slow us down. We did not ascend the peak, we had no need to but that meant we could not see Ulf's home from our position below the peak. I was counting on the scouting skills of my son and Snorri. I heard Sigtrygg and Cnut urging the men on at the rear.

"Move your legs Ulf! I could have brought women they would have moved faster!"

"Karl, I have a wolf skin on my back with more life in it than you! Our friends are dying!"

In truth we were moving as fast as we could. Had we all had ponies or horses then we would have already reached Ulf's Water. That was just something else for me to ponder upon.

The ground grew gentler and, in the distance I could heard the clash of arms and screams. The sun was setting behind us and I could see the other side of the valley and the Water itself but Ulf's stad was hidden. My scouts appeared.

"Jarl Dragon Heart, there is a warband of over two hundred Saxons. They are pressing against the ramparts. Ulf still holds but I fear it will not be for long."

"You have done well. Arturus, when the boys and archers arrive take them and keep them raining death on the Saxons. Keep them safe."

"But I am Ulfheonar!"

"Then you will do as I say will you not?"

He bit his lip and nodded. I waited until we had fifty men. "Snorri, you bring the others when they are all here. You are our reserve." I saw that most of the boys and archers had reached us. They had no armour and it was easier for them.

I raised my sword and led my men down the slope towards the side of the Water. There was a road of sorts. In places it had stone but it was mainly trodden earth. It merged, in places, with the shingle on the beach. We could approach in five lines of ten. The noise of battle was louder and I led my lines forward. I had ten men with spears behind my first line. They would afford us some protection.

As we turned around a rocky outcrop I saw the battle ahead. Part of the wall had been breached. Soon we would be too late. We needed to attract their attention. I began to howl like a wolf. Suddenly it was taken up by the men who followed me. I felt the hairs on the back of my neck prickle. We moved down the slope to close with the enemy the men still howling in the darkening hills.

I raised my sword. "Ulfheonar!"

All fifty men shouted the same battle cry. "Ragnar's Spirit goes to war! Charge!"

It was my best Ulfheonar in the front rank and we ran at the same speed. We had learned to do so under Prince Butar. The ones behind picked up the rhythm and we moved as five solid lines. The Northumbrians had turned to face the threat to their rear and they ran at us.

Viking Wolf

I held my shield at a slight angle and I protected Cnut's left side. Ragnar's Spirit was held high ready to strike down. It was almost dark now and we were a line of black, demonic, red eyed wolves which raced towards them. The ones in the front of our line had the same blackened mail as me. The white faces of the Saxons stood out in the fading light.

I knew which warrior would try to kill me. He held his spear high and was staring at me for I was the centre of the line. We closed at pace and I saw the spear as it darted at my head. I turned my head slightly and felt the spear head bite and tug at my face mask. I stabbed down with my sword and the spearman impaled himself upon it as he lunged forward. The spear fell from his lifeless hands. Our solid line rebuffed the Northumbrians who came at us individually.

We had, perforce, slowed down and the next warriors who came at us were more cautious and they were more numerous. We struck their line. The spears from our second rank darted out to strike unguarded flesh and I swung Ragnar's Spirit overhand to smash down on poorly made helmets. We drove deep into their lines and that proved our undoing. We were surrounded and I felt the others moving backwards as the press of warriors forced them back.

We had done what we intended. They were no longer attacking Ulf but they had turned their attention to us. "Make a circle!" Even as I shouted it I knew that many of those in the rear would die as they attempted to make a shield ring but a circle would aid us until Snorri arrived with my reserves.

It was Arturus and the slingers who gave us a lifeline. I heard the whoosh of arrows and the crack of slings. He and his boys were on the hillside and they were attacking the rear of the Saxons before them. It enabled us to complete the circle. We were now a ring of death. The Northumbrians attacked us relentlessly. So long as our shields held then so would we. The ones at my side were the best of the best and soon there was a wall of bodies before us but I felt pressure from the rear as those warriors were forced back.

I shouted to the ones facing the Saxons. "Time to go forward! Now!"

Stepping over the wall of Saxon dead I brought Ragnar's Spirit down to sink into the shoulder and neck of the mailed warrior who faced me. I found myself in a space and I swung my sword horizontally. It connected and, in the dark, warriors screamed. One of those I had wounded was so enraged he threw himself at me. I barely had time to jab Ragnar's Spirit forward. His impetus impaled him on my sword. I could not remove it. I was forced to drop it and grab the spear head which came from the dark at my head. I pulled and tugged it from the Northumbrian's hand. I quickly turned it and jabbed it forward. I felt it sink into flesh and then it was torn from my grip.

I reached down and my hand searched in the dark. Almost immediately I felt a pommel and I knew that it was Ragnar's Spirit. Just in time I pulled it from the dead Saxon and deflected the blade which suddenly lunged at my face. Cnut's sword ended the warrior's life.

Behind me I heard a wail. It must be Snorri and the reserves. The pressure on my back lessened. Then there was a shout from the front and Windar and his men arrived to pour through the gap in the ramparts. The Northumbrians were caught between two fresh warbands and an island of Ulfheonar. The victory, which had briefly been in their grasp, disappeared in a heartbeat. Had it not been night then we might have slaughtered them all. As it was, many died. Some disappeared along the edge of the Water while others feigned death as my men passed over them and vanished before they could be despatched. There was confusion as our warriors milled over the field looking for the Saxons who had dared to come to our land. We knew that our people had suffered and those that we found paid a heavy price. Even though some escaped to take the tale back to the east it was a mighty slaughter. King Eanred's attack had failed. He had gambled and failed. He would never again try to wrest my land from my hands.

175

Chapter 17

Windar, bloodied but unwounded, found me. "I have failed you, Jarl Dragon Heart. We took too long to reach you. I fear Ulf and his brother have died."

"It could not be helped. At least we held the Northumbrians here."

Up the valley we could hear the shouts and the screams as the fleeing Saxons were caught. Haaken shouted me over, "Jarl Dragon Heart, we have a prisoner."

I went over, taking a torch which Windar thrust into my hand. There was a mailed warrior kneeling at the edge of the lake. His right hand and arm had been badly cut and he would lose it.

"You are truly evil! I did not believe the priests when they told me that you could turn into a wolf and back. Now I have seen it with my own eyes. You are shape shifters. You are cursed!"

"Who are you?"

"I am Eorl Oswald of Bebbanburgh."

"You follow the White Christ?"

"I have been baptised."

"Then you would not welcome a warrior's death?"

"It matters not for when I die I shall go to heaven."

"And that is filled with the priests of the White Christ?"

He nodded, "It is."

"Then I shall stay a pagan and go to Valhalla. Your arm is useless. I have a healer but he is not here." I gave the torch to Windar. "You will not die but you shall be my messenger. Hold out his damaged arm." Cnut held the bloody mangled limb. He moved the mail up so that the bare flesh could be seen. I swung down Ragnar's Spirit swiftly and the arm was cleanly severed. Windar thrust the burning torch into the wound. The air was filled with Oswald's screams and the smell of burning flesh but he remained conscious; he was a warrior.

"Take off his mail. He will not need it now. Did they bring any beasts?"

Viking Wolf

One of Windar's men said, "Aye Jarl. There are five ponies."

"Bring one for him." My men stripped his armour from him and they were none too gentle. I took a cloak from one of the other dead leaders and fastened it about his shoulders. "My men will escort you to our borders. Return to your king and tell him this; I will not visit death upon him this time. If, however, he ever sends warriors west then I will appear with my wolves and we will feast upon Northumbrian flesh. This is my land. This is the land of the wolf. This is Úlfarrland."

I had not taken off my helmet and my red eyes burned into him. I saw true terror at that moment. He believed I was a shape shifter. He mounted his pony with help from Haaken. "I will deliver your message and I swear this to you. I will never leave my burgh again." Oswald kept his oath. I heard that he never moved out of sight of his fort on the rock.

"Escort him to the borders."

By the time dawn broke the survivors had either fled or were slain. We gathered the weapons first and then the bodies. We made a pyre of the bodies close to the place where the battle had taken place in the dark. The smoke spiralled high into the sky. Our own dead, and there were too many, were laid on the rocky slopes of Úlfarrberg. We laid many rocks above them until they almost made a mount themselves. We cut turf and laid it over the mound.

"This marks our land. Let the dead guard our border. Let their spirits walk this land."

They did for no enemy ever risked crossing that mound and that blackened piece of earth during my lifetime. Ulf and Ulla's children prospered and hunted north of their land to stop any enemy, Saxon or Pict from despoiling their fathers' graves.

It was late afternoon when we had finished and too late to return home. We were exhausted and were hungry. Thorir Ulfsson was now the headman and he slaughtered animals to feed the remnants of our army. The only one who appeared to be in high spirits was Haaken for he had a fine song to sing. He sang of the men who became wolves and slaughtered the Northumbrians at the battle of the Úlfarrberg. It was a momentous occasion. We did not know it at the time but Northumbria grew smaller year by year. It had cost us some fine warriors but our eastern border was now secure. We trudged home the following day.

The voyage and the battle had eaten into the time we might have spent preparing for the winter. Autumn was close and we all had to work collecting in the crops, salting fish and repairing halls and homes before the winter. Our craftsmen were kept busy making weapons and fine jewellery. Much of the jewellery was given by me as reward for good service but we had a surplus and they would make fine trades. We had decided not to trade weapons with any save the men of Gwent. When we had an excess then we might but until then the better weapons we produced were reserved for us alone.

Thorkell's ship was also finished before the autumn storms. There were some who wished to join my jarl. He was ever popular and many remembered his time at Wyddfa. I used some of my men to crew her and I escorted the 'Oarsteed' north. Bolli and I had come up with the name after her trials. She was like a lively young horse. If Thorkell wanted to rename her then he could. The ship had been paid for by my crew. Thorkell had been one of us. He would have to create his own wealth now. The ship would enable him to raid whilst protecting our land.

I saw that he had not been idle since we had left. He even had a ditch around his wooden wall. As a gift from Bjorn we had brought some new swords and spear heads. The settlers were, however, the most welcome addition. There were some widows as well as orphaned girls. Our last battle had left some empty halls. Happy with his ship he led me to the river to show me his next task. "We will build a wood jetty here so that we can moor my fine new ship."

"That is good." It was still pleasant to sit outside and we sat on a small mound. I told him of the men of Gwent and the battle with the Northumbrians.

"It has been quiet here, Jarl Dragon Heart. I make sure that my men patrol the river and they are armed. Those who see us from across the river flee at the sight of us." He chuckled, "They are terrified of Lochlannach. The men of the north have always plagued them."

"We will be trading when we return. Have your people anything that they can trade yet?"

He shook his head. "We have salted fish and collected as many animals as we can but we will need them for the winter."

"Perhaps it will not be as bad as the last one."

He shrugged, "If it is then you may just find our bones here in the spring."

"No, that cannot happen now, Thorkell the Tall. You have a ship and you could return to Úlfarrston if you found life too hard."

"We will persevere. Besides if Pasgen survived at Úlfarrston, then we should manage that here."

I clasped his arm. "Take a wife, Thorkell. None of us are getting any younger. We need to leave our mark on this land after we are gone. Our children are the future of this land."

"I will. I have spent my life as a warrior. I should like to pass something on to someone else."

When we left for our Frisian and Gwent trades I only took some of my Ulfheonar. Haaken, Cnut, Snorri and Arturus were the only ones who accompanied me. I think the others were a little disappointed to be left behind until I pointed out that we had had unwelcome news when we had returned from our last two voyages. It would not happen again. I needed our home protecting. I would sail with Trygg and Sigtrygg as far as Gwent and then I and my ship would visit Frisia. Aiden, of course would accompany me. For the rest I took those who wished to become my warriors. It would help to test them and give Haaken and Cnut the opportunity to see them rowing and working together.

During the voyage south we endured poor weather but we sailed on empty seas. It was as though we ruled the waves for we saw not a single ship. For Haaken and Cnut they were perfect conditions to observe the men. It also allowed me to see if Magnus could sail alone and make the correct decisions. He did so. Erik Short Toe and Ketil also showed me that they were seamen and not warriors.

King Selfyn's men had spotted us when we were still at sea and he and Iago awaited us on the jetty.

"We hoped you would return but we were not certain."

As we walked to his hall Iago said, innocently, "We heard that the monastery at St.David's was raided not long after you left."

I stopped and turned to face him. "It was us. You do not have to be delicate around either me or my men. If you wish to ask something then do so. We do not lie."

"I am sorry, Jarl Dragon Heart. I meant no offence."

"I know and none was taken. Too many people think that they know the Norse and the Dane. They do not! Only a man who has gone a-Viking can ever truly understand another Viking."

Iago remained silent. I think he was a little afraid of upsetting me again. As we passed the Roman fort, now a ruin, I asked. "Did you know anything of the Romans?"

The king shook his head. We use some of their stone for our buildings and we occasionally find things they have buried but that is all. Have you examined their buildings?"

King Selfyn looked confused, "Why? They are just full of Roman ghosts."

I shook my head, "Would you mind if my healer and I explored them. Come with us if you wish."

I could see that he was intrigued. "Very well."

The five of us went. Iago and Arturus accompanied me while the rest of my people arranged the trade for the iron ore. This was not the first Roman fort I had explored and I was amazed at the similar layout. Some were larger than others but the proportions appeared to be identical. I could see that some of the stone had been taken. There was evidence that people had sheltered there; we could see evidence of burning. The people of Gwent appeared to fear the spirits of the Romans who had lived at this Imperial outpost.

We headed for the main building. It looked much the same as the others we had visited. It had been ransacked and anything of value taken. The king and Iago looked at us with a look which suggested we were wasting our time. When the three of us dropped to our knees and began to examine the ground they stared at us in amazement.

This time it was Arturus who found it. "Here!" He pulled his dagger and began to scrape away the dirt. As we joined him I saw the number II carved into the stone. We knew now that they were the names of the Roman legions that had built and garrisoned this fort. This flagstone looked to be larger than the one we had found in the monastery. It took us longer to clear it. Three of us were not going to be able to lift it. I looked at a bemused Iago. "If you have a knife then you can help us lift this stone."

He knelt and took out his dagger. "What do you seek?"

"We know not but more times than not we find treasure."

He did not look convinced but he put his blade into the cleaned crevice. Aiden said, "Lift, gently."

As we had found before it was difficult at first and we had to strain but gradually, slowly, inexorably, it began to rise. I saw a broken piece of wood. "Your majesty, when this clears, jam that wood underneath to stop it falling back into place."

As the stone emerged he did so. The four of us sat down, exhausted by the effort. Aiden sniffed. "That smells worse than the others."

"I know. Light a brand, Aiden." He went outside to find something which would burn.

"Why did the Romans build holes in their buildings?"

"From what Aiden has read they kept the soldiers' money in them and other valuable documents. We have found coins before." Aiden returned with a candle he had in his satchel.

It was not a good one and the light was yellow, barely illuminating anything.

He placed it on the ground and then we manhandled the stone to reveal the hole. Aiden was our expert in Roman holes and he took the candle and lowered the upper half of his body into the hole. "Arturus, hold my legs." Arturus sat on his legs. Suddenly Aiden started and lifted his body back out of the hole. "It is a body, or the bones from one, at least. I think it is a soldier."

Arturus laughed, "Do you wish me to go down?" Aiden had been like a big brother to Arturus when growing up. This was the first chance that Arturus had had to tease the healer. "No. It came as a shock that was all." He put his head back in. "I think I can climb inside this one." Arturus released his legs and Aiden slipped down into the dark hole. His head was above the top. He handed me a short fat sword. I had seen one before. It was the kind of sword used by Roman soldiers. It was plainly finished and heavy.

I handed it to Iago. "Not treasure but useful."

Next came a dagger, followed by a belt and a rotting piece of leather covered in metal medals or coins of some description. Finally he handed a gold crown of leaves to me. It was a fine piece of work. It was obviously Roman for there was a Roman eagle on it and the letters SPQR again.

The king was impressed. "This is a surprise."

"Anything else Aiden?"

His disembodied voice came from beneath us. "There are fragments of parchment but they crumble when I touch them." There was silence. "There is a small chest." His head emerged and he lifted a heavy wooden chest. Arturus pulled himself from the hole and we replaced the stone.

"Sleep in peace Roman. Your bones will remain where you died."

Aiden did his magic and unpicked the lock. He had made various keys and picks now and he was quite adept. We opened it and found the usual gold and silver coins. King Selfyn could not contain himself. "You are all truly magicians. Let us take this back to my hall and you can tell me how you learned of this hidden treasure."

As we walked back we told him of our earlier experiences. We had not finished when we reached his hall. It was more of a roundhouse than a hall but it was well made and spacious. Our men were busy trading with the merchants of the town. We continued our tale including the finding of the sword. It was at that point that Iago became excited.

"We have heard tales of a mounted warrior who led his men to hold back the Saxons. It was said he had a sword which was magic and as long as he bore it he would never be defeated. He lived by the holy mountain." He pointed to the king. "We still have mounted warriors to protect the king."

"What happened to him?"

"The stories say he was betrayed by one of his own family and slain but his death drove the Saxons from his land."

"They have returned."

King Selfyn looked at me. "The stories are that he had the wolf symbol on his shield." He pointed at my shield which rested on the wall. "Like yours. Are you descended from him?"

I shook my head, "In truth I do not know. I may be but..."

Iago clapped me about the shoulders. "You are." He smacked his chest, "I feel it here. Your coming halted the Saxons much as your ancestor did. He was the wolf the Saxons feared and you are the Viking wolf."

For some reason it seemed to make him happy. I was uncomfortable with the attention. "Let us divide the treasure up, your majesty."

He seemed surprised. "But you found it!"

"On your land. Keep the sword for we need it not but we will take the torc to Frisia. We will get a better trade there. You are a richer king now. With the gold we gave you for your iron you will soon be able to buy better armour for your men. That is the best defence against Saxons!"

The feast, that night, was a joyous affair. Iago became roaring drunk and swore undying friendship to all of my men. We had sore heads the next day.

The king, Iago and all of his horsemen came to see us off. I bade farewell to Sigtrygg and Trygg. They would sail home with the iron. We would head for Frisia. I was as excited as Iago had been the night before. I had left a home safely protected and with the iron and the wheat we had traded, we would be both secure and well fed over the winter.

We left the other ships at the mouth of the estuary. As I put the steer board over the wind changed a little to come from the north east. The Allfather was smiling on us and giving us his blessing. Our discovery of the dead Roman had not been an ill omen.

Chapter 18

We approached the dangerous seas towards dusk at the end of the first day. The sea air and the wind had cleared all of our heads. The treasures, all of them, had been safely stored beneath the pine deck. When we had sailed north this had been the point where we had felt safe. Now we sensed the danger in the malevolent maelstrom which whirled around the islands and rocks.

We approached the islands of Syllingar and I had the sails reduced to barely sticks. "Oars!"

We would have to edge our way through the jumble of islands, and the precocious wind sent by the Allfather now prevented us from making headway east. Ketil raced down the deck. "My lord, it is too dark to see. There are rocks all around us."

He was right. I should have anchored closer to the mainland and risked these savage rocks during the day. My mind had been distracted. I had wanted to sail close to here. I knew not why. "Find me a beach then or at least some shelter from the wind."

"Aye my lord," He scurried up the mast like a squirrel.

"Cnut, just give us headway until Ketil can find somewhere safe."

He had swarmed up the mast and was now clinging precariously to the yard. He shouted down and pointed to the south, "There, Jarl Dragon Heart. It is not far."

"Magnus, go to the bow with Erik Short Toe and watch for rocks."

I edged the steer board over to a southerly direction. The oars were barely touching the water. Magnus' hand came up and I nudged the board a little more to steer board. Aiden shouted, "I can see it; white sand and less than two hundred paces from us."

I allowed the wind to bring us beam on to the beach and we stopped just short of the sand and shingle. Magnus and Erik leapt ashore with their ropes and tethered us, fore and aft to two large rocks. I took my sword and jumped into the water. It came up to my waist. The ship would not ground.

"Haaken, Aiden and Arturus come with me. Cnut, take charge."

We wore no armour for I had seen no sign of life but it paid to be cautious. There was a rocky hill rising in the middle of the island and we headed there the better to see the other side. Worryingly there was a well worn path leading from the beach and I saw footprints. People used this island. It was not tiny but I had not thought it to be inhabited. These were strange islands. We had heard tales of women luring ships on to the rocks and then devouring their flesh. I did not believe the stories but there must have been something which happened to cause the stories to be told.

We reached the top and I saw that it was indeed a small island. It was less than a mile long and just over half a mile wide. There were, however trees, and Aiden's sharp ears picked out the sound of water. We followed the noise and discovered a small spring which spurted from the rocks.

"We can fill our water skins here."

Suddenly a voice came from beneath our feet. "You would steal my water?"

Our swords were out in an instant. I could see nothing. Haaken grabbed his amulet and kissed it. It had been a female voice. Were we doomed to be eaten by the women who lured sailors to their deaths? The voice began to laugh and it chilled my blood. I could still see no-one. We stood back to back. Aiden's seax seemed a little inadequate but we would fight to the last to preserve our lives.

The voice came again. "Three Norsemen and a Hibernian and they are afraid of an old woman." She laughed again and I gripped Ragnar's Spirit even tighter. She was hidden yet she knew all about us. I closed my eyes. In my head I implored Erika, my mother and Ragnar for help.

Suddenly the laughing stopped and the silence which followed was almost as bad. I was hardly breathing. I saw a glow appear some ten paces from where we stood. A rock seemed to be on fire. The glow grew. None of us could move. It was as though we were frozen to the spot. A shape appeared out of the glow. Something had come from the bowels of the earth. I could face any man and be confident that I would beat him. This was supernatural and even Aiden seemed afraid. The shape grew closer and I debated attacking it before it came too close. How do you kill a spirit?

Then the shape spoke. "Your mother and your wife say you will be safe, Dragon Heart. You can sheath your swords. No harm will come to you here."

"Do not believe her, jarl. She is bewitching us!"

The cackling laugh came again, "Haaken One Eye, would you kill me and lose the chance of a story to tell?"

She knew too much and the fact that she had spoken of Erika and my mother convinced me. "Sheathe your swords. She is right."

"Thank you Dragon Heart; your mother is right you are a wise warrior."

She was the oldest woman I had ever seen. Her wrinkled flesh seemed to hang from her bones like a shift which was too big. Her blue veins seemed like small mountains on her arm. And yet her voice was clear and her eyes were as sharp as Aiden's.

"I am Eawynn and I am what you call a volva. I am a witch. I see the future and I remember the past. Your mother and your wife have spoken with me. I have been expecting you."

My mouth must have fallen open for she laughed again. "You who have spoken with the spirits all of your life should not be surprised. Come, it is too cold out here for my old bones."

We followed her down into her cave. The light we had seen was from lamps burning oil. There was also a fire burning in the sand. There was a cosy feel to it but I was still reeling from the knowledge that we were expected. I had not chosen this island; Ketil had just seen a beach. Then I remembered that the Norns are the weird sisters. They do nothing which is simple. Was this one of the Norns, had we just met a Weird Sister?

She took a ladle and poured a liquid into a beaker. She handed it to me and then repeated it for the others. Haaken looked at it with suspicion while the other two looked at me. The old woman said not a word but I heard, in my head, '*drink*'. I drank. Aiden and Arturus looked at each other and they drank. I laughed as Haaken watched us for a sign that the drink was drugged. He sipped and then drank. It was a pleasant drink.

"Tell me, Eawynn, why did we need to speak with you?"

She inclined her head and said to the ceiling, "You are right about him." Then she looked at me. "You need to go to Miklagård. Your destiny lies there."

Haaken snorted, "That is the other side of the world!"

Eawynn ignored him. "You will go to Frisia and you will try to sell the eagle and the torc. Do not. They will try to rob you. If you go to Miklagård then your people will rule your land for generations to come. It is *wyrd* and you cannot fight it."

It seemed to me that my whole life had been determined by the sisters. "You can see beyond today, Eawynn. What of my people now while we are far from them? Will they come to harm? My wife and my mother both came to harm when I was not there. Will Kara and my people be safe?"

She seemed happy with my questions. "No harm will come to your people while you are away." The smile left her face, "That does not mean that you will not face hardship, danger and death. But I will answer your question; your people will be safe. They will see the spring."

Aiden suddenly said, "And if we are not returned by spring then they will not be safe."

"And you have the gift. You have powers within you that you are not yet aware of. You too, need to go to Miklagård. There your mind will be opened. You need to train your mind as much as the Dragon Heart trains his body. You, Aiden, are part of this journey." She waved her arms. "And now you had better go for your men worry!"

We had heard nothing but we stood. As we went towards the door we heard our names being called. Eawynn laughed, "Men! They have so little faith." Her thin, blue veined hand came out to grab my arm. "Your mother and your wife are there for you always." She handed me a small jug with a cork stopper. "A few drops of this, mixed with wine or beer will help you to communicate with them but do not waste it. Use it only when necessary."

"Thank you, Eawynn."

She shrugged. "I serve the spirits. It is my purpose in life."

When I stepped outside Cnut, Snorri and the rest of my warriors were standing with drawn blades.

"We thought you had been taken!"

"By whom?"

"We heard strange noises and saw flickering lights. We thought you had been lured to your death."

"We are quite safe and very hungry. I hope that there is food ready or we shall all be angry."

Cnut, with a confused look upon his face, led the way. I was lost in my own thoughts. Miklagård! It was *wyrd* for it had been in my mind to go and I had been seeking an excuse. Perhaps this was all a dream and I would wake up. Arturus voice told me it was not, "Will we go to Miklagård then?"

I smiled and put my arm around his shoulder. "It seems your mother and your grandmother decided that already son; first Frisia and then Miklagård."

Haaken regaled the men with the story as we ate on the beach. I could see where Eawynn gathered her food for the waters abounded with shellfish and sea weed. I had seen no boat. I wondered how she moved from the island. Perhaps she did not. Aiden and Arturus sat on either side of me.

"This is powerful magic, father. How did she know of mother?"

"I sometimes know events which have yet to occur but you are right, this is powerful magic. Your mother did not display such powers."

Aiden said, quietly, "Perhaps not while she was alive but since she has died..." He looked at me nervously. "Perhaps she needed to die to gain her powers."

"You may be right. My mother's powers became greater after her death. We will follow this course and see where it leads. I take comfort from the spirits watching over us."

We headed across the grey autumn waters, east to Frisia. It was a much easier journey than our previous one and it proved to be almost dull. We did not mind for we were still thinking of the seer of Scillonia. When we sailed we stood off from the shore. We were alone and we needed to be wary. We were a powerful ship but we could be outnumbered. Just as a mighty stag can be brought down by a pack of dogs so we could succumb to smaller boats. We saw none and that pleased me.

We avoided the Rinaz. I had no doubt that they would remember us from our last visit. As we sailed through the islands I had my men keep a weapon close to hand. We sailed slowly for I wanted a more central berth this time. We were lucky, or, perhaps it was meant to be for we found one close to the main square. We tied up and I detailed four young strong warriors to guard the gangplank. To his obvious annoyance I left Haaken in charge of the boat while I took Cnut, Arturus and Aiden to meet with Rorik. I would not hide from a confrontation. Although we had neither helmet nor mail we had our leather byrnies beneath our kyrtles. If there was to be bloodshed then I was sure we could handle it.

We received some sour looks as we wandered through the narrow streets. I daresay some of the ones we passed we had fought and there were others we had robbed of family members. That was the price you paid for attacking the Ulfheonar. We headed for Agnetha's ale shop. It was not busy when we entered. She still had no smile upon her face but she approached us.

"Four wheat beers!" I put the copper coins on the crudely made table.

She whisked them away. "You have nerve returning here. You were roundly cursed after your last visit."

I shrugged, "If people poke the sleeping wolf then they can expect to be bitten."

She laughed, "And you showed your teeth right enough, Viking wolf."

I had no doubt that Rorik would hear of our arrival and he would come. I knew not if he would fight or talk but I was ready for both. As we drank we listened to the conversations around us. We had arrived on the day of a slave auction. We had none to sell but it would be interesting to see what slaves were available and the prices they earned.

Rorik came in flanked by two warriors. I noticed that he had a new scar running from one eye down to his neck. I did not remember him receiving that from us. I watched him as he approached. I had my hand on my dagger in case he tried anything. My long sword would be of little use in such a confined space. A smile appeared on his face. Thanks to his new wound it appeared lopsided and almost comical. He held out his hand in friendship. I slipped my dagger into my left hand as I took it.

"It is good to see you again, Jarl Dragon Heart. Have you more slaves to sell?"

"Not this time. We may be in the market to buy." I shrugged as though it was of little interest."

He pulled a chair over and sat down. Agnetha brought him a beer and held her hand out. Once again Rorik appeared irritated that he had to pay. I suspect he was given goods elsewhere.

Arturus was still young and he stared at Rorik's face. Rorik smiled his lopsided smile again, "I see your son has seen my gift from Charlemagne. The Emperor sent some of his men here to try to tax us. They received none."

"That is a little risky is it not; taking on such a powerful army?" In my mind I was imagining the wharf rats he had to fight for him.

"We are more powerful than you think. Since you were here many other Norse and Danes have settled. We have a large army if we need it." Agnetha handed him his beer and gave him a look of disgust as she left. She obviously did not think much of him and his Norsemen. "Why do you not join us? We know that you can fight and your sword would attract many warriors."

"I thank you for your compliment but we are happy in our homeland."

"If you change your mind you are always welcome." He spread his arms, "There is a slave auction this afternoon and we now have halls for merchants to use. If you take your goods to one then trade takes place during the hours of daylight."

"I understand why. The nights can be very dangerous here, can they not?"

"They are only dangerous for the sheep and you, Jarl Dragon Heart, are no sheep."

As we walked back to the boat I asked the others for their opinions. "We still need supplies for our voyage but I am not certain we will receive a good price for the eagle and the torc."

"You are right, Jarl Dragon Heart. They would command a higher price in the land from which they came. Remember Eawynn and her prophesy. She told us to go to Miklagård and to sell them there rather than to the robbers here."

"You are right Aiden. We will take some of the silver and copper and buy supplies. What else do we need?"

"A map would be useful but I am not certain that we will find one here."

"You never know. Cnut, you and Arturus stay aboard with Snorri. You saw the men with Rorik. If you see them again you can be on your guard."

There was a time when Arturus would have objected but each day he was changing and becoming a man. "Aye father."

I split the money we would take between the three of us. I left much of the gold on board the ship. If we needed it then we would return. The slaves were being brought from the slave pens and so we went to buy produce which we could take on board our ship. There were a vast array of preserved meats and fish. Haaken chose wisely. Despite a search we found no one offering maps for sale. We did buy two good oak barrels for water. On our way to the slave auction we called in at Agnetha's and bought a barrel of her wheat beer. It would only last ten days or so but it would delay the time we had to begin drinking stale water.

We did not need slaves but I was keen to see the prices. They began with some young Saxon girls. I heard them speak and knew that they came from the southern coast of Britannia. They pleaded for someone to save them before the overseer cracked them about the rump with his whip. I knew why they were so upset. They would be bought by the whorehouses of this place. They were more valuable than gold and it was reflected in their prices.

Next came two tonsured priests. They remained stoic, anticipating, I do not doubt, some benefactor like the Count buying them and freeing them. Sadly for them the Count was not present and they were bought by a Frank who did not look as though generosity of nature was one of his characteristics. They were sold for a gold piece each. We had done far better with the Count. The two priests looked less than happy as they were led away.

I was going to leave when a voice in my head told me to stay. The next ten slaves were a consignment of Saxon boys. They were older than the girls who had been sold. The prettier ones were sold for high prices by the same men who had bought the girls but the other eight were sold for silver coins. Slaves did not have the value they once had.

Finally the older slaves were brought up. The auctioneer tried to make them sound like an attractive purchase but it was obvious he was only going to receive copper for them. He would want them off his hands to save the expense of feeding them.

The first three were older women. He extolled their virtues pointing out that they did not eat much and had many skills such as cooking and cleaning. Two more even older women were brought out and the five were all bought by

Agnetha. She had an eye for a bargain. Her ale house was always busy and slaves who could serve would free her to find other ways to make money. She did not need pretty girls. She wanted experienced women.

The last five were men. Three of them were a little older than me but all looked ill used. They were sold as herdsmen. It would be a harsh life for them. They would have to live alone and protect their herds from wolves and raiders. The three of them would not have a long life.

The last two were ancient. One was whole while the other had no left arm below the elbow. The first one, it turned out, could read. The auctioneer did not tell us that, the slave blurted it out before being silenced by the auctioneer. I thought that the auctioneer was being foolish for a bidding war began and the man ended being sold for a silver coin. He had gone for more than the three herdsmen added together. The second was dressed in rags and he was thin and emaciated. He carried himself with a little dignity. I was intrigued at him and his story. Once again my voices told me to stay.

Haaken was keen to leave. "We have seen enough, Dragon Heart. Do we want to see an old cripple humiliated when no-one bids for him? He is a man and deserves some respect."

"No, we have seen the others, we will wait and see."

"What am I bid for this old sailor? He only has one good arm but he can mend nets. I know he is from far away but he can speak our language too. Come now. Shall we say, a single silver Imperial?"

There were hoots of laughter and I saw what Haaken meant. The man was old but he deserved more than this. He reminded me of Ragnar even though Ragnar had two arms one was almost useless. My own days as a slave came to mind.

"Ten copper pieces? Five?" There were still howls of derision from the crowd who were enjoying the humiliation both men were enduring. "A copper piece then? Surely he is worth that? Even if you only get seven days work from him you will have your money back."

"Two silver pieces!"

My voice silenced the crowd who turned to look at this fool who obviously did not know the rites and rules of an auction. Aiden and Haaken kept faces of stone although I do not doubt that they thought I had lost my mind.

The auctioneer showed that he was no fool. He roared, "Sold!" before I could change my mind. The silence was replaced by a buzz of noise as people discussed my action.

I went to the table where the tallyman waited to take our coins. I stood behind Agnetha. She turned and gave a rare smile. "You are like me, Norseman, you see beneath the skin although I do not know why you paid in silver."

"The man deserves dignity."

"Those are the words of a noble man; a noble man who has money. You have a bargain there. Josephus can speak many languages and he was a captain until he was captured by Rorik and his pirates. He was a good sailor. If you had not bought him then I fear he would have had his throat cut. You certainly make life interesting when you visit."

This was *wyrd*. The man was a captain. His name did not sound as though he came from the north. Could it be that he knew the seas through which we would travel? Had the voice been the spirits in my ear?

Having paid I went to collect my purchase. When I arrived they were fitting a thrall collar. "Do not bother with that?"

"But he is a slave and he might run!"

I turned to the auctioneer. "Do you think he could out run us? Come Josephus. Let us get you clothed." I gestured for him to follow.

He spoke in our language. It sounded awkward but he could be clearly understood. "Thank you, master. I will serve you well in the time left to me."

"That is out of our hands, Josephus. If the Allfather wills it any of us could make the last journey now."

There was a stall selling clothes and I spent some coppers to buy him not only clean and usable clothes but some for cold weather. He looked as though he would not last a strong breeze.

He made to dress in the street. "No Josephus, your days of such indignities are over. We have a shelter on the ship you can change there." I noticed the eyes on us as we headed for my ship. I trusted no one in this town, none save, perhaps, Agnetha. She alone had not tried to rob us.

Once dressed Aiden made sure that the old man ate. Then, with the five of us sat around him I questioned him. "The auctioneer said that you were a sailor."

He stuck his scrawny chest out proudly. I was a captain. I had my own ship and I sailed the seas from Constantinopolis to the Rinaz. I had money."

"Until you were captured?"

"Until I was captured. It was Rorik the devil who captured me." He held out his stump. He did this after I was in chains and after he had butchered my crew."

"That is strange. Why did he not sell them? He struck me as a man who likes a profit."

"He is also a cruel man. I had a small crew of Greeks. They were fine boys but they were young and there were but four of them. When he took my arm they objected and they died."

"Why did he take your arm? It reduced your value."

"He wanted me for my knowledge of the seas. I have sailed these seas since I was a boy. I followed my father and my grandfather. There was a time when we sailed to the island of Mona and traded there."

Haaken frowned and Aiden said, "Anglesey."

"Yes it has become the island of the Angles now but my father sailed there when it was a powerful kingdom."

"You know the Middle Sea then?"

He smiled, "Like the back of my hand." He chuckled, "My right hand that is."

"Good for we sail there. Is that your home?"

"I was born a day from the walls of Constantine. I will die there." We all clutched our amulets. It was a bad omen when a man foretold his own death.

"Will you guide us there?"

He looked surprised at the question. "I am your slave as I have been for the last ten years."

"I will grant you your freedom when we reach your home. How say you to that?"

His eyes welled up. "They say you are a wild and cruel man, Jarl Dragon Heart but I see something noble in you. I will guide you." He patted the deck with his good hand. "It will be good to sail south again and feel warmth on my face for the final time."

"Could you teach me Greek?"

He seemed to see Aiden for the first time. "Of course. We will have time."

"And how to speak Latin? I can read it but I have never spoken it."

"Of course."

"And can you help me make maps?"

He nodded and began to laugh. "When I stood there waiting to be sold the three of you frightened me. I did not want you to buy me for I thought that you were like Rorik. Now I see that you are more like the nobles of Charlemagne. Yes, I can help you make maps. I was brought up to make them by my father."

"Then get some rest, we shall sail on the next tide."

His face became serious. "I would sail sooner. Rorik and his sea rats covet your sword and your ship."

It confirmed my suspicions. "Can we sail now?"

"What does this vessel draw?"

"Laden as we are, the height of a tall warrior."

"Then we can sail. There is a passage to the north we can use." He hesitated, "If you can trust a one armed man to steer."

Haaken laughed, "Well he trusts a one eyed man to fight next to him so the answer will be yes."

197

"Cnut, have the men put their bows within easy reach. I
want Ketil on the mast head and Magnus and Erik Short Toe
at the prow. Do not make it obvious that we are preparing to
leave." I turned to Arturus. "Come we will prepare to slip
our cables. We will walk along the jetty as though we are out
for a stroll. Keep your sword handy. The rest of you, be
ready for when we return. As soon as our ties are severed we
sail north!"

We headed towards Rorik's ships. They were two drekar
at the end of the jetty. I wanted to be able to recognise them
and see how prepared they were for sea. As soon as we drew
close I could see men boarding as quickly as they could.
They were preparing for sea. They had thirteen oars on each
side. I had sailed a threttanessa and I knew how fast they
could be. However, like my old ship, *'Wolf'*, they both had a
low freeboard.

We were about to return to our ship when Rorik and his
two warriors appeared. "Do not believe everything that old
dog tells you! He is a liar! I should have cut his tongue out
and not his hand."

"Thank you for your advice. I will give it the
consideration it deserves."

"Why did you pay so much for him? Have you so much
gold that you can throw it away?"

"Let us just say he reminded me of two old men who
were kind to me. I was repaying their kindness."

He snorted, "And I thought you were a warrior! The wolf
indeed! You are weak if you show kindness! It is for fools
and women."

For the first time he had dropped his mask and I saw
beneath the skin. It was also clear to me that Josephus was
correct. He desired my ship.

"Come Arturus, let us have another wheat beer at
Agnetha's while we may and then we can return home!"

I was not sure if he believed me but I wanted doubt in his
mind about our destination. He was sure to have spies on the
jetty and they would report that, when we left, we headed
north.

It was hard not to rush as we strolled back to our ship. "Take the forward rope and I will take the stern. As soon as it is untied, board. I will follow."

I saw Rorik's spies. The two scrawny looking men were pretending to play dice while watching our ship. I nodded to Arturus. He slipped the rope. I watched the two spies. They were little bigger than Erik Short Toe although they were grown men. As I expected they both jumped to their feet. Before they could turn away I grabbed one under each arm. I took two strides and when I reached the jetty, hurled them into the water. There were two splashes and shouts. Everyone looked around and then began to laugh. Without bothering to see if they could swim I slipped the rope and leapt aboard. I only just made it. Aiden and Haaken reached for my arms. My crew had taken me at my word and obeyed me. The bow was already moving away from the land as the sail caught the breeze.

Aiden and Haaken laughed as they pulled me aboard."That could have been embarrassing my friend. But it will make a good line for my latest saga!"

As I stood at the stern I saw the two wharf rats scrambling ashore. Rorik would get the news but it would be delayed somewhat!

Chapter 19

I saw a wide grin appear on the face of Josephus as he edged us into the channel. His eyes flicked from the sea to the mast to the shore and back. "Aiden stay here with Josephus in case he needs anything."

"Aye my lord. Do you think Eawynn foresaw this?"

I smiled, "Probably. We are just following a path already laid out for us. It is best not to worry overmuch."

I picked up my bow and slung my quiver over my shoulder so that it hung by my left hand. Haaken and Cnut picked theirs up too. "Are we expecting trouble then?"

"Yes, Cnut. Rorik's ships were ready to sail. They will be swift and he knows these waters as well as our pilot. Our best defence will be our bows. We can keep showering him with arrows whilst we row. Make sure our best archers are not used for rowing."

The islands around us looked very close to me. Josephus seemed unconcerned. There were islands and patches of marches as far as the eye could see. I returned to the stern. The island we had left was receding in the distance and I could see no sign of pursuit. Of course the threttanessa was a smaller boat and the two we had seen were not laden. They could take the southern passage easier than we could. Our size dictated our course.

Eventually the land cleared and we could see the open sea. Josephus shouted, "What course, master?"

"Miklagård!"

He put the steer board over and watched the pennant on the mast head to check the wind. He seemed satisfied and nodded. "It is with us."

That was good news. We would not have to row. I felt that I could rely on my new crew member but I wanted Magnus, as well as Aiden, to benefit from his skills. "Magnus, go and watch the new steersman. He is an experienced captain and you can learn much. He is also old so spell him now and then."

"Aye captain."

I went to the prow. It was a luxury I would take. I wanted to see the sea before me. I knew that Rorik would come for us. He had two ships and we were a tempting prize. The weapons my men owned would be the envy of any warrior. Rorik would assume that he had the advantage for he knew these waters. I would have to outwit him. It was also pleasant to watch my ship sailing from the prow. I could see the way her prow cut through the water. It was clean and it was smooth. It was important to see how your ship sailed. I knew from the other end that she was very responsive to the touch. I looked forward to speaking with Josephus to learn his opinion and headed back to the stern.

I noticed he kept us further from the coast than I would have done. I saw that he had allowed Magnus to steer, under his direction. Magnus appeared to be hanging on to his every word.

"You keep us further out to sea captain. Why is that?"

"More wind and fewer rocks, master. You have a fine spread of canvas aloft it would be a shame to waste any of it." He patted the rail once more. "She is a fine ship. I have never sailed in one as fast or as responsive." He touched Magnus gently on the shoulder. "Look at the mast head; a point or two to steer board. Magnus made the adjustment and we all felt the increase in power as the mast creaked a little and we heeled slightly more.

He smiled at Magnus who beamed. "And the other reason for sailing further from the coast is that it keeps us from the likes of Rorik." He pointed to the south. "He will come from one of the inlets further south and attack us. He will have his men rowing all night to reach us by the morning. There are many places and islands further south where he can wait and ambush us. He knows the lairs well."

"I wondered where he acquired his power."

"He has built up a fleet of ten or more ships. They are never all in port at once. The two he has in port are his biggest ones. Some of the others only have six oars a side but he uses them to herd ships to where he wants them. He is like a giant spider and he controls many weaker men. He is

very cruel. I would rather die than fall into his hands again."
He looked astern and then up at the mast. "This will be a
little too big for him I hope."

"And my men are resting. If he has his men rowing all
night they will be tired."

"Aye he will. Do you intend to sail all night?"

"That depends upon you, pilot. Do you think we can?"

"If we keep a good watch and stand out to sea then I see
no reason why not. Aiden here has told me that he has a
rough map he has made. We can add detail once I am sure of
our course and Magnus here has this powerful beast under
control."

"Magnus is a good sailor and he will captain this before
too long."

"This is how I learned my trade and my son before he and
the others were butchered by Rorik."

"Your son was in your crew?"

"He was and my nephew too. If they are alive then I have
my brother and my wife to face when I reach
Constantinopolis."

The sun began to sink into the west. Josephus looked at
me with a question in his eyes, I nodded. He could command
the crew. "Ketil, Eric Short Toe, take a reef or two out of the
sail." When the sun dropped behind the horizon Josephus
said, "You see that star yonder." He pointed and Magnus
nodded. "Keep the prow pointed at it. When I have helped
Aiden with his map and had a sleep I will relieve you."

"I can stay awake all night."

"I know but this old man is enjoying captaining again. Do
not deprive me of that pleasure." He went to the small shelter
we had rigged on the other side of the stern. Aiden had a
candle lit and the rough map before him. As the two sat and
began to talk, in a mixture of Norse and Greek, I realised that
this old man had come seamlessly into our lives and was
now one of the family. He knew the sea like Olaf had but he
was gentler and more considerate. Olaf had been a little
abrasive. Like me he had been a slave and that made you
behave differently to other men. Your freedom is more

precious; having lost it once you are loath to do so a second time.

I left them and went to speak with Haaken and Cnut. "We will be attacked in the morning. I want a six man watch all night. I will take the first, Haaken the second, Cnut the third. I will take the fourth and so on. Josephus is working wonders but he is old and he has not been well treated. We must nurse him along. He is the key to Miklagård. The spirits have sent him; of that I am certain." I nodded towards him. "Keep him well fed and he may live to see his home."

The men were soon asleep; their snores providing a counterpoint to the creaking of the ropes and the swish of the seas at the prow. On land the noises would have kept men awake; at sea they were like a lullaby. I went to the stern. "Magnus you can rest for an hour or so if you wish. I have the watch."

"No, Jarl Dragon Heart, I promised Josephus that I would steer her."

"You like him do you not?"

He nodded, "I never knew my grandfather. I would like to think he was like Josephus."

Wyrd! I had never known my grandfather and Ragnar had become the grandfather I had never known. I was pleased that I had been drawn to the islands of Syllingar. We were meant to do this. It was no longer about the treasure, it was about the voyage and our journey. Aiden would learn languages and have his maps and Magnus would become a captain. I did not know yet what Arturus and I would gain from it but that did not matter. We would change and that change would be for the better. The adventure was in not knowing what lay ahead.

I saw Aiden and Josephus as they curled up in their blankets. I suspected that this was the first blanket the slave had had in many a year. Arturus had fallen asleep long before. I knew that he was keen to learn Greek as well as Aiden. He might have the intention but I feared he did not have the resolve. Still, if he learned a few words it might help.

When it came my turn to sleep I found that my mind was filled with too many thoughts for it to be a restful one. The Otherworld seemed much closer to our world than I expected. It was an uncomfortable thought. And I know that I was excited. Once we passed Navarre it would be as far south as I had ever travelled. I knew that it would be hot and I would see strange sights. Would it change me forever? I had heard of Vikings who had sailed south in search of treasure and adventure. None had returned home. Would I be the first?

I was roused before dawn by Cnut. Josephus was steering and Magnus, Arturus and Aiden lay asleep at his feet. He could barely move they were so close and curled together.

"You should have said something, I will move them."

"No master. This is a joy to me. I have three young minds. They are like the sponges of the middle sea. They soak up knowledge. I wish to pass on what I know before I die. Rorik tore my knowledge from me and my child that is why he will find a watery grave. The Allfather does not like such behaviour. He will be punished."

"You are not a follower of the White Christ then?"

"I was baptised and all of those in Byzantium are Christians but when I was captured I lost my faith and I went back to the old ways. I do not like to turn the other cheek. I want vengeance. I want Rorik to suffer."

I could hear the passion in his voice. "If it is in my power then he will pay." I saw the thin line of dawn on the eastern horizon. "Haaken, have the men stand to and prepare their oars. Let us eat before dawn in case our new friends from Frisia await us."

Josephus nodded, "There are islands coming up and we have to sail close to them. He will be amongst them. His small ships mean he can hide and they will have watchers. He will see us."

I nodded and thought about the sea battle to come. Torin One Shoe handed me and Josephus some of yesterday's bread, some cheese and he sliced an onion in two. Josephus said, "That is more food than I would have seen in four days when I worked for Rorik!"

"Eat, I need you well for this voyage. Tell me, Rorik will try to attack on both sides at once will he not?" His mouth was full of bread and he nodded. "How many men does he have on each ship?"

He swallowed and washed it down with a little of Agnetha's beer. He has a crew of about thirty on each ship."

"Archers?"

"A few, not many."

"And which will be his ship?"

"The one which stands off; he likes others to do his dying for him."

I had the measure of this man now. I would not wear my mail. I did not intend to allow him to board. If I did so then we would lose. I would win this battle before it had even begun.

With the whole crew fed and prepared we waited for dawn to break. There was little point in running out the oars and rowing. It would slow us down and tire our men. I would wait. I went to the stern where Josephus had the steer board. He was teaching Aiden Greek by pointing to the things on the ship. I smiled as I saw Magnus mouthing the words. He was learning just by being close to the two of them.

Ketil was at the mast head, his legs dangling down as he sat astride the yard and the mast. Erik Short Toe was watching for rocks although we were still some two miles from the coast. The islands that Josephus had mentioned were ahead. We would pass within a mile of them and there appeared to be a cluster of them. We thought that Rorik might be there but, equally he could have found another ambush site. I could feel the tension getting to me. I wanted this threat gone so that we could concentrate on the voyage to Miklagård. This was the past come to haunt me and I wanted the future.

I saw the islands grow closer and I stared, looking for a mast head. I saw nothing. We had passed two when Ketil shouted, "Masts to the east!"

The two threttanessa came hurtling out like greyhounds released after hares. "Take her to steer board. Rowers prepare; archers at the ready." I glanced up at the wind which was coming from the south west. My move had slowed us down for it took us into the wind. Josephus compensated by sailing as close to the wind as he dared. He did not look worried.

The two ships were now a mile away and they had separated. There was one to the south and one to the north. I thought that the southern one would be the one which would reach us first. "Josephus, which is Rorik's?"

"The one to the north."

"Rowers to your oars. Archers on me." I strode to the shore side of my ship. Snorri would organise the archers. This would all require careful timing. Cnut set the men rowing at a steady pace. The two drekar were still catching us but less quickly. The southern one was trying to cut off our escape. Rorik had a similar problem to us, the wind was against him. I allowed the southern ship to close with our beam. My men were just warming up at their oars. When I chose they would be able to row much faster and for a longer time.

"Josephus, hard to shore! Erik, Ketil to the sail!"

The '**Heart of the Dragon**' suddenly changed direction. The wind was now coming from our quarter and we raced towards the closer of the two drekar.

"Cnut, full speed!"

We were but three hundred paces from the drekar. The captain tried to turn and head towards us but he ran into the wind and only his oars kept his forward momentum.

"Archers at the ready. I want death to visit this drekar. Half speed!" As we slowed and the drekar's captain struggled to work out what I was up to I shouted, "Release!"

Twenty arrows soared across the short distance to the drekar. A second and a third followed a heartbeat later. The dragon prow was just twenty paces from our oars. I hoped I had judged it well. Aiden shouted, "The other drekar is two hundred paces from our stern!"

Our ship was now passing across the prow and I heard Snorri order the release of another two flights. The oars were in disarray as our arrows had struck rowers and the steersman. Rorik was so keen to catch us that he took his eye off his companion. The ship's way kept her moving so that she crossed our stern. My archers riddled the stern with arrows and I saw the captain and steersman fall to their deaths. The drekar slewed to steer board just as Rorik tried to reach us. The two ships cracked into each other. I heard oars shear and men scream as they were skewered by broken oars. Rorik's ship began to sink.

"Steer board Josephus!" I did not want to risk running aground and I wanted to see what happened to the two ships.

Rorik's vessel was doomed. I saw his men trying to cross to the drekar of death. It was still afloat but I suspected it had sprung strakes. My men cheered as Rorik's drekar sank to its gunwales. I watched as mailed warriors, ready to board us when they caught us, sank beneath the waves. We were going more slowly now as we turned back into the wind. I saw Rorik climb aboard his surviving ship and shake his fist at us. If I had wanted to I could have turned and destroyed him and his crew. I did not. He would struggle to make it to shore with the damaged drekar.

I turned to Josephus. He was smiling. "Thank you, master. My son and my nephew are avenged."

Once we returned to a southern course we were able to rest the rowers. I took the opportunity of speaking with Josephus. "Can you manage her, Magnus?"

"Aye, Jarl Dragon Heart."

We went to the leeward side of the ship. "How long will it take us and what dangers can we expect? Now that we have rid ourselves of our problem I need to know what to expect."

"If the winds are favourable and we rest each night then it would take a month, perhaps more."

"If we sailed at night?"

"We could possibly make it in twenty days. But why risk it?"

"I am just working out the time. I have a land to watch over. I trust those who are there but you must know, Josephus, that we would all rather be with our families."

"You are right. As for the troubles? The Pillars of Hercules can be tricky but it is once we pass there that the real danger comes. There are Barbary pirates who plague the southern waterways and if we head north then the waters are tricky. Once we are in Imperial waters then life should be easier except…"

He looked at the deck. "Go on Josephus, tell me."

"You are a Norseman. You will be taken for a pirate."

"So when we reach Imperial waters we should try to avoid the shipping and the main routes?"

"I am afraid so."

He looked sad. I was not. "Then the gods sent have you to me for you shall help us to sneak in to the Miklagård."

"Constantinopolis ."

"What?"

"They call it Constantinopolis. It is only the Norse who name it Miklagård."

"You see, I am learning already."

Chapter 20

We were all able to relax a little once the threat of Rorik was past. The winds were not the best but they were steady and, as Josephus told me, my ship was the fastest he had ever sailed and used every puff of wind. We did not need to use the rowers. Apart from the daily maintenance of the ship the men occupied themselves making intricate carved bone items. Some would become handles for knives while others would be given as gifts for those at home. Some might even use them for trade when we reached our destination.

Of course Arturus and Aiden used all the spare time they had to learn Greek. I even managed to learn a word or two and we discovered much about the Empire. What Josephus could not tell us was who the Emperor would be. From what he told us it sounded like a ruthless culture of political and religious intrigue. Emperors did not necessarily rule for a long time.

On our fourth night after the fight we were on a beach a half a day from the Pillars of Hercules. Josephus told us that we were now in the land of the Arab and the Moor but the beach we found was secluded and far from any people. My men had hunted and we enjoyed hot food on the beach while we finished the last of Agnetha's beer.

We showed Josephus our treasures and he told us what they were. "This is the eagle that the legions of the ancient Romans carried into battle. To lose one would be a great disgrace. The golden torc, I believe would have been given to a general who had been successful; I would not know which general. I was a sailor and not a scholar. There are vast libraries in Constantinopolis if you sought the information then it would be there." He held up the metal discs. "These were called phalerae and were medals given to soldiers for brave deeds in battle. Whoever you found he was a hero. Why do you wish to learn about him?"

"We don't. We just thought that these might be valuable to your people."

He laughed, "There may be some who might pay for them just to make a link with the past. Rome's glories are often used by those who seek power."

"Is not the Emperor a great warrior?"

"Some lead our armies into battle and are good strategoi but others wouldn't know one end of a sword from the other and are only interested in money."

Haaken, Cnut and I could not understand that. Haaken scratched his head. "But coin is only useful for trading for the things you need."

"You will have your eyes opened in Constantinopolis."

Haaken pointed to his one good eye, "You mean keep my one eye open."

We all laughed but Josephus seemed worried that he had offended the warrior. "I am sorry for my offence, master."

"You have offended no one. Haaken lost the eye in a battle long ago. It gained him great glory and he would not wish its return if it meant he did not have the glory."

"Besides my one eye works perfectly well; why should I worry?"

Josephus shook his head. "You are Norsemen but you are not like the Norsemen of Rorik. They were cruel and wanted only treasure."

"But they were not led by Dragon Heart and the sword touched by the gods."

Josephus had not been told the story. Haaken had a new audience and he told the story of the creation of the sword. When he had finished the old Greek nodded approvingly. "That is a treasure which would fetch a high price in Constantinopolis. Your blade looks like the sword of St.Michael and he is the most revered saint in Byzantium."

That gave me much to think on. We were going to Byzantium for trade and to learn. I suddenly realised that Josephus was doubly valuable. He had been a sailor and a trader.

"We have gold coins, Josephus, what could we trade for in Constantinopolis which is more valuable?"

"Spices! They are light and expensive. That was where we made most of our profit." His face warmed as he remembered the old days. "The courts of the Franks could not get enough of the spices." He pointed to the satchel carried by Aiden. "That much spice could be sold for hundreds if not thousands of golden coins. They are brought from the distant corners of the Empire. In Constantinopolis there are many markets where you could buy them. There they are relatively cheap but if you take them to the west then they become fantastically valuable."

I had thought to bring back weapons but perhaps I could bring back goods of a greater value. Haaken and I spoke with Josephus about the armies of Byzantium while Arturus and Aiden wandered off to find shell fish.

They both came back and were highly excited, "We have found stones and they contain minerals."

Haaken became interested, "Gold? Silver?"

"I think not but they may be a new ore that we can mine. There are just three stones. I would like to take them to the ship and examine them."

I shrugged. Aiden had a quest for knowledge and hitherto it had not let us down. "Very well, show them to us."

We wandered along the beach and saw the three stones. They were huge. I laughed, "Aye you may have them if you can pick them up."

He walked over and tried to lift one. He managed to lift the stone the height of a thumb above the sand and then he was forced to drop it. I was about to leave it there when his crestfallen look made me relent. "Come Haaken, we will carry them aboard. It will give us ballast if naught else."

We picked it up, Haaken grumbling. "I hope we get something from this or I will take it out of the gladramenn's hide." We managed to manhandle the three stones aboard and Aiden was like a pleased puppy with his effusive thanks. We placed them at the stern where Josephus could use them as a seat.

The following day we set sail before dawn for we would have the famous Pillars of Hercules to navigate. This was the

portal between the Middle Sea and the Western Sea.
Josephus told us that it could be treacherous and we wanted
as much daylight as possible if we were to pass through it. I
knew how serious it was from the attention on the face of
Josephus. He was concentrating totally on the sail and steer
board. His normal smile was missing.

My normally stable drekar pitched and tossed alarmingly
as the two seas fought a battle and we were caught up in the
middle of it. It demanded the attention of my whole crew and
then, after a morning's hard sailing, we were through and the
waters changed to azure blue gentle waters of the Middle
Sea. It was as though we had entered a different world. The
air was warmer and the sea looked to have been painted by
the gods.

I shook my head as I clapped Josephus on the back.
"Well done, old man, but I cannot understand why you
forsook such a land for the cold Western Sea."

He smiled sadly, "Had I known my fate then I would
never have left but I followed my father and I followed the
trade. I have paid my dues." I saw him gazing east and knew
that he was thinking of his family and his dead crew.

"What problems do we face now?"

He pointed to the south. "There are Arabs to the south.
They have small fast little ships and they fill them with
warriors. Because there are few large waves here they have a
low freeboard and they are very quick. They do not use a
square sail but a triangular one they call a lateen. The do not
operate alone but in packs; they are like dogs."

"Why does the Emperor tolerate them?"

"They only became dangerous in the last thirty years. It is
the rise of the Muslims which has caused it. They conquered
much of the land called Hispania. It is only recently that
Charlemagne recaptured some of it. They are fanatics."

Haaken shook his head, "I have never heard of this
religion. Is it like that of the White Christ? Do they turn the
other cheek?"

"No it is the opposite. They either convert you or kill you.
They call it Jihad, Holy War."

"A strange religion."

"Aye, they keep their women covered and do not drink."

"What is the point of that? The Gods made women more beautiful than men so we may look on them. That is why they do not have beards!"

Cnut snorted, "I have seen some Hibernians and Pictish women who had better beards than Arturus here!"

We laughed. Haaken spat over the side, "And why would a man not drink? Imagine waking in the morning and knowing that was as good as you would feel all day!" He shook his head and looked to the skies, "I will still follow the Allfather!"

We sailed east across an empty ocean. The gentle breeze from the south west took us ever eastward, steadily. Aiden took the opportunity to examine the rocks we had brought aboard. He used his tiny hammer and chisel which he had forged himself to chip away at the reddish mineral which he had found. After an hour's work he shook his head in disgust. "Copper! And it is of a lower grade than Olaf's mountain!"

We all laughed and Haaken said, "Well they stay there until you have the strength to lift them. I carried them aboard, you can carry them off. It is a lesson for you gladramenn!"

Josephus began to look anxiously at the darkening sky. "We have a choice, Jarl Dragon Heart: we can either find a beach for the night or keep sailing."

I was curious about these Arabs but, equally, I wanted to reach Miklagård as soon as possible. "We will sail tonight and tomorrow night we will venture inshore for we will need provisions. Are there small settlements by the coast?"

"Aye master." He looked incredulous, "You would raid the Arabs?"

"Why not? They are men and they have both food and drink although not the drink we might crave. It is what we have always done."

"But they are fierce warriors."

I grinned, "And they call us wolves, for we feast on fierce warriors!"

Josephus slept for a few hours while Magnus and I sailed alone. Then I sat with Josephus for a couple of hours after he took the steer board. Aiden awoke and listened in to our conversation. "Do not underestimate these Arabs, master."

"I will not. How do they fight?"

"On land they are the masters of the horse but at sea they fight half naked and use their numbers to swarm over a ship. They always outnumber the crew and they slaughter them. They take no prisoners."

"And their weapons?"

"They use spears and a curved blade called a scimitar. If I tell you that there will be no Imperial ships within a hundred miles of the coast then you will know how feared they are."

"And how far away are we?"

"Probably thirty miles or so."

Aiden pulled out his map and lit a candle. He pointed with his dagger to a point on the map. "I estimate that we are here."

Josephus glanced at it and nodded, "I agree."

"And what is this island here?"

"That is Melita. It is part of Byzantium. We have to pass close by the island."

"Then tomorrow we will head to the shore and see these people from close up. And now I will sleep."

As I curled up beneath my wolf cloak I heard Josephus say to Aiden, "I have never met his like. He is fearless. He will poke the Arab with a stick! That is dangerous."

"He believes, as we all do, that he is protected by the spirits and the gods. We would follow him to the edge of the world if he asked for we know that we would return!"

We awoke to a glorious day but a stiffer breeze than we were used to. Magnus was steering while Josephus ate. He pointed to the north east. "Melita is a day away to the north. There will be ships patrolling."

"Then my plan to land in Africa is still a good one."

He nodded grudgingly. "It is but it is risky."

It was noon when Ketil shouted from the mast head. "Sails from the north west!"

I looked at Josephus. "Byzantine?"

"You will only know when we get closer. The Byzantine ships ride higher in the water and are bigger than the pirates."

"Then we will head further south. Cnut, have the oars run out. The men have been getting lazy lately. It is time to exercise."

The wind aided us as we turned slightly and, as soon as the oars began their stroke we fairly flew through the azure blue water."

"Are we losing the ships?"

"No, Jarl Dragon Heart. There are two of them and they are closing."

That worried Josephus. "Then they are Barbary pirates. We would have outrun an Imperial ship," He pointed south. "I would watch to the south. This is a typical pirate trap."

"Haaken, have the men not rowing get their bows and their weapons."

Cnut and the rowers were still taking it easy. There was little point in exhausting them if the pirates were catching us. Better to let them think they had us and we had nothing in reserve.

"Sails to the south east!"

Snorri and Erik Short Toe were at the prow and they both had good eyes. I shielded my eyes and I could just make out the dark shapes. "Josephus, head for them. Cnut, let us up the rate."

Josephus was incredulous. "You would go towards them? You should flee!"

"But where to? They are catching us already and the ships ahead can cut us off. Better to meet them separately than let them join forces."

I donned my helmet and my sword before picking up my bow. I hoped that surprise would win the day. I wanted them to believe we had not seen their plan. The two ships were now clearly visible. They were approaching rapidly despite the unfavourable wind. Their sails helped them to sail very close to the wind.

A gap had appeared between the two small boats ahead. I could now see that they were very low in the water. "Sail as close as you can to the southernmost ship. I want to be alongside them."

"But they will board!"

"They will try to. Cnut, when I give the word I want the oars in and every bow aimed at the ship to the north!"

Even Cnut was surprised. "The north?"

"Aye I have a surprise for the other. I want you and Haaken with me at the stern." I handed my shield to Aiden. "When the fight starts then I want you, Arturus and Magnus to protect Josephus. He is the treasure we must watch! Snorri, command the archers."

"Aye Jarl Dragon Heart."

The southern ship was now less than fifty paces away while the other was over a hundred paces to the north and was turning to reach us. "In oars. Snorri, I want every warrior on that ship killing."

I saw the southern boat as it headed towards our stern. "Haaken, Cnut, grab Aiden's precious stones." They grinned as they realised what I intended. We went to the side as the grappling hooks were hurled up. I saw a cloaked figure at the stern and the rest were gleaming half naked ebony bodies which glistened with sweat. There looked to be over twenty warriors assembled. They had colourful earrings and wicked swords. With teeth bared they prepared to board us. Behind me I heard the whoosh of arrows. "Now!" As one we lifted the stones and dropped them to the boat below. They were heavy rocks and we were higher than the lean little ship. One stone struck a warrior on the head which opened like a ripe red plum the others crashed to the deck and through to the blue sea below. The tiny boat immediately filled with water and capsized. I drew my sword and severed the grappling hooks. Our speed took us away from the men who were either drowned already or would soon be.

The three of us ran to the other side. The small boat was a floating coffin. Its speed had brought it so close that my archers could not miss. I saw that the two other ships were now less than four hundred paces from us. Flight was impossible.

"Josephus, put the steer board hard over. Take us towards them." As we turned, our bow cracked and creaked through and over the doomed pirate ship. The planking sprung and it began to fill with water taking the dead down to the deep.

Cnut turned to me as he donned his helmet, "We have no more rocks to throw."

"No, but we have arrows aplenty, and now we have three more archers. If we destroy one crew then the other may leave."

There was a gap between the two ships as they sought to flank us. "Head for the northern ship. Ulfheonar, let us show these pirates that they fight the finest warriors the world has ever seen! Ulfheonar!"

They all took up the chant and then began to howl like wolves. It was eerie. Remembering how we had crushed one ship I shouted, "Ram him, Josephus!"

My captain turned the steer board and I saw the panic on the crew of the nearest ship, now just fifty paces away. Haaken shouted, "Loose!" and we all released our arrows. We were so close we could aim and my arrow took the cloaked warrior at the steer board in the chest. He pitched overboard and the ship swung beneath our bows. Snorri's arrow took the helmsman next to him. The small ship had no one left to steer.

"Hard over, let us close with the other. Archers loose!"

We all headed for the stern. The second ship was closing. Our arrows were more ragged but I saw warriors falling overboard. The grappling hooks struck the steer board side and I saw black arms grasping our gunwale. Drawing my sword I launched myself at the huge warrior who climbed aboard. He had a dagger in his teeth and he wielded a double handed scimitar. He swung it at one of my men who threw himself backwards to avoid the blow. As the warrior raised his weapon to finish off Thorgill the Unlucky I stabbed at him. Ragnar's Spirit pierced his arm and he spun to face me. Despite the blood flowing from the wound he lunged at me. I realised I had to treat the scimitar as an axe. I ducked beneath it and as I felt it whoosh above my head I jabbed forward and felt my sword sink into layers of flesh. He roared his pain but this was a hard warrior to kill. He looked as though the wound, which would have killed a lesser man was merely a scratch. I met his next blow with my sword and I held mine with two hands too. His grin told me that he expected me to be forced back. I was not and sparks flew as the blades met.

I lifted my right foot and smashed it against his left knee. I heard a crack and he dropped to the ground. Before he could recover I swung my blade and decapitated him. He might have been a hard warrior to kill but no man can fight without his head.

I turned just in time for there were three men trying to get at Josephus. Aiden was defending him with my shield. I brought Ragnar's Spirit down on to the back of the nearest warrior's head. I split his head and laid his backbone open. He slumped to the ground. At the same moment Arturus stabbed upwards and his sword emerged from the warrior's back. As the last warrior glanced at his two dead companions Aided ripped his seax across his throat and he fell in a heap.

I whirled around but the deck was devoid of any warriors who still lived. I glanced over the side and saw that the pirate ship was slowly sinking. I raised my sword and my whole crew erupted into a cheer. We had won. Four pirate ships had been sunk and their crews slaughtered.

We had suffered no deaths but there were some badly wounded warriors. Aiden set to healing them. We stripped the bodies of everything we could and threw the pirates overboard. Already larger fish were gathering for a feast.

We had a fine haul of weapons and jewellery. Many of the warriors had rings of gold studded with rubies and emeralds. Most of them had earrings of gold and golden bracelets and all of them had sported at least three weapons.

We were not delicate when we removed the earrings and the rings; the pirates were dead. We had gathered much from the fifteen who had boarded us.

Josephus shook his head as I approached. "The gods favour you master. To take on four pirate ships and not lose a man is truly heroic. And I owe my life to you and your son. I have two lives to give you now."

"You have repaid me already. It was your knowledge which saved us this day." I looked south. "They will have come from the coast will they not?"

"Aye, they will live close by."

"Then we will visit and provision ourselves at their expense."

He shook his head, "Nothing will surprise me anymore." He put the steer board over and we headed south.

I was hungry; fighting always made me so. I looked forward to a hot meal cooked ashore.

Chapter 21

We sailed due south until we saw the land grow from a smudge to a brown strip dotted with strange trees which Josephus told us were called palms. We headed east along the coast. We stopped when we saw smoke rising in the distance. Lowering the sail we moved under oar power only. Ahead we saw a rocky promontory. We stopped and I went ashore with Snorri and Arturus.

"We will spy out the land. Have the men prepare for a raid. If we are not close enough then I will return and we will sail closer." Haaken and Cnut resented being left behind but I needed them to organise the men. These were not Ulfheonar. Someone would need to ensure that they were prepared.

The sand felt hot, even beneath our boots. I regretted both my mail and my wolf cloak. By the time we had climbed the dunes and discovered the coastal road I was bathed in sweat. I noticed that it was paved. It was Roman. Snorri and Arturus were much fitter than I was. I waved them forward. "I will come at my own pace."

I did not have far to go. A stand of the palm trees we had seen obscured the road ahead. Before I reached them Snorri waved me to the ground and I was forced to crawl the last twenty paces. There, beyond the trees no more than five hundred paces away, was the town. It was made of what looked like crumbling stone and I later discovered was mud. There was a primitive gate and a tower but I only saw four men on the walls. There was a harbour, of sorts and within were four fishing boats; no more.

I backed away from the palm trees. "Snorri, return to the ship. I want Haaken and twenty warriors. The rest should sail slowly around to the harbour. I want to be in position before they race ashore." He nodded and left.

Arturus pointed inland. "Will we attack from that direction?"

"Aye. We will move quickly for their attention will be on the ship." He nodded, "Remember son, these warriors are fanatical pirates. That is a strange combination. They will fight like berserkers. Take no chances."

He pouted a little. "I have killed men before!"

"As I have." There was steel in my voice. "When I fought that African on the ship I stabbed him twice and he felt it not. Had I not taken his head he would be fighting yet. You have never seen a berserker fight. I have and they terrify me."

He remained silent. He was not sulking. I had taught him too well for that but he was reflecting on my words. I realised how thirsty I was and I regretted not bringing a water skin. This was not Britannia. The sun was so hot that I had to be wary of touching the metal. I could have cooked an egg on my helmet it was so hot!

It seemed an age before Snorri and Haaken returned. I knew that it had not been that long but I do not wait well. Snorri handed me a water skin with a grin. "I thought you might need this!"

I drank deeply and handed it to Arturus. He had not complained but I knew that he too was thirsty. I noticed that both Snorri and Haaken had removed their wolf cloaks. It was not just me who was feeling the heat.

"We will head into the desert and approach the town from the south."

We trotted across the road and made for the little cover that there was. I assumed that the guards would be more likely to be watching the sea. If they saw us now it would be too late for those in the village. When we had travelled half a mile I turned and we ran east towards the town. The ground was rough scrubby desert and I wondered what creatures they had here in Africa. It would be cruel to die from a creature whose name we did not know. I wished I had asked Josephus about the animals. I could see now that the walls of the fort were not high. They were less than the height of two men.

We were finally spotted and the alarm was sounded. I saw men on the walls pointing at us. I hoped that this was the village which had sent the men after us. We would find it hard to fight a large number of warriors. We had spread out in a long line. I was in the centre with Arturus and Haaken next to me. Snorri was ahead of me and he stopped abruptly and threw up his shield. An arrow thudded into it. They were defending their town. As we turned to approach the walls I saw the mast of my ship on the other side. We had managed to surround it.

Suddenly the gate was thrown open and people began flooding out. "Let them go, it is what they have in their fort that we want!"

One warrior rushed at us as we raced towards the gate. He clumsily swung his axe and Snorri hacked his body in two with one mighty blow. Once inside I shouted to Arne and Hilvand. "Close the gate and guard it!"

I sheathed my sword. I did not think I would need it. By the time the gate had been closed the narrow streets had emptied and doors were slammed. "Snorri, open the northern gate; the one near to the sea. The rest of you collect any animals you see and take them to the ship."

It was a poor town but the jewels and the weapons on the dead pirate spoke of treasures here. "Arturus, let us find the finest building in this town."

People fled when they saw us. I now know that we were the first Vikings they had seen and we must have terrified them. My black armour and wolf skin must have made me appear like some creature from the place they called hell. We were certainly different.

Most of the buildings were poor mud huts but we spied one stone built building. We headed towards it. As we approached we saw three black skinned Africans climbing the village wall to escape into the desert. They were almost naked. I had seen Africans before but they had always been clothed. These seemed to gleam in the sun as the light reflected from their sweating bodies. They appeared to be the direct opposite of us!

The door was ajar and we entered. There were fine tables and chairs which surprised me. Sadly we could not take them. However there were fine curtains and wall hangings.

Erika would have loved them. "Take down the hangings. I will continue my search."

There was a cooking area and I found strange powders and foods. We would take those too and ask Josephus what they were. Sadly there were no weapons and, I suspected, all the gold and jewels had already been looted by the three men I had seen fleeing.

When I returned to the main room Arturus had a pile of the curtains and hangings. "There is much food in the back. Go to the ship with the hangings and return with others to help carry it all. I will continue to search."

I went to the upstairs. I had never been in a home with stairs. I began to wonder about both the building and the owner. The bed was enormous and had fine and soft bed linen. This was a find! I found another room with clothes within. They appeared to be robes which were made of thin material but they were finely made. I almost tripped over the box which was at the back of the clothes room. I would have missed it had I not caught it with my foot. I dragged it out into the light. It was locked. I had learned my lesson and I would leave its opening for Aiden.

"Jarl Dragon Heart!"

I heard my men calling for me. "I am upstairs."

Aiden, Cnut and Arturus joined me. "We have the town although it is a poor place. I cannot see much treasure here."

I spread my arms. "And what of this?"

Cnut nodded grudgingly, "It is not the treasure I would have hoped but it will sell."

"Or we could take it back with us. I would sleep on such linens."

"And the clothes?"

"I think that they may be the most valuable treasure of all. I long to wear something light and cool. I think that they would do."

Aiden suddenly spied the box. "This may be your treasure Cnut." He knelt down and took out his tools. His keys did not work but his picks and his dagger popped open the lid. Within it there was another ancient wooden box as well as coins and rings. I wondered if we had disturbed the thieves before they could take all of the riches.

"That is better."

Aiden took out the box. He traced some letters which were on the lid; they looked to be Greek, 'Cephas'. Aiden slowly opened the box for the lock had been broken. Inside were the bones of a hand.

Arturus snorted in disgust, "Who would want to keep bones?"

Aiden closed the lid and returned it to the chest. "The followers of the White Christ come to mind. These will be the bones of one of their holy men. This may be worth more than all of the rest."

"And why would an African pirate want them?"

"He was a pirate. Perhaps he robbed them and was waiting for a buyer. Remember the Count your father sold the holy book of the White Christ to? There are some buyers and collectors who will pay the best price for such relics."

I spied an empty chest. "Put the linens and clothes in there. Then we will gather the food from downstairs."

We lugged the treasures down to the ship which was tied to the tiny jetty. We passed those who had fought my men. There were huddles of bodies close to doorways. I could see that they had been searched. With their men dead I doubted that the people of this village would return.

My men had managed to gather one old cow and four sheep as well as a host of smaller, noisy birds. They were in good spirits. "Get some cages for the birds. They will feed us at sea. Slaughter these larger beasts and we will cook them. There is no danger here now. We will rest here tonight and enjoy the fruits of our victory."

Josephus came ashore and told us what some of the powders were. "These," he pointed to a cedar box containing many smaller boxes, "are the spices of which I spoke. This box would be worth a hundred golden talents in Frankia!"

I showed him the garments I had obtained. Josephus became excited when I showed him two of them. "These are made of silk." He frowned, "The man who had these was not a true Muslim for they are forbidden to wear silk but it is a wonderful material. It is the material worn by the Emperor himself. Take care of that Jarl Dragon Heart for it is more valuable than you can know."

Aiden produced the small chest containing the bones. "And this?"

He gasped when he read the name, "That is Simon Peter. They worship him as one of the followers of the White Christ. He is the one they call St.Peter." He smiled, "You now have your way into Constantinopolis! The Emperor will welcome anyone who brings such a relic into the city. They believe the relics of the saints protect them from the infidel and the barbarian."

I handed the box to Aiden. "Then guard this well." I began to strip. "And I shall bathe and then put on some cool cloth. I have had enough of sweating like a pig!"

I walked, naked, into the sea and enjoyed the refreshing salty water. As I swam around the ship I saw my men removing the deck planks to put the chests and the amphorae in the hull. Anything which might rot we kept on deck. I swam around the ship to inspect any damage from the fight. Ragnar Bollison had built well. There were a few grazes on the prow but naught else. Her hull was sound. Just to make sure I dived beneath her. The water was so clear that I was able to examine her completely. She was undamaged.

After I had dressed in the borrowed robes I felt much better. The material Josephus had called silk was both soft and cool. It felt like the touch of Erika's fingers on my body. "If I were you I would find garments such as this. I do not think it will get any cooler."

Some of my warriors ran back to the town to find other items of clothing. They had not seen them as treasure now they knew better. Josephus advised the cooks on the use of some of the herbs and the air was soon filled with the most aromatic smells. Cnut and Haaken sat counting out the coins we had collected.

"You were right, Jarl Dragon Heart, there was more treasure than we first thought. There were many of those we slew who had coins about them. Not many but when you add them and the ones which they had hidden in their home we collected together then it became a sizeable sum. We are all rich men now!"

When we had eaten I wandered with Haaken to look at this small settlement. The fishing boats were very small and looked like miniature versions of the pirates we had fought. We stood on the beach at the eastern end of the huts and looked towards the setting sun.

"These people have much in common with us Dragon Heart. They have not much in the way of land to grow things and they raid the ships which pass by."

"If this were my home I would have defended it far better. Those mud walls were not even as strong as our wooden walls."

We strolled back to our camp. "It is a strange land. I could not live here. It is too hot."

I lifted my arms to show the garment I was wearing. "I am cool!"

"Then I shall have to wear the same."

We had noticed that there were no tides here in the Middle Sea. Perhaps Ran did not rule the blue waters. Josephus told us that there was a Roman god called Neptune. It might have meant that he was more powerful here. The gods were complicated.

We left at dawn. We had stripped the dead animals clean and their bones were now bleaching on the deck. They would provide materials for the ship and for carving once they had dried out.

Josephus thought that we had passed Melita and we could head north east towards the jumble of Greek islands. Josephus was confident that, with our shallow draught, we could avoid large Imperial ships. Once we reached Miklagård then we could explain ourselves but any warships we met would assume we were a threat and deal with us accordingly. Thanks to the water and the food we did not need to stop again and we pushed on for as long as there was daylight. It took us a whole day and a night to reach the islands.

Once we reached them then we were totally in Josephus' hands. He knew the coastline well and he took us through channels which I did not think could accommodate us. He assured me that we would save time. Aiden was busy adding all this information to the maps he had drawn. I had promised Josephus his freedom and I would not be forsworn but we would miss his skills. The maps were our only chance of reaching home safely. He and Aiden now spoke only in Greek. Aiden told me that it was the best way to learn and improve his Greek. I had picked up some words as had Arturus. We could speak with any Byzantine we met but it would be a basic conversation. It would be down to Aiden to make the trades and conclude any deals.

Once we reached the islands we moved very cautiously; this was partly to avoid detection and to ensure we did not rip the hull out of our ship. It allowed us to marvel at the clarity of the water. We could see the fish swimming round the ship.

"This is not like the waters of home, Jarl Dragon Heart. They are dark and hidden waters. The blue waters here invite you in." Aiden and Arturus were quite taken with the seas.

"Well, Josephus, you will soon be home."

He looked sadly at me, "I never thought, when I was placed on the auction block, that my life would move in this direction. I anticipated a cold end to my life herding pigs and stealing their food. Even if my family have all gone to the Otherworld I would not change my last voyage. I have sailed a wondrous ship and seen warriors who change their world. Thank you."

"No, thank you, captain. We would never have reached these seas were it not for you. It has been a good arrangement. We have both benefitted." I stood back at him. "And now you do not look like a bag of bones held together by dirty rags!" He laughed with us. He laughed more these days.

Once we had cleared the islands Josephus set a northerly course. We were heading for the Sea of Marmara and Miklagård. We were within touching distance of our destination.

The last day of sailing saw us in congested waters. We could not avoid it for we had to pass through the Sea of Marmara as did every other ship sailing to the centre of the world. We were far longer and sleeker than any that we saw. We could see them all steering well clear of us but, miraculously, we did not see any Byzantine warships and we woke one morning to see the skyline of Miklagård in the distance. It seemed to glow and rise from the blue sea like a white and golden crown. We had finally reached the most powerful city in the world and the one in which we hoped we would make our fortune.

Chapter 22

Josephus was nervous as we rowed in towards the city which towered above walls so high I could not imagine how men had built them. They dwarfed every Roman fort we had seen. They were the height of at least six men and more. As we slowly approached I could see no end to the walls.

"We will head to the Langa Harbour. We will not be seen as much of a threat there." He looked at me with a pleading look on his face. "Do not expect to be made welcome."

I laughed, "A Viking is never welcome anywhere. We learn to grow a thick skin."

Josephus shouted the commands to the crew. It was as it should be. He knew the harbour and he knew the rituals. "Slow, Cnut. Barely keep her way. Magnus and Ketil, be ready to leap ashore and tie us up."

The harbour wall was fortified and I saw that there were weapons and soldiers guarding it. It had a narrow entrance and I saw war machines and warriors guarding it. We had got in but we would never leave without permission.

He was a fine seaman and he knew my ship now as well, if not better, than me. He shouted, "Oars in!" We gently spun with the slight breeze and nudged the stone harbour. Magnus and Ketil had us tied up faster than I had ever seen.

Six spearmen with mail shirts and conical helmets raced down the steps and spread out in a half circle. On the walls, some thirty paces from the harbour I saw bows aimed at us.

"Keep your hands from your weapons. This is an occasion for words and not action. Aiden and Josephus will speak for us. Magnus run out the gangplank."

I saw more armed men approach and behind them came, what I assumed was an official. He was dressed in white and had a wax tablet clutched in his hand.

"This is where you and Josephus speak, Aiden. I will be with you."

Of the three of us I was the only one armed and that was with a sword. I was wearing one of the garments we had found in the village and, on Josephus' advice I had tidied and washed my hair as well as trimming my unruly beard. I walked behind the other two and I saw the spears of all thirty soldiers remained pointed at us. The weapons on the wall would have slaughtered us all had they been released.

Josephus bowed and began to speak. I caught one word in three. The official spoke and Josephus spoke again and then pointed to Aiden who spoke. After he had finished there was a pause and then the official spoke to the soldiers who lowered their spears. They still stood before us but I took it to be a good sign. The official spoke one last time and then Josephus and Aiden turned to me. "We are to return on board while the clerk seeks advice. We are ordered not to move or we will be destroyed." I saw some powerful weapons on the walls and I believed him.

It was something of an anti climax. My men had expected either a battle or a welcome. They did not like what we had received. I shook my head as they complained, "Are you women? This is an adventure. You cannot predict how it will turn out. Haaken you will have tales to tell that people will pay a fortune to hear and if we are successful then none of us will ever need to raid again. Have a little patience and remember that the witch Eawynn prophesied that we would come here and, against the odds, we have made it!"

No-one came near us for a whole day. The guards changed; boats bobbed around our stern and bow looking at us but no one approached us. We were lucky to be still well provisioned with food and water but I knew that my men were restless.

Finally, at noon on the second day in port the official we had seen arrived with another two important looking men. Behind them was a slave. I thought, for a moment, that it was Olaf the Toothless for he looked to be his double. He looked to be just as old as Olaf had been. One of the richly dressed men was a warrior. He had a mail shirt which was topped with lamellar armour. On his head he wore a fine golden helmet and he had a sword hanging from his baldric. His face showed the scars of combat. The other man was more effete and seemed so slight I worried that he would blow away in the slight breeze from the Sea of Marmara.

They stood and waited at the gangplank. The armed guards had levelled weapons. Josephus led the three of us down once more. Our Greek began to speak. The effete man said something to him and he bowed and stepped back. The slave stepped forward.

He spoke our language although I did not understand some of the words he used. "This is the Hetaereiarch, Strategos John Cantacuzenus. He apologises to your translator but he wishes to be certain that his words are translated as he would wish."

I stepped forward. "I understand and what is your name?"

He seemed nonplussed that he had been noticed, "Er I am a slave of the household; Tostig Olafson. I was chosen because I am Norse." He looked at me with sadness in his old eyes. "I was a Viking."

The warrior said something and the old man replied. "The Hetaereiarch asks why a barbarian, I am sorry, it is his word not mine, dares to come to Constantinopolis? He wants to know if you wish to die."

I laughed, "Tell him that I have sailed from one end of the world to the other and I fear no man nor do I fear death."

He translated although he had a worried look on his face. Before the general could reply I continued, "I came here to trade because I have things of value aboard my ship and I had heard that Miklagård welcomed traders. Was I wrong? If so I can go further east and trade with the Muslims."

When he translated I saw the ghost of a smile play upon the lips of the warrior while the two officials looked shocked at my lack of respect. I was playing a game with them. I gambled that the warrior would want me to act as a warrior.

Tostig licked his lips nervously, "The Hetaereiarch asks what you can possibly have to trade that the Emperor might desire?"

I allowed silence to descend. I smiled and said, "A Roman Legionary eagle and the bones of St.Peter."

Had I slapped the three of them in the face I could not have had a better reaction. The warrior became serious and spoke with Tostig. "The Hetaereiarch asks if this is true or are you boasting to impress him."

I carefully drew Ragnar's Spirit. I saw arrows being notched behind them. I held it by the blade like a cross of the White Christ. "I will say this only once. When I say something it is the truth. I am never foresworn. I swear by the sword touched by the gods that I speak the truth but if the Hetaereiarch disputes it then he and I will cross swords here and blood will be spilled." A look of horror spread across the slave's face. "Translate it Tostig. Word for word! Josephus tell me if he does not and he shall die too."

I watched the three of them as he did so. The two courtiers stepped back while the eyes of the Hetaereiarch narrowed briefly before he began to laugh. Tostig seemed relieved when the Hetaereiarch spoke. "He says he believes you. He will go and speak with the Emperor and asks if there is anything you need."

"Food, and if you have it some beer."

The Hetaereiarch laughed again and Tostig smiled as he said. "He will send some." They all left leaving the archers on the walls and the twenty spearmen to watch us. Josephus said, as he shook his head, "You speak of poking the wolf, you have poked a pack of lions. I will grant you this, Jarl Dragon Heart, you have no fear."

When Aiden told the rest of the crew of my words they were all on my side.

"Jarl Dragon Heart, if they do not wish to trade then let us fight our way out. '*The Heart of the Dragon*' is a nimble vessel and we can row as fast as any!"

"Thank you for your confidence Haaken One Eye but we will see if I have read this Byzantine aright. I believe he will return and with better news."

Within a short space of time food and drink was sent to the dock although the slaves who brought them looked fearfully at us. I suppose we were terrifying. As my crew brought the much needed supplies on board I noticed how

232

wild they looked. None had groomed themselves since we had left Cyninges-tūn. Had I not trimmed by beard and hair then I would have looked as wild.

"Aiden, I will wash myself when I return try to make my beard and hair less wild."

I walked to the side of the ship away from the harbour and took off my clothes. I jumped into the water. It was not as clean as the sea close to the African village but it felt good. I heard a shout from Magnus and saw four of the spearmen standing at the dockside and waving their spears at me. They were shouting something.

Aiden said, "They are ordering you out of the water, Jarl Dragon Heart."

"Tell them I will return to the ship when I am clean."

Aiden spoke and I continued to scull around the stern. Their spears were lowered but I saw puzzled looks upon their faces. When I was happy I shouted, "Throw me a rope!"

I climbed up the side feeling much fresher and cleaner. After drying and dressing I sat while Aiden ran a horn comb through my beard and my hair. He hacked some of the wilder parts of both. "I am sorry, Jarl, that is the best that I can do."

He held up Ragnar's Spirit so that I could see myself in the polished blade. It looked a little neater. It would have to do. I had just strapped my sword on when Arturus said, "They have returned, father."

I went to the side and saw different warriors with the Hetaereiarch. These looked to be better armed and armoured warriors. Their armour gleamed. They had no spears but their swords were long ones like mine. The three of us descended to the dock.

Tostig spoke again, "You three are to come with us. The Emperor would like to see the treasure and then he will decide your fate."

I nodded and then pointed to Josephus. "This man is one of your people. He was a slave and we have returned him to his home. I would like him to be able to find his family."

Tostig frowned and then translated. Josephus looked at me with a grateful smile. The Hetaereiarch spoke to Josephus who answered. They had a long conversation during which the Hetaereiarch kept glancing at me. Finally he nodded and Tostig said, "The captain may go. You will come and bring the treasure."

I turned, "Arturus fetch the bones and the eagle."

"Yes father." Tostig turned and said something to the Hetaereiarch.

As Arturus went to retrieve the boxes I took a small purse I had with me. It contained some of the coins we had found in the African village. I gave it to Josephus. "I hope you find your family. Here is money for you. I know not what will happen to us but if you need more or you wish to return then, the Allfather willing, we will be here."

He took the bag. "I do not deserve this but I will take it for I know not what the Gods have waiting for me. Take care, Viking, and remember this is Byzantium. Beware the daggers in men's smiles."

"I will and I hope you find your family."

He turned. The Hetaereiarch said something and the guards parted allowing him to ascend towards the gate. Arturus ran up. He handed the two boxes to Aiden. The Hetaereiarch spoke and Tostig said, "The Hetaereiarch says just your son should accompany you." My eyes narrowed as I stared at Tostig. He had heard my son call me father. He quailed before my gaze. "I am sorry Jarl. Had I not told him and he had discovered my deception I would have paid the price."

I knew he could do nothing else. I had been a slave once. I nodded. "Aiden, tell Haaken he is in command but do not let him do anything foolish! Even if they hold us for some time then he should do nothing. If we die then he can make the decisions but keep a good watch."

"I will Jarl Dragon Heart." He lowered his voice. "I heard the Hetaereiarch speak. He wants your son as a hostage and a surety for your good behaviour."

Viking Wolf

I laughed, "You learn well my gladramenn! I will return. Come Arturus, we are the first to see this wondrous city! Tell the Hetaereiarch to lead on, Tostig Olafson."

He spoke quickly and the Hetaereiarch snapped an order. The guards formed two lines on either side of us. As we set off towards the gate in the wall my whole crew began to howl and then they began banging their swords on their shields and chanted, "Ulfheonar! Ulfheonar! Ulfheonar!"

Our guards stopped and levelled their weapons at me. I said, quietly to Tostig, "They are just saying farewell."

Tostig translated and we continued on our way. I saw the warrior shake his head and smile. The chanting continued until we passed through the gate. My senses were assaulted as I passed into the ancient city. Every building was stone and there were paved roads beneath my feet. The smells were ones I had never experienced before. There were sweet smells of food as well as the pungent smell of urine. I saw two men relieving themselves in a trough outside a house and that explained the smell. There were colours all around us from the clothes of the people to the walls of the houses and the statues that we saw.

I felt a hand in my back as I dawdled. The guards had cleared a path for us through the maelstrom of humanity but it seemed to me that the people were backing away as these two barbarians were paraded through their city. I was taken back to the time when I had been captured and led through Harold One Eye's village when everyone had stared at me. Then I had been afraid and hung my head. Now I stared back and examined the people we passed. There were women, and some men with deep blue eye shadow painted above their eyes and lips painted the same red as my war eyes. The hair of many was oiled and some of the women had it coiled above their heads like some black serpent. I touched the hilt of my sword for this felt like we had gone to the Otherworld; this was like nothing I had ever seen before. I had entered a new world.

The Hetaereiarch spoke to Tostig, as we ascended to a building which rose above all of the others. When he answered he looked at me. Tostig asked, "Did your men call you Ulfheonar?"

I nodded, "We are the men of the wolf."

Tostig said, "Shape shifters?"

In answer I smiled enigmatically and I saw his hand go to his amulet. Tostig did not follow the White Christ. He spoke to the Hetaereiarch who nodded after he had heard what I had to say.

I could see that we were heading for the Imperial palace. There were warriors such as the ones around us and they guarded the huge gate. They stared belligerently as we entered. Once inside the heat of the city disappeared. It was cool, peaceful and vast. This was even bigger than the walls we had seen running along the sea. I wondered if I ought to leave a trail of breadcrumbs to find our way out and then I realised that we would only leave if the Emperor permitted it.

We entered a door and ascended a magnificent staircase. We reached a landing and we were taken into a room which had a table and six chairs. On the walls were magnificent curtains which depicted warriors fighting monsters. Tostig said, "We are to wait here. The door will be guarded!"

The Greeks all left and there were just the three of us in the room. Arturus laid his burden on the table and began to look at the figures on the tapestry. I knew what was going through his mind. How could anything so beautiful be made by man?

I turned to Tostig. "What is your story?"

"I lived in the north in the land of the Norse. We were raided by another drekar while our men were out hunting. I was taken to Frankia where I learned to be a servant. As I had knowledge of ships my master took me with him when he went to trade with the men of Hispania. We were captured by the Moors and were taken to Africa." He shrugged, "I suppose I would have ended my life there had we not been attacked by a Byzantine ship. I was the only survivor. When I arrived here I was bought by one of the Emperor's courtiers as a curiosity." He pointed to his red hair. "They had never seen a red headed man before. They use me to speak with the men of the Rus that they capture."

"The Rus?"

"They are like us and speak a similar language. They live even further north than we did and travel down the rivers where they raid. I question them before..." He left the sentence deliberately unfinished.

"Before they are executed?" Arturus turned at those words. I smiled at him. "And that will be our fate?"

Tostig looked unhappy, "I do not know. So many warriors have never arrived at the same time before. We have only had one or two prisoners at the most and they were usually wounded. They all wished to die with their swords in their hands."

"And that was denied them." He nodded. "I see, interesting. And this Hetaereiarch, what of him? He seemed almost like us."

"He was a mercenary. He came from Italy and proved himself brave. The new Emperor likes him. He is not Greek."

A number of the comments interested me. "A new Emperor?"

"Aye the Emperor Nikephoros," he lowered his voice, "he took the throne from the Empress Irene. He rules now."

"Did the guards and oathsworn of the Empress not defend her to the death?"

Tostig smiled for the first time. "The guards here are oathsworn to their pay and not their mistress."

"You said the Hetaereiarch was not Greek, what did you mean by that?"

"The Greeks can be treacherous. The Hetaereiarch is a man of his word."

That echoed the words of Josephus. This was a nest of vipers. I resolved to trust only myself until I had learned more. Tostig might have been Norse once but now he was tainted by the attitude of the Greeks. He had shown fear at tiny things. This Italian Hetaereiarch might prove to be an ally but I would have to judge him when I saw more of him.

"The treasures," I pointed to the two boxes. "Are they valuable?" I opened the lids. We had just brought the bones and the eagle. The others I would hold on to.

He pointed to the bones. "They will be worth a king's ransom if they are truly the bones of St.Peter. Here St.Michael is the supreme saint but the bones would be worth its box filled with gold."

"And the eagle?"

He shrugged, "I do not think that the Emperor would find it valuable. He was the minister of finance but there are those who yearn for the glory of Rome. The strategos, Bardanes Tourkos, would pay a high price for it." He hesitated, "However he would be just as likely to take it by force he is an ambitious and cruel man."

"How do you know so much about the politics here?"

"The slaves in the palace live together and it is all we have to talk of. We know we will never leave and will end our days here. Knowledge of the politics of Constantinople and the palace can save our lives."

I went very close to him and lowered my voice. "Then think on this Tostig the Norse do not betray me. I am you worst nightmare. I am Ulfheonar and you know what that means."

He was shaking so much I thought that he would wet himself. There was not a trace of the Viking left in him. "I promise you I will not." He fell to his knees, "Buy me Jarl and take me home. If I stay here I will lose my life to the next Emperor."

I raised him to his feet. "A Viking does not kneel! If I can I will take you home. I just need to make sure that I can get home too."

Chapter 22

We were left alone for some time until a guard came and we were summoned into the presence of the Emperor. We had to wait at a beautifully carved and decorated door. As we went in our swords were taken from us. Arturus looked ready to react. "Not yet, my son. It is to be expected." I turned to the soldier who took them. I said to Tostig, "Tell him that if anything happens to them then I will rip his heart from his chest."

I stared at the soldier while Tostig translated. He must have realised that I meant what I said for he nodded and spoke to Tostig.

"He says he will guard them for he can see that they mean much to you." I watched as he placed them in a chest by the door.

The Emperor was seated on a magnificent throne atop a raised dais. All the trappings suggested that he was to be revered if not actually worshipped. The Hetaereiarch was on one side of the Emperor, a drawn sword in his hand, and a large warrior dressed completely in mail held a mace on the other side of the Emperor. Ten other guards, with weapons drawn, lined the small chamber.

He waved his hand for us to approach. When we were at the foot of the dais Tostig prostrated himself upon the floor. I looked at Arturus and we both gave a half bow. I saw the glimmer of a smile on the face of the Italian Hetaereiarch. The Emperor and the other soldier looked nonplussed. The Emperor said some sharp words. Tostig rose to his feet.

"The Emperor wishes to know why you do not kneel."

"I am a Viking and I kneel to no man. I have no king to whom I owe fealty and I rule my own land."

My response took them all by surprise.

"And where is your land?"

"In the north of the island the Romans called Britannia."

There was a conversation between the three of them and Tostig turned to me his eyes pleading for me to behave. "Just translate everything I say and you shall come with us."

At my words they turned and the Emperor spoke again. "You and your son will be held hostage here as a surety to the good behaviour of your crew. If they cause trouble then you will both die."

I laughed. The Emperor looked as though I had slapped him in the face. "I have ordered them to behave and so long as we live then your city will be safe. If anything happens to us then your city will be bathed in blood."

When the words were translated the Hetaereiarch asked, mildly, "Are you threatening the Emperor?"

"Of course not. I am telling him of the consequences which would result from my death. We came here to trade and if you do not wish to trade then let us go and we will travel east."

"You leave if I say you can leave." If the Emperor thought to intimidate me he was wrong. I smiled at him and he appeared to be confused. The Hetaereiarch leaned in and whispered in his ear. "Where are these so called treasures you wish to trade?"

I nodded to Arturus who took them and laid them on the floor by the Emperor's feet. The Hetaereiarch took the box with the bones and examined it. When he opened it the Emperor looked amazed.

"Where did you get this? Britannia?"

"No, we were attacked by African pirates. After we killed them we raided their town and found this."

The Hetaereiarch looked amazed then. "You destroyed pirates and their town? And you only had one dragon ship?"

"It was all that I needed."

The Emperor closed the box. "If I chose to keep this treasure without paying you there is little you could do about it."

Again I smiled to disconcert him, "You could but I could lay a curse on you and after you had killed me my spirit could come back as a wolf and destroy all of you."

He paled, "We do not believe in pagan curses and spirits."

"Really? I thought your whole faith was based on the White Christ dying and coming back as a spirit."

This time the Hetaereiarch had to cover his mouth to hide his grin. The Emperor nodded, "So you are not an ignorant savage as I was led to believe. You can play the political game I see. I will pay you for the bones although I do not guarantee that you will either live or leave here."

I nodded, "It is pleasant here and I do not wish to leave just yet. I am keen to learn about your culture."

"And this other box?"

I spread my arms, "We found this in Britannia. We thought it was gold but we see it is base metal. It means nothing to us but we were told that there were some who revered the symbol."

The Emperor opened it and when the mailed warrior saw it his eyes lit up. The Emperor did not seem impressed. "It has no value to me." He looked up as the mailed warrior took it out, "However, it seems that Strategos Bardanes Tourkos is taken with it. You may have a buyer."

"We sell to any who have the coin, Emperor."

I could see, as he translated the latest words that Tostig was feeling the pressure. He was translating exactly what I said. He did not like it for it was erring on insolence but he did it.

Strategos Bardanes Tourkos spoke for the first time and as he spoke I heard the authority in his voice. This man was used to command. The Emperor's voice had not commanded; it had negotiated.

"I would buy this from you. What other items do you have?"

"We found a torc and something we were told was a collection of phalerae."

"And where are they?"

"On my ship."

"Then send for them and I will buy them."

"We will fetch them when our visit is finished."

"I could have you killed out of hand."

"Strategos you could try but if you succeed you would never have the other treasures. Surely the few coins they would cost would be worth it. It would be better than risking death."

As my words were translated he launched himself at me. I had angered his honour. I pushed Tostig out of the way. The strategos swung his mace at my head. I ducked and put my right leg out while I used both my arms to throw him to the floor. I had his dagger out and held at his throat before anyone else could move.

I only had a little Greek but I had enough for this. "Move and you die."

I felt a hand on my shoulder and looked up at the Hetaereiarch. He shook his head and raised me up. He spoke to a shaking Tostig.

"The strategos was a little hasty Viking Wolf. Pull in your claws."

The strategos was helped to his feet. The box with the eagle had fallen when he had attacked me and now Arturus clutched it to his chest; his eyes glaring defiance at the strategos. The Emperor spoke to him. He nodded and then spoke to Tostig.

Tostig translated although I could hear the fear in his voice. "I will pay for the eagle." I looked at him. "I swear." I nodded to Arturus who gave the box to him. He clutched it, bowed to the throne and backed out of the room.

For some reason both the Italian and the Emperor appeared to find it amusing. The Hetaereiarch spoke through Tostig. "You have courage, Viking, but you have made an enemy of the general. The Emperor will pay your price but you will be our guests here for a few more days."

I nodded, "Then I would suggest that you send Tostig here to tell my crew of the arrangement. It will make life simpler for your sentries on the wall and I would advise that you feed them. If they are hungry they may go looking for food themselves. You do not want a boat load of Vikings loose in your city!"

He nodded and smiled, "A full wolf is less likely to go hunting. We will do so."

We were led away down the corridor and up another flight of stairs. We were taken to a small room with two tiny and narrow windows. There was a table and two chairs and on the floor were three straw mattresses. Tostig seemed relieved to be away from the throne room. "These are our quarters. I have been told to tell your crew what has happened."

"Tell them everything that you saw and we did. Haaken is my leader, tell him and the others that we are safe and you will let them know if I need help."

He looked surprised, "You trust me?"

"You have little choice now if I made an enemy of Bardanes Tourkos then so did you. The weird sisters have bound us together in their web. *Wyrd*!"

He smiled, "I have lived here so long that I had forgotten about the sisters. You are right. There are guards outside."

"How many?"

"Two."

"Then fear not for we can leave whenever we like if there are but two of them. However, we will stay for the spirits have not yet told me to leave."

As a confused Tostig left I lay down on the mattress. It was true I had not heard the voices for some time. That did not worry me. I only heard the voices when I was in danger. The last time had been before the pirates had attacked us. I was about to close my eyes and enter the dream world when Arturus said, "Are we in danger here?"

I opened my eyes and looked at him. I sometimes forgot, because he had killed men, just how young he still was. "No, my son, I know where the swords are and there are two guards only. We are Ulfheonar and we could kill the guards, take our swords and disappear. The sentries on the walls are to keep men out not stop others escaping. We will see what the Norns have planned for us. If this is a cage then it is a gilded one." I pointed to the table where there was wine, bread, cheese and some small green and black fruits which looked like tiny plums. "I will sleep and then we will eat."

I do not know if it was the strange room or perhaps I had put the thought into my head but the voices came. At one time they had always been old Ragnar's voice I had heard but it had been some time since I had heard him. Now it was just my mother and my wife whose sweet voices filled the dark places of my dreams. The voices were soothing as they sang to me. It was the lullaby my mother had sung me and Erika had used for Arturus and Kara. There were flashing images which randomly popped up behind their words.

'Beware the knife in the night.' A glowing candle appeared and then disappeared. 'Keep our son close.' A serpent slithered out of the darkness and then vanished. 'Be the wolf'. Suddenly a wolf leapt at me and I jumped.

Then I woke. Arturus stared at me. "What is amiss?"

"I dreamed."

"The spirits?"

"Aye your mother and grandmother." I rose. I am famished. What is the wine like?"

He shrugged, "It is wine." I laughed he was not used to such drinks. He smiled, "But the cheese and the bread are good."

I held up one of the small green fruits. "And what of these?"

"I did not know what they were."

I did not know either but I put one between my teeth and bit. It was slightly bitter and there was a stone within. I spat it out and drank some of the wine. The fruit I had tasted suddenly became more palatable and I picked up another one and cautiously bit into it. The wine and the fruit went well together. I discovered that the bread, the cheese and the fruits combined to improve the taste of each part. The cheese was quite soft and salty. I thought, from the taste, that it might be sheep's cheese. The Byzantines had not just given us a random selection of food. We were guests and not prisoners. Or at least we were prisoners who were being treated well.

I was not certain if Tostig would have eaten and we saved some for him. He arrived, by the light in the room, during late afternoon. We had been in the palace all day. Tostig reported to me first. "Your men were all set to come and rescue you," he shook his head. "Are they all berserkers? The young one called Aiden counselled them and persuaded them to heed your words. They have been sent more food and they were busy preparing the ship in case you need to leave quickly."

"You have done well, now eat. We are safe for a while. But we need weapons."

He stopped eating. "It would mean my life if I were to get you weapons."

"All we need are a couple of daggers. Surely you could lay your hands on those?"

"Possibly but it might be dangerous."

"Just try."

Arturus took out some bone dice he had made and we amused ourselves with a game to while away the hours. This room had no fine tapestries and the walls were plain plaster. I suspected it had been a store room of some description.

"What do we do when we need to make water?"

Tostig pointed to a hole close to the wall. "You use that and it gets goes down gullies and pipes and ends up in the sea." I went over and saw that there was a gap below the hole and the marks on the stone pipe beneath showed its use. That explained the room; it was a store room and a place for the guards to relieve themselves. Although not built as a cell the hole was too small for anything larger than a cat.

The windows were quite high but we saw the light flickering from the setting sun. The door had no lock but Tostig had told us that the two guards still remained. The door opened and two slaves brought in three plates of food and fresh water and wine. Behind them came the Hetaereiarch. The empty plates were whisked away and the door closed.

The Hetaereiarch spoke with Tostig who translated. "I hope you do not mind if I stay with you for a while. I am keen to learn more about you."

It was at that point that I wished I had paid more attention to Josephus as Aiden had. I would have liked to speak to this warrior in his own language rather than having a translator take my words and make them his own.

"Make yourself welcome. I will eat when these two have finished."

That proved more difficult than I had thought for Tostig could not translate and eat. The Hetaereiarch realised this before me and he indicated that I should eat. I did so. The lamb was succulent but it also had some of the spices we had encountered in Africa. It gave it a different taste. Aware that he had a job to do Tostig finished his first and, after wiping his mouth stood ready to translate. I had had enough food but I continued to nibble on the meat while we talked.

"You are the first Viking who has survived in the palace this long. That is quite a feat."

I smiled, "But it is barely a day!"

"I know and that is why it is such a feat. I met some of your warriors while serving in Italy. You surprised me for you had a sword. They had axes."

"Then they were Danes and not the Norse. Our land is even more inhospitable than theirs. We have snow and ice for almost half a year."

"And it makes hard and hardy warriors. Your ship is a hunter is she not?"

"Aye, I bet she would have the legs of any of your ships no matter how big."

"And you have done well to sail this far."

"The Allfather was with us."

He shook his head, "You see it comes down to being a pagan again. The Emperor cannot understand it."

"Will he pay what we ask and then let us trade? It is all we wish."

"I believe you. I went to your ship and spoke with the one called Aiden. He has our language and is a bright youth. He convinced me that you are a man of your word but the Emperor fears that you are here with an ulterior motive. He has only recently gained the throne and there are those, some closer than is comfortable, who would like to wrest it from him. He will need a longer time to be convinced."

I nibbled again on the sweet meat and washed it down with the earthy red wine. A sly smile appeared on his face, "Do not try to escape. I know that you could but I would be forced to catch you and, probably, kill you."

"Many have tried."

"That I can believe." He stood, "Anyway the reason I came was to tell you that tomorrow the Emperor wishes you to speak with his council of ministers and tell them of the world beyond the Pillars of Hercules. Our merchants tell us of their ports but you can tell us of the world beyond." He turned to go and then he put down a leather purse. "Bardanes Tourkos pays his debts." I was surprised and it showed on my face. "I would be worried rather than excited, my Viking wolf, it means he thinks he will be getting it back soon. My quarters are on this corridor and I have good men at your door but sleep lightly."

He left. *Wyrd*. It was what my spirits had said, '*Beware the knife in the night*'. I would heed such sage advice. The slaves did not return for the dishes. Before we went to bed I placed them all behind the door. If anyone tried to open the door in the night then we would hear the metal dishes being scraped along the floor.

"I will sleep just behind the door. I am a light sleeper."

In the event we had an incident free night and when the guard tried to open the door in the morning he was surprised to encounter resistance. I quickly stood. He came in with his sword drawn but when he saw the dishes he smiled and nodded.

The slaves brought us not only food but bowls to wash ourselves and soft cloths to dry us. After they had finished two nervous looking men came in with some bottles and combs. They spoke with Tostig who ventured, nervously,

"They are barbers Jarl. They are here to try to tame your hair and your beards and to make you smell better."

"Do not worry, Tostig, we understand. Tell them we will not eat them… yet!"

He laughed as he told them and their look of relief almost made me burst out laughing too. They were good at their job and they held a polished piece of metal so that we could see the improvement. Even in the distorted reflection I could see that it was neater. Then they used perfumed oils on our faces and hands to make us smell sweeter. We must have offended them the day before.

We were taken down to the ground floor and a large room which had an oval table and chairs. There were ten Greeks, the Hetaereiarch and a scribe seated around it. Our guards followed us in. We were stood before the table. The guard at the door opened it and Emperor Nikephoros entered. He sat at the middle of the table. We were bombarded with questions. They wished to know how far west we had travelled and how far north. They appeared to have a good picture of the lands to the east of Britannia. The Emperor was most interested in Charlemagne and his hold in Frankia. I told him what I knew which was not a great deal.

Finally we were questioned about the Norse, the Danes and the Rus. I told them that I could only speak knowledgeably about the Norse. They appeared happy with that. They were less happy when I told them how we raided their churches and sold their priests. They could not understand our pagan culture. After a morning of intense questioning the Emperor clapped his hands and my sword was brought in. Poor Tostig was grateful for the relief and drank deeply from the water jug.

"This is a fine weapon. As good as one of ours; where did you steal it?"

"I did not steal it. I bought the blank from Frankia and our smith made it." I saw the doubt on their faces as Tostig translated, "But this one is particularly special for it was touched by the gods."

For some reason, that seemed to upset them. The Hetaereiarch held up his hand and asked us, "Explain what you mean."

I told them of the tower and the thunderstorm and the lightning which had struck the sword. The Hetaereiarch smiled as he spoke to them. Tostig said, quietly, "He has just explained that lightning striking a sword would make it stronger and that, as a primitive people we would see that as supernatural."

I was not certain if I like being called primitive.

The Hetaereiarch led us back to our room. "Where is Bardanes Tourkos?"

"He left the palace last night. Perhaps you upset him."

I shrugged. "I find I do that with many people like him."

"You did well there Norseman. I think the Emperor is warming to you."

"Then we can return to our ship?"

He shook his head as Tostig translated my words, "It will take some time longer I am afraid."

When we were alone in our room I hoped that my men would be patient. They would not like to be ship bound.

Chapter 23

The voices of the spirits were rarely wrong. We had had no problems the night before but that did not mean that I could be complacent. "Did you get any weapons, Tostig?"

"I am sorry Jarl. I tried but I was worried. They searched me when I left and when I returned."

"No matter. I shall sleep behind the door again."

I could not sleep. Perhaps it was the food. We had eaten a meal with tiny red flakes in it. Although they tasted good they were hot when you swallowed them. My insides seemed to be churned up. I went over to the hole in the wall to try to rid myself of the slight pain. I seemed to squat forever but it saved my life. I saw a sliver of light as the door was opened. The guards had avoided doing so before and I wondered why they were doing it now.

Then I realised it was not the guards. It was our executioners. I had no weapons save my hands. They would have to do. Chopping trees and firewood as a boy, rowing when I was a youth and training for war when I was a man had made my hands like knotted oaks. They would have to do.

The first of the killers slipped through the door. I saw immediately that he was not one of the guards. He had no mail on and he had a blade which was curved even more than a scimitar and he was holding it in two hands. I dared not make a sound; I could not wake the other two. I would have to deal with him myself. He was good. He paused once in the room to allow his eyes to grow used to the dark. By that time I had moved to the wall in which the door had opened. I was behind him. He moved forward to the sleeping forms of Tostig and Arturus. As he did so the second man entered with the same weapon. He paused once inside and I took my chance. I hit him on the side of the head with my fist. I put all my weight behind it and I heard his cheekbone crack. Before he could raise his weapon I grabbed it with my right hand and stepped behind him so that my left hand was around his neck.

His companion turned and sought me out. The man I was holding was using both hands to wrench free his hand and his weapon. So long as I was behind him I was safe. I pulled back hard with my left arm. I heard him begin to choke. The first killer was even closer now and I put my foot against the back wall and pushed us both forward. His curved weapon sank in to the side of the first killer and its design helped it to rip into the man's body. I pulled back hard on the man's neck and heard the snap as it broke.

Arturus was awake and on his feet. "Tostig, make sure these killers are both dead."

I opened the door and saw our two guards dead in ever widening pools of blood. "Grab a sword!" I hissed to my son. "Tostig, stay in the room!" We were warriors; the slave would only get in the way. I picked up a sword and I listened.

I remembered that the Hetaereiarch had said he had a room on this corridor. We headed down. I saw another two bodies and then heard the sound of fighting. We burst into the room which had the bodies outside. There were three warriors attacking the Hetaereiarch with the two handed curved weapons. I launched myself at the nearest one and felt the sword grate off his backbone as it slid into his heart. Arturus lifted his and brought it down two handed just as one of the killers was turning. It shattered his head in two. The Hetaereiarch finished his opponent off. I saw that his left arm had been badly cut. I tore one of the sheets off the bed and ripped a piece with which to bind it. It was a crude job and Aiden would have been unhappy with it but it stopped the bleeding.

He waved us to follow him. I saw his look of anger when he saw the dead guards and he led us down stairs. As we passed the first room we had been taken to I saw the chest. Opening it I took out our swords and handed Arturus his. Ragnar's Spirit almost sang as I gripped it.

We could hear the sound of combat now and the Hetaereiarch urged us on by waving at us. We moved down the corridor towards the Emperor's quarters. There were more of the killers now and they were forcing back the ever diminishing number of guards. I could see that they had defended the Emperor with their lives. I saw him cowering behind them. I remembered that he was no warrior. If he had been he would have wielded a sword and sold his life dearly.

Sometimes the power of battle is upon you. I had been frustrated for days and now I had the chance to fight. "Ragnar's Spirit!"

I leapt forward and passed the surprised Hetaereiarch. The killers at the rear turned to face me. They had the same double handed long curved weapon as the others had. I swung my blade with all my force as I closed with them. As my sword struck the first weapon it shattered it and knocked the second one to the side. I rammed my shoulder into the first warrior and, when he fell to the floor I stamped hard on his neck. I did not wait to see if he was dead. Before the second man could raise his weapon again I swung it horizontally and took his head off.

I felt Arturus next to me. I knew that no one would approach from my right. I changed to a one handed grip and I jumped towards the next warrior. He pulled his arms back to swing his vicious blade at me I stepped in and held his two arms with my left. I plunged my sword through his middle as a blade swung at my head. Arturus' sword sliced through the two arms and the warrior fell at his feet bleeding to death.

A dead sentry was at my feet and I knelt down to pick up his dagger. I had no shield but I now had something better than my fists to defend myself. Blood lust was upon me and I had the measure of these weapons now. I could see that the Emperor's guards were now fewer. I swung my sword at a warrior who was swinging his own blade at me while I sank the dagger into the side of a warrior fighting a guard. I pulled out the dagger and ripped it across the throat of the man whose weapon was blocked by Ragnar's Spirit. I sensed, rather than saw the axe which was swung at my left side. I spun around on my left leg and watched it slide dangerously close to my right leg. I brought Ragnar's Spirit around horizontally; it cracked through his ribs and sliced into his vital organs. The axe fell to the floor. I saw that the Hetaereiarch was wounded. I could not help him and the Emperor.

I turned and saw Arturus struggling to fight two killers. I hurled the dagger. It spun through the air and buried itself in the eye of one of them. I was on him one stride later and I sliced through his throat as Arturus finished off the other. There was just the captain of the guard defending the Emperor now and he was badly wounded. The three men who were advancing could see that they would soon kill the Emperor.

Arturus and I leapt at them. One turned as he heard us coming at him. His weapon came directly for my head. I barely managed to bring Ragnar's Spirit to block the blow. I punched him in the right side with my left fist and head butted him at the same time. We fell to the ground as he grabbed my tunic. As I lay on top of him I brought up my knee between his legs while holding my sword horizontally. His head jerked up and he sliced his own throat on my sword.

I saw the last killer raise his weapon to finish off the Captain of the guard. I swung my sword with all my strength and chopped his left leg in two. The wounded Captain of the Guard took his chance and sank his sword into his chest.

I leapt to my feet. "Arturus!"

He stood, bloodied but unwounded. "I am safe. "

"Protect the Emperor."

I ran back to the Hetaereiarch. He had a wicked looking cut to his leg. I tore one of the tunics from a dead warrior and, after I had bound it, I helped him to his feet. I led him to the Captain of the Guard. Arturus was binding his wounds. The Emperor said something but I did not catch any of it. The Hetaereiarch answered. It seemed the Emperor had been deserted. He had two Vikings and two wounded soldiers left to protect him.

Silence was no longer necessary and I yelled, "Tostig! Get down here now!" As a warrior he might be useless but he could watch the wounded and translate.

I took the opportunity to pick up another sword. The Hetaereiarch weakly smiled at me and said something. I guessed it was 'thanks'. I inclined my head; we were not out of the woods yet. Tostig raced down the corridor with a sword in his hand. I almost laughed for he looked like he could barely lift it. "Ask the Hetaereiarch what we should do."

After he had translated I saw the relief on the face of the Hetaereiarch and his Emperor. His only two defenders could now talk to him.

"These men here are the men of Bardanes Tourkos. They favour the rhompeia. It explains why he is not here in the city. We need to get to my men. They are at the Contascalion Harbour."

"Is it far?"

"Five hundred paces from the main gate of the palace."

"That might as well be five hundred miles. Arturus, you guard the Emperor. Tostig help the Captain. Ask the Hetaereiarch if he can walk."

In answer he picked up a spear and began to use it as a crutch. He pointed down the stairs and I led. This might be the longest five hundred paces I would ever walk.

The evidence for the attempted insurrection was everywhere. Guards and their attackers lay in untidy bloody huddles. My worry was that they would have secured the gate first to prevent reinforcements. I had two of us who would be able to fight and we had neither armour nor helmet. I assumed that our opponents would.

When we had descended the stairs I made everyone wait. I picked up a sword from a dead guard and handed it to the Emperor. He might not be able to use it but it would make the enemy think we had more warriors than we actually had. I slipped silently out of the door and looked towards the main gate. As I had feared there were six warriors there. There were the sounds of battle in the far reaches of the

Grand Palace. I assumed that would be the barracks being assaulted. We had to escape now or reinforcements would soon arrive. The odds were bad but they would get worse.

I returned to the others and spoke to Tostig. "Tell them that my son and I will have to deal with the guards at the gate. You will need to watch the gate and when you see your chance you and the Emperor must help the other two to escape."

Before he translated he said, "I am a slave. I cannot tell the Emperor what to do."

"Tonight you are a man and a warrior and you will tell the Emperor. Remember, Tostig, Viking blood courses through your veins."

He nodded and translated. The Emperor seemed to accept it but the Hetaereiarch said something. "The Hetaereiarch says we must leave him and the captain and get the Emperor to safety."

I grinned and said, "So long as I am in charge we will do it my way!" I turned to my son. "Come, Arturus, I know it is asking much of you but you are Ulfheonar and you are my son. If this is our time to die it will be a glorious death. Even if you are struck continue fighting and we will prevail."

"I will not let you down, Jarl." We both picked up a second weapon from those lying with the dead men. I had a spear in my left hand. It was better than the sword I had had and easier to use in my left hand.

We moved quickly across the open space. Two of the guards had the rhompeia while the other four had swords. None had shields. We had trained to run without making a noise and we were just ten paces from them when they saw our shadows emerging from the dark. The barbers' attempts to tidy our appearance had not worked and I suspect we must have terrified them. They froze for just a heartbeat. It was enough.

I swept my spear to the left to keep the two men there at bay while I slashed down with Ragnar's Spirit. The edge was still sharp enough to rip across the neck and throat of the warrior with the rhompeia. I felt a sharp pain in my side as a soldier from my left jabbed his spear at me. I jabbed forward with my own spear and felt it sink into the other warrior and, dropping the spear I grabbed the spear which had just scored a wound on my side. He did not expect it and he kept hold of the weapon. I brought my sword around and struck him on the side of the head just below his helmet. I cracked into his skull and he dropped like a stone.

Arturus had felled one and the other two were trying to surround him. I saw his second sword fall as I struggled to reach him. The gods gave my legs a power I did not know they possessed and I stabbed one of my son's assailants through the back while he despatched the other.

"Go and fetch the others while I check the gate."

As he padded off I opened the huge gate. Outside there was darkness and silence. I fully opened the gate as Arturus and Tostig helped the two wounded warriors across the open space. The Emperor reached me first and said something. I had no idea what. I waved him through; he needed to move quickly.

Suddenly there was a shout from the palace walls and an arrow thudded into the gate. "Hurry!"

The Emperor left. Arturus followed with the Captain. It was when Tostig reached me with the Hetaereiarch that arrows began to rain down. I saw a shield and picked it up. As I did so one of the men I had hit before rose to his feet and stabbed at me with his spear. Tostig tried to come to my aid. He weakly waved his sword at the guard. I watched, in horror, as the spear came through him. I took the head from his killer. Waving the Hetaereiarch to follow the others I knelt.

Tostig was smiling, "I will not see my home after all, Jarl Dragon Heart, but I died with a sword in my hand and I will go to Valhalla. Thank you for giving me the chance to be a warrior and to gain some honour. At the end I remembered my Norse blood. May the Allfather..." He died. I put both his hands around the hilt.

"I will see you, my friend, in the Otherworld." As I stood two keener warriors had raced across from the palace to reach me. I took one blow on the shield which I had just picked up. I swept my long sword in an arc and felt it bite on flesh. I punched with my shield and as the surprised warrior reeled back I skewered him with my sword. The spear from the other warrior bit into my leg. I sliced down and his right arm fell to the floor. He dropped to his knees and tried to halt the spurting blood with his left arm. I turned and ran from the gate.

Ahead of me, down the slope, I saw the others as they struggled along. I found the Hetaereiarch sitting on a water trough. He tried to wave me away. I dropped the shield and sheathed my sword. I hoisted him across my shoulders and followed the others. Had there not been a slight slope I would not have managed but I saw hope when a gate opened and Arturus, the Emperor and the Captain of the Guard were admitted. I could hear footsteps behind me but I could go no faster. I waited for the blade in my back but then the Hetaereiarch's men erupted from the barracks and hurtled towards us. Two of them took him from me. The wounds I had suffered had taken their toll and I slumped to my knees. I could go no further.

I had travelled to Miklagård and seen wonders. Was I doomed to die here? Arturus grabbed me and helped me to struggle the last hundred paces to the safety of the barracks. We had survived. The weird sisters were still weaving their webs.

Once safely inside the building we were totally isolated. We had no means of communicating with the others. Their healers came to look at the Hetaereiarch and the Captain of the Guard. The Hetaereiarch said something in a sharp voice and another healer came to dress my wounds. They removed all my clothes and I saw that the two wounds had been deeper than I had thought. The tunic was sodden with blood. The healers gave me something to drink. It warmed me and eased the pain. I began to feel sleepy and the next thing I knew I was in the dream world. I heard nothing but I saw my mother and Erika as they drifted in and out of view. I did not need their words; to see them was a comfort. I wondered if this was the start of the journey to the Otherworld.

When I awoke Aiden and Arturus stood over me with one of the Greek healers. I could see the relief on Arturus' face. "You had us worried. They were deep cuts. The healers had to use many stitches."

"How are Haaken and the others?"

"Itching to be at your side and defend you against your enemies." Aiden looked up. "I have spoken with the Emperor. He is pleased with you. We are no longer prisoners." He leaned and said, "I think that he will ask you and our men to become his personal guards. The two of you impressed him last night. He said he had never seen two such ferocious fighters before."

I smiled, "You were able to talk with him then?"

"Josephus was a good teacher."

I tried to get to my feet. Arturus held his hands to restrain me. "Where do you think you are going?"

"I am Jarl and I have to see to our men." As I stood I felt a little dizzy and I put my hand on my son's shoulder. I saw that we were in a small room with a tiny window. "Where is the Hetaereiarch?"

"He is next door."

"We will see him and return to our ship." A sudden thought struck me. "The insurrection?"

"The men of the Hetaereiarch's thema retook the palace and reinstated the Emperor. Before they were executed they admitted that they had been paid to kill the Emperor by Bardanes Tourkos. Loyal troops now guard all the gates."

"Good." Tostig had not died in vain. His sacrifice had enabled us to escape. The guard at the door of the Hetaereiarch frowned as we approached. Aiden said something and he smiled and opened the door for us. The Hetaereiarch was sat up in bed.

He spoke and Aiden translated.

"The Hetaereiarch says that you should be resting as he is but he says you must be a wolf and cannot be caged."

"Tell him that I was not meant to be imprisoned behind stone walls, no matter how beautiful. I would return to my men."

As it was translated I saw him nod, "He says that he owes you his life and the Empire owes you a great debt. He will try to repay it before we leave."

I limped over and clasped his arm in the warrior's handshake. I used my limited Greek. "You are my friend. I would fight alongside you again."

He smiled and spoke again, "He says that the Emperor wishes you and your men to serve him. He will pay you each a fortune."

"Tell him that I am honoured but I must return to my people. It is no Empire but it is mine and my people need me."

He nodded and we parted. As we made our way out of the barracks we had to endure many questions but as soon as Aiden mentioned who we were the scowls changed to smiles and we were accorded bows.

It was daylight when we emerged and the brightness almost blinded me. We had had limited light for three days in our little cell and I had forgotten where we were. As we wound our way down to the harbour I noticed that there were far fewer people around. I suppose a rebellion makes everyone nervous. The sentries at the gate recognised us and bowed. As soon as we stepped through I saw that the guards had gone and my men were taking advantage of their freedom and were strolling along the harbour wall. As soon as they saw us they raced towards us.

"Have I enough material for another saga, Jarl Dragon Heart?"

Arturus laughed, "At least two and they will be requested over and over my friend."

"Then let us get you back on board and then we can sail home."

"You forget, Haaken One Eye, that we have yet to trade and to be paid for our treasures. We did not sail all the way around the world just so that I could gain another two wounds. We came for profit."

Once I was aboard all that I wanted to do was to sleep. Magnus and Aiden rigged up a shelter at the stern and I slept. I slept a sleep without dreams. I just fell into a deep black hole and when I awoke I felt refreshed. It was just turning from dark to light. I must have slept all day and night. I was starving. As I rose Aiden appeared at my side with a candle. "The gods send sleep to heal warriors. You have a better colour, Jarl Dragon Heart. I will get you some food."

I relieved myself over the stern and watched the sun rise over the turrets and towers of the city. I was pleased that we had seen it but I would be glad to leave. When I had eaten I felt much better. I rubbed my hands, "Now we can begin to trade!"

Arturus and Aiden laughed. "I am afraid, father, that we have already done so. Haaken and the crew were so desperate for activity that they went to the spice market yesterday to buy some of the precious powders."

Aiden laughed, "The merchants were terrified for the story of the two wolves that defended the Emperor had spread. There was a mixture of gratitude and terror when we bartered. We bought a huge quantity and did not spend much of the gold. We have the money from Bardanes Tourkos and we have been told that the Emperor will give us our payment for the bones later today."

"Then we can sail tomorrow?"

"We can indeed. Haaken and Cnut just need to provision the ship and then we can sail west."

"Go with them now, Aiden, I would that we were ready to go sooner rather than later. I miss my cold northern home. You will need to use your new maps."

After he had gone I asked Arturus to get us some coins. "I think we will go and buy some more of these fine garments. We will be comfortable while we sail the Middle Sea."

"But the language?"

"We will use the language of gold!"

Snorri insisted upon accompanying us. "You are still injured Jarl and although he will not tell you, Arturus was also wounded in the fight."

"Is this true? You were hurt?"

He nodded, "I took a spear thrust to the leg but it was a scratch only."

I nodded. Each day my son became more of a man and less of a boy. "Magnus, take charge of the ship."

It must have been *wyrd*, for as we entered the gate to the city we saw Josephus standing there. He bowed, "I am pleased that you live, master. The talk all over the city is of the foreigners who saved the Emperor."

"And you Josephus, did you find your family?"

I saw his eyes well up with tears. "My brother died many years ago but my wife finally gave up hope and passed over less than a month ago. Even as we set off from Frisia she was in the Otherworld."

There was little I could say. I put my arm around his shoulder. I understood his pain and his loss. I had suffered the same. "And have you a home?"

He shook his head, "No master, and I am here to ask to be your slave again."

"No Josephus, that is not possible." His face fell as though I had struck him. "You can be part of the crew and share in the profits." He dropped to his knee and kissed my hand. "Enough of that, my men kneel to no-one! Come to the market and you can help us to strike bargains."

When we returned we had had to hire men to carry all the goods that we had bought. I traded for all the things I thought Erika would have liked. Kara would enjoy them. Then we found a stall selling medicines and we bought those for Kara too. Finally we bought the finest weapons that the city had to offer. When the gold I carried was gone we returned to the ship.

A messenger awaited us. We were expected at the palace. I took Aiden, Arturus and Josephus with me. We dressed in our new clothes and I left Haaken to prepare the ship for sea. The palace guards cleared our way but we were recognised and cheered all the way to the palace. This time it was no antechamber we were taken to, it was the large hall where we had addressed the council. The Hetaereiarch was seated and I saw that there were four heavily armed warriors behind the Emperor. As we entered we were applauded.

I stood before him and bowed. He began to speak and Josephus translated. "The Empire owes a debt to Jarl Dragon Heart and his men of the Norse. They will ever be welcome in Byzantium. He pays his debts first." Two slaves carried a huge chest. Their straining muscles told me of its weight. "And to the two heroes who fought off an army he gives these suits of mail." Two more slaves brought forth complete sets of mail. I had seen them on Bardanes Tourkos and knew of their efficacy.

The Emperor smiled and descended to speak with me. I knew that I was still a barbarian in his eyes but he took my arm as a warrior would and spoke some Greek. The whole crowd applauded and cheered.

I looked at Josephus, "He said, Jarl, that the Viking wolf will ever be welcome in Constantinopolis!"

I nodded, "Then we can sail home. I have fulfilled my destiny!"

The End

Glossary

Áed Oirdnide –King of Tara 797
Afon Hafron- River Severn in Welsh
Bardanes Tourkos- Rebel Byzantine General
Bebbanburgh- Bamburgh Castle, Northumbria
Blót – a blood sacrifice made by a jarl
Byrnie- a mail shirt reaching down to the knees
Caerlleon- Welsh for Chester
Casnewydd –Newport, Wales
Cephas- Greek for Simon Peter (St.Peter)
Chape- the tip of a scabbard
Charlemagne- Holy Roman Emperor at the end of the
8th and beginning of the 9th centuries
Cherestanc- Garstang (Lancashire)
Cymri- Welsh
Cymru- Wales
Cyninges-tūn – Coniston. It means the estate of the
king (Cumbria)
Drekar- a Dragon ship (a Viking warship)
Duboglassio –Douglas, Isle of Man
Dyflin- Old Norse for Dublin
Ein-mánuðr- middle of March to the middle of April
Fey- having second sight
Frankia- France and part of Germany
Garth- Dragon heart
Gaill- Irish for foreigners
Gladramenn- wizard
Glaesum –amber
Gói- the end of February to the middle of March
Haughs- small hills in Norse (As in Tarn Hows)
Heels- when a ship leans to one side under the pressure
of the wind
Hel - Queen of Niflheim, the Norse underworld.
Hetaereiarch – Byzantine general
Hoggs or Hogging- when the pressure of the wind
causes the stern or the bow to droop
Hrams-a – Ramsey, Isle of Man

263

Itouna- River Eden Cumbria
Jarl- Norse earl or lord
Joro-goddess of the earth
Knarr- a merchant ship or a coastal vessel
Kyrtle-woven top
Lochlannach – Irish for Northerners (Vikings)
Legacaestir- Anglo Saxon for Chester
Mammceaster- Manchester
Manau – The Isle of Man (Saxon)
Marcia Hispanic- Spanish Marches (the land around
Barcelona)
Mast fish- two large racks on a ship for the mast
Melita- Malta
Midden- a place where they dumped human waste
Nikephoros- Emperor of Byzantium 802-811
Njoror- God of the sea
Nithing- A man without honour (Saxon)
Odin - The "All Father" God of war, also associated
with wisdom, poetry, and magic (The Ruler of the
gods).
On Corn Walum –Cornwall
Orkneyjar-Orkney
Pillars of Hercules- Straits of Gibraltar
Ran- Goddess of the sea
Roof rock- slate
Rinaz –The Rhine
Sabrina- Latin and Celtic for the River Severn. Also
the name of a female Celtic deity
St.Cybi- Holyhead
Scillonia Insula- Scilly Isles
Seax – short sword
Skeggox – an axe with a shorter beard on one side of
the blade
Sheerstrake- the uppermost strake in the hull
Sheet- a rope fastened to the lower corner of a sail
Shroud- a rope from the masthead to the hull
amidships
Stad- Norse settlement

Viking Wolf

Stays- ropes running from the mast-head to the bow
Strake- the wood on the side of a drekar
Syllingar- Scilly Isles
Tarn- small lake (Norse)
The Norns- The three sisters who weave webs of
intrigue for men
Thing-Norse for a parliament or a debate (Tynwald)
Thor's day- Thursday
Threttanessa- a drekar with 13 oars on each side.
Thrall- slave
Trenail- a round wooden peg used to secure strakes
Tynwald- the Parliament on the Isle of Man
Úlfarrberg- Helvellyn
Úlfarrland- Cumbria
Úlfarr- Wolf Warrior
Úlfarrston- Ulverston
Ullr-Norse God of Hunting
Ulfheonar-an elite Norse warrior who wore a wolf skin
over his armour
Volva- a witch or healing woman in Norse culture
Woden's day- Wednesday
Wulfhere-Old English for Wolf Army
Wyrd- Fate
Yard- a timber from which the sail is suspended

Maps

Northumbria circa 800 AD

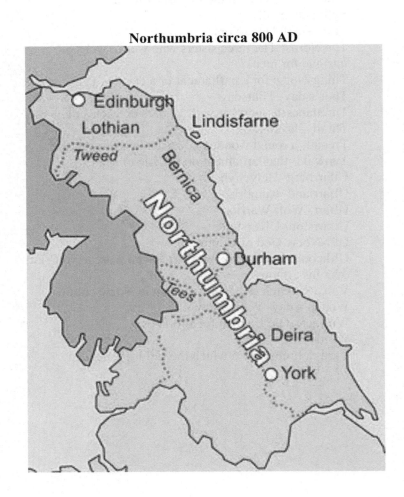

Historical note

The Viking raids began, according to records left by the monks, in the 790s when Lindisfarne was pillaged. However there were many small settlements along the east coast and most were undefended. I have chosen a fictitious village on the Tees as the home of Garth who is enslaved and then, when he gains his freedom, becomes Dragon Heart. As buildings were all made of wood then any evidence of their existence would have rotted long ago, save for a few post holes. The Norse began to raid well before 790. There was a rise in the populations of Norway and Denmark and Britain was not well prepared for defence against such random attacks.

My raiders represent the Norse warriors who wanted the plunder of the soft Saxon kingdom. There is a myth that the Vikings raided in large numbers but this is not so. It was only in the tenth and eleventh centuries that the numbers grew. They also did not have allegiances to kings. The Norse settlements were often isolated family groups. The term Viking was not used in what we now term the Viking age beyond the lands of Norway and Denmark. Warriors went a-Viking which meant that they sailed for adventure or pirating. Their lives were hard. Slavery was commonplace. The Norse for slave is thrall and I have used both terms.

The ship, '***Dragon Heart***' is based on the Gokstad ship which was found in 1880 in Norway. It is 23.24 metres long and 5.25 metres wide at its widest point. It was made entirely of oak except for the pine decking. There are 16 strakes on each side and from the base to the gunwale is 2.02 metres giving it a high freeboard. The keel is cut from a piece of oak 17.6 metres long. There are 19 ribs. The pine mast was 13 metres high. The ship could carry 70 men although there were just sixteen oars on each side. This meant that half the crew could rest while the other half rowed. Sea battles could be brutal.

The Vikings raided far and wide. They raided and subsequently conquered much of Western France and made serious inroads into Spain. They even travelled up the Rhone River as well as raiding North Africa. The sailors and warriors we call Vikings were very adaptable and could, indeed, carry their long ships over hills to travel from one river to the next. The Viking ships are quite remarkable. Replicas of the smaller ones have managed speeds of 8-10 knots. The sea going ferries, which ply the Bay of Biscay, travel at 14-16 knots. The journey the *'Heart of the Dragon'* makes from Santander to the Isles of Scilly in a day and a half would have been possible with the oars and a favourable wind and, of course, the cooperation of the Goddess of the sea, Ran! The journey from the Rhine to Istanbul is 1188 nautical miles. If the *'Heart of the Dragon'* had had favourable winds and travelled nonstop she might have made the journey in 6 days! Sailing during the day only and with some adverse winds means that 18 or 20 days would be more realistic.

Nikephoros was Emperor from 802-811. Bardanes Tourkos did revolt although he did not attempt a coup in the palace as I used in my book. He was later defeated, blinded and sent to a monastery. Nikephoros did well until he went to war with Krum, the Khan of Bulgaria. He died in battle and Krum made a drinking vessel from his skull!

I have recently used the British Museum book and research about the Vikings. Apparently, rather like punks and Goths, the men did wear eye makeup. It would make them appear more frightening. There is also evidence that they filed their teeth. The leaders of warriors built up a large retinue by paying them and giving them gifts such as the wolf arm ring. This was seen as a sort of bond between leader and warrior. There was no national identity. They operated in small bands of free booters loyal to their leader. The idea of sword killing was to render a weapon unusable by anyone else. On a simplistic level this could just be a bend but I have seen examples which are tightly curled like a spring.

The length of the swords in this period was not the same as in the later medieval period. By the year 850 they were only 76cm long and in the eighth century they were shorter still. The first sword Dragon Heart used, Ragnar's, was probably only 60-65cm long. This would only have been slightly longer than a Roman gladius. At this time the sword, not the axe was the main weapon. The best swords came from Frankia, and were probably German in origin. A sword was considered a special weapon and a good one would be handed from father to son. A warrior with a famous blade would be sought out on the battlefield. There was little mail around at the time and warriors learned to be agile to avoid being struck. A skeggox was an axe with a shorter edge on one side. The use of an aventail (a chain mail extension of a helmet) began at about this time. The highly decorated scabbard also began at this time.

The blood eagle was performed by cutting the skin of the victim by the spine, breaking the ribs so they resembled blood-stained wings, and pulling the lungs out through the wounds in the victim's back.

It was more dangerous to drink the water in those times and so most people, including children drank beer or ale. The process killed the bacteria which could hurt them. It might sound as though they were on a permanent pub crawl but in reality they were drinking the healthiest drink that was available to them. Honey was used as an antiseptic in both ancient and modern times. Yarrow was a widely used herb. It had a variety of uses in ancient times. It was frequently mixed with other herbs as well as being used with honey to treat wounds. Its Latin name is *Achillea millefolium*. Achilles was reported to have carried the herb with him in battle to treat wounds. Its traditional names include arrowroot, bad man's plaything, bloodwort, carpenter's weed, death flower, devil's nettle, eerie, field hops, gearwe, hundred leaved grass, knight's milefoil, knyghten, milefolium, milfoil, millefoil, noble yarrow, nosebleed, old man's mustard, old man's pepper, sanguinary, seven year's love, snake's grass, soldier, soldier's woundwort, stanchweed, thousand seal, woundwort, yarroway, yerw. I suspect Tolkien used it in the Lord of the Rings books as

Kingsfoil, another ubiquitous and often overlooked herb in Middle Earth.

The Vikings were not sentimental about their children. A son would expect nothing from his father once he became a man. He had more chance of reward from his jarl than his father. Leaders gave gifts to their followers. It was expected. Therefore the more successful you were as a leader the more loyal followers you might have.

The word lake is a French/Norman word. The Norse called lakes either waters or meres. They sometimes used the old English term, tarn. The Irish and the Scots call them Lough/lochs. There is only one actual lake in the Lake District. All the rest are waters, meres or tarns.

The Latin inscription MATRIB TEMPL CVM ARA VEX COH I VARD INSTANTE P D V VSLM I have transposed from Hadrian's wall. Translated it says: '*To the Mother Goddesses, this temple with its altar stone [was built by] a detachment of the First Cohort of Vardulli, under P[ublius] D[omitius?] V[...], willingly and deservedly fulfilling their vow*'.

When writing about the raids I have tried to recreate those early days of the Viking raider. The Saxons had driven the native inhabitants to the extremes of Wales, Cornwall and Scotland. The Irish were always too busy fighting amongst themselves. It must have come as a real shock to be attacked in their own settlements. By the time of King Alfred almost sixty years later they were better prepared. This was also about the time that Saxon England converted completely to Christianity. The last place to do so was the Isle of Wight. There is no reason to believe that the Vikings would have had any sympathy for their religion and would, in fact, have taken advantage of their ceremonies and rituals not to mention their riches.

There was a warrior called Ragnar Hairy-Breeches. Although he lived a little later than my book is set I could not resist using the name of such an interesting sounding character. Most of the names such as Silkbeard, Hairy-Breeches etc are genuine Viking names. I have merely transported them all into one book. I also amended some of my names- I used Eric in the earlier books and it should have been Erik. I have now changed the later editions of the first two books in the series.

Eardwulf was king of Northumbria twice: first from 796-806 and from 808-810. The king who deposed him was Elfwald II. This period was a turbulent one for the kings of Northumbria and marked a decline in their fortunes until it was taken over by the Danes in 867. This was the time of power for Mercia and East Anglia. Coenwulf ruled East Anglia and his son Cynhelm, Mercia. Wessex had yet to rise.

Slavery was far more common in the ancient world. When the Normans finally made England their own they showed that they understood the power of words and propaganda by making the slaves into serfs. This was a brilliant strategy as it forced their former slaves to provide their own food whilst still working for their lords and masters for nothing. Manumission was possible as Garth showed in the first book in this series. Scanlan's training is also a sign that not all of the slaves suffered. It was a hard and cruel time- it was ruled by the strong.

The Vikings did use trickery when besieging their enemies and would use any means possible. They did not have siege weapons and had to rely on guile and courage to prevail. The siege of Paris in 845 A.D. was one such example.

The Isle of Man is reputed to have the earliest surviving Parliament, the Tynwald although there is evidence that there were others amongst the Viking colonies on Orkney and in Iceland. I have used this idea for Prince Butar's meetings of Jarls.

The blue stone they seek is Aquamarine or beryl. It is found in granite. The rocks around the Mawddach are largely granite and although I have no evidence of beryl being found there, I have used the idea of a small deposit being found to tie the story together.

There was a famous witch who lived on one of the islands of Scilly. Famously Olaf Tryggvasson, who became King

Olaf 1 of Norway, visited her. She told him that if he converted to Christianity then he would become king of Norway.

The early ninth century saw Britain converted to Christianity and there were many monasteries which flourished. These were often mixed. These were not the huge stone edifices such as Whitby and Fountain's Abbey; these were wooden structures. As such their remains have disappeared, along with the bones of those early Christian priests. Hexham was a major monastery in the early Saxon period. I do not know if they had warriors to protect the priests but having given them a treasure to watch over I thought that some warriors might be useful too.

I use Roman forts in all of my books. Although we now see ruins when they were abandoned the only things which would have been damaged would have been the gates. Anything of value would have been buried in case they wished to return. By 'of value' I do not mean coins but things such as nails and weapons. Such objects have been discovered. Many of the forts were abandoned in a hurry. Hardknott fort, for example, was built in the 120s but abandoned twenty or so years later. When the Antonine Wall was abandoned in the 180s Hardknott was reoccupied until Roman soldiers finally withdrew from northern Britain. I think that, until the late Saxon period and early Norman period, there would have been many forts which would have looked habitable. The Vikings and the Saxons did not build in stone. It was only when the castle builders, the Normans, arrived that stone would be robbed from Roman forts and those defences destroyed by an invader who was in the minority. The Vikings also liked to move their homes every few years; this was, perhaps, only a few miles, but it explains how difficult it is to find the remains of early Viking settlements.

The place names are accurate and the mountain above Coniston is called the Old Man. The river is not navigable up to Windermere but I have allowed my warriors to carry their drekar as the Vikings did in the land of the Rus when travelling to Miklagård. The ninth century saw the beginning of the reign of the Viking. They raided Spain, the Rhone, Africa and even Constantinople. They believed they could beat anyone!

I used the following books for research
British Museum - 'Vikings- Life and Legends'
'Saxon, Norman and Viking' by Terence Wise (Osprey)
Ian Heath - 'The Vikings'. (Osprey)
Ian Heath- 'Byzantine Armies 668-1118 (Osprey)
David Nicholle- 'Romano-Byzantine Armies 4th-9th Century (Osprey)
Stephen Turnbull- 'The Walls of Constantinople AD 324-1453' (Osprey)
Keith Durham- 'Viking Longship' (Osprey)

Griff Hosker **October 2014**

Other books by Griff Hosker

If you enjoyed reading this book, then why not read
another one by the author?

Ancient History

The Sword of Cartimandua Series
(Germania and Britannia 50 A.D. – 128 A.D.)
Ulpius Felix- Roman Warrior (prequel)
The Sword of Cartimandua
The Horse Warriors
Invasion Caledonia
Roman Retreat
Revolt of the Red Witch
Druid's Gold
Trajan's Hunters
The Last Frontier
Hero of Rome
Roman Hawk
Roman Treachery
Roman Wall
Roman Courage

The Wolf Warrior series
(Britain in the late 6th Century)
Saxon Dawn
Saxon Revenge
Saxon England
Saxon Blood
Saxon Slayer
Saxon Slaughter
Saxon Bane
Saxon Fall: Rise of the Warlord
Saxon Throne
Saxon Sword

Viking Wolf

Medieval History

The Dragon Heart Series
Viking Slave
Viking Warrior
Viking Jarl
Viking Kingdom
Viking Wolf
Viking War
Viking Sword
Viking Wrath
Viking Raid
Viking Legend
Viking Vengeance
Viking Dragon
Viking Treasure
Viking Enemy
Viking Witch
Viking Blood
Viking Weregeld
Viking Storm
Viking Warband
Viking Shadow
Viking Legacy
Viking Clan
Viking Bravery

The Norman Genesis Series
Hrolf the Viking
Horseman
The Battle for a Home
Revenge of the Franks
The Land of the Northmen
Ragnvald Hrolfsson
Brothers in Blood
Lord of Rouen
Drekar in the Seine
Duke of Normandy

Viking Wolf

The Duke and the King

Danelaw
(England and Denmark in the 11th Century)
Dragon Sword
Oathsword
Bloodsword
Danish Sword

New World Series
Blood on the Blade
Across the Seas
The Savage Wilderness
The Bear and the Wolf
Erik The Navigator
Erik's Clan
The Last Viking

The Vengeance Trail

The Conquest Series
(Normandy and England 1050-1100)
Hastings

The Aelfraed Series
(Britain and Byzantium 1050 A.D. - 1085 A.D.)
Housecarl
Outlaw
Varangian

The Reconquista Chronicles
Castilian Knight
El Campeador
The Lord of Valencia

**The Anarchy Series England
1120-1180**
English Knight

Viking Wolf

Knight of the Empress
Northern Knight
Baron of the North
Earl
King Henry's Champion
The King is Dead
Warlord of the North
Enemy at the Gate
The Fallen Crown
Warlord's War
Kingmaker
Henry II
Crusader
The Welsh Marches
Irish War
Poisonous Plots
The Princes' Revolt
Earl Marshal
The Perfect Knight

Border Knight
1182-1300
Sword for Hire
Return of the Knight
Baron's War
Magna Carta
Welsh Wars
Henry III
The Bloody Border
Baron's Crusade
Sentinel of the North
War in the West
Debt of Honour
The Blood of the Warlord
The Fettered King
de Montfort's Crown

Sir John Hawkwood Series

Viking Wolf

France and Italy 1339- 1387
Crécy: The Age of the Archer
Man At Arms
The White Company
Leader of Men
Tuscan Warlord
Condottiere

Lord Edward's Archer
Lord Edward's Archer
King in Waiting
An Archer's Crusade
Targets of Treachery
The Great Cause
Wallace's War

**Struggle for a Crown
1360- 1485**
Blood on the Crown
To Murder a King
The Throne
King Henry IV
The Road to Agincourt
St Crispin's Day
The Battle for France
The Last Knight
Queen's Knight

Tales from the Sword I
(Short stories from the Medieval period)

**Tudor Warrior series
England and Scotland in the late 14th and early 15th
century**
Tudor Warrior
Tudor Spy
Flodden

Viking Wolf

Conquistador
England and America in the 16th Century
Conquistador
The English Adventurer

Modern History

The Napoleonic Horseman Series
Chasseur à Cheval
Napoleon's Guard
British Light Dragoon
Soldier Spy
1808: The Road to Coruña
Talavera
The Lines of Torres Vedras
Bloody Badajoz
The Road to France
Waterloo

The Lucky Jack American Civil War series
Rebel Raiders
Confederate Rangers
The Road to Gettysburg

Soldier of the Queen series
Soldier of the Queen
Redcoat's Rifle

The British Ace Series
1914
1915 Fokker Scourge
1916 Angels over the Somme
1917 Eagles Fall
1918 We will remember them
From Arctic Snow to Desert Sand
Wings over Persia

Combined Operations series

Viking Wolf

1940-1945
Commando
Raider
Behind Enemy Lines
Dieppe
Toehold in Europe
Sword Beach
Breakout
The Battle for Antwerp
King Tiger
Beyond the Rhine
Korea
Korean Winter

Tales from the Sword II
(Short stories from the Modern period)

Other Books
Great Granny's Ghost (Aimed at 9-14-year-old young
people)

For more information on all of the books then please visit
the author's website at www.griffhosker.com where there is
a link to contact him or visit his Facebook page: GriffHosker
at Sword Books or follow him on Twitter: @HoskerGriff